Cleopatra, Immortal Queen

by

Cleo Fellers Kocol

Order this book online at www.trafford.com
or email orders@trafford.com

Most Trafford titles are also available at major online book retailers.

Printed in Victoria, BC, Canada.

ISBN: 978-1-4269-1539-0

*Our mission is to efficiently provide the world's finest, most comprehensive book publishing
service, enabling every author to experience success. To find out how to publish your book, your
way, and have it available worldwide, visit us online at www.trafford.com*

Trafford rev. 12/02/09

 www.trafford.com

North America & international
toll-free: 1 888 232 4444 (USA & Canada)
phone: 250 383 6864 ✦ fax: 812 355 4082

Introductory Notes by Cleo Fellers Kocol

Historian Michael Grant wrote Cleopatra was the most maligned woman in history. The Romans, afraid of her power, blackened her name. Subsequently she's been identified as a courtesan, a temptress, a woman of loose morals. Grant argues that if there had been even a hint of sexual immorality the Romans would have broadcast it far and wide. In Egyptian eyes she was wed first to Caesar and then to Antony. Using her womanly wiles to keep Caesar and Antony enamored with her did not keep her from being educated and ambitious, a feminist of her day.

To make this ancient story easier reading for today's reader, I call Marcus Antony, Marc Anthony, and use terms like miles instead of cubits. I've also streamlined Cleopatra's family. She had two older sisters, Berenice and Cleopatra Tryphaena, a younger sister, Arsinoe, and two younger brothers, Ptolemy XIII and Ptolemy XIV. For the sake of clarity, I left the two older sisters out of the novel. Chosen by her father to succeed him, our queen was the seventh Cleopatra, the immortal queen. But all the characters in the novel really lived except for the fictional characters Laknefer, Nicodemus and his family. The poetry, excerpted in the novel, is ancient Egyptian. After the era of the book, Octavian became Caesar Augustus.

While writing the novel I consulted thirty-five histories including Michael Grant's biography, **CLEOPATRA** and Alice Curtis's **CLEOPATRA'S CHILDREN.** I also read **CLEOPATRA, GODDESS/ QUEEN,** *by* Kristin Zambucka, **WOMEN IN HELLENISTIC EGYP**T, **From Alexander to Cleopatra,** by Sarah B. Pomeroy, and, of course **PLUTARCH** *and* **SEUTONIUS** in translation. I read everything that told me what it was like to live in Alexandria, Egypt, in Rome, and the other important cities of Cleopatra's world. I read books about, how people traveled, ate, dressed, and thought in an attempt to bring that ancient time to life.

Chapter I

48 BCE

ALEXANDRIA'S LIGHTS WERE dim against the cloud-filled sky as the prow of the small ship ground onto the sand. The two-man crew jumped out and began pulling the boat higher onto the beach while Cleopatra allowed Nicodemus to carry her beyond the waves to drier land. In the dark he was a shadowy form, but familiar, someone she could trust. During her early years, attending classes at the palace with her, his sweet manners had charmed everyone. The last time she'd seen him the soft lines of youth had disappeared. Now, three years later, he was a man, but she barely noticed, the next few hours paramount in her mind.

Faint lights pricked the hillside, but on top of the hill the palace – *her palace* – blazed with light, and the sounds of Roman soldiers patrolling the perimeter of the gardens carried to her, increasing the anger she felt. "What is it like, Nicodemus?" she whispered, her feet sinking into damp sand as he set her down. The night had turned cold, and she shivered. With difficulty she moved toward the softer, drier ground barely visible near the wall. "Is my city the same as when I left?" If Arsinoe got to the palace first, she would spread her legs for the Roman. Delay could mean defeat even if her sister could never satisfy Caesar's taste for literature, poetry, and word play like she could.

"Not quite, My Lady." He pointed toward the city proper. "Some of the buildings have been razed, others fortified."

She tried not to picture the destruction. While she was in exile, Alexandria's royal image had sustained her, her palace the jewel at the top of the hill. "And my people?" She spoke to stop inner trembling.

Caesar could be compassionate, but he could wipe out whole cities without compunction, including babies at the breast. Born into an impoverished branch of a noble family, his mother devoted her life to his education. As a young man he'd married Cornelia, marrying twice more, the third wife recently. It was clear he did not look askance at women.

She smoothed the folds of her dress. He would like her magnificent eyes, her shapely body, but she must make him like her. Even though he was old enough to be her father, she had much in common with him. She could speak nine languages, recite ancient poetry and literature, all of which would appeal to him. His pedagogue had been educated in Alexandria and Caesar had studied many of the same subjects she had. But Egypt had lived under the Roman thumb for decades. The Romans had patronized her father, bled him dry and then let him borrow money so they could hold the debt over his head like a blade to plunge into soft flesh. She hated the thought of Rome, but to save Egypt, it had to be placated.

"Some of our people have fled. Others stay in their homes. Others welcome Caesar." Nicodemus held out a hand. "Come. We must hurry. Apollodorus, the Sicilian merchant helping us, waits in his shop." He led her up the beach.

Nicodemus's voice brought her back to the present. She nodded, hating to sneak through the streets like a thief. She'd been queen since her father died, chosen over her siblings, and every day of her exile, she'd chafed. She belonged on Egypt's throne, not her half sister, Arsinoe, not her half brother, Ptolemy XIII, and certainly not Caesar of Rome.

Holding her cloak tightly about her, she hesitated near the Moon Gate. Her gown and jewels covered, her feet in papyrus sandals, she looked far from queenly. She'd almost worn a pair of leopard earrings painted black, the leopard's eyes blazing with green feldspar, but it would not do to tempt destiny with signs of the underworld. The pearls she'd selected were one of the costliest jewels in the world and would enhance the image she wished to project. Plus, the ribbons of gold and beads of lapis lazuli threaded through her hair added to the splendor. She 'd look like a queen.

She glanced around. Although most people would be sleeping, someone could be returning from a drunken revel or clandestine assignation. "If we get stopped, I'll pretend you're my husband, and we're returning home after a party with friends," she whispered. Nicodemus had become a very successful architect; many Alexandrians would recognize him on sight, hardly glance at her. "You can pretend marriage to me was a sudden decision." She smiled. Acting out dramatic scenarios was a game they had played with Iras and Charmion many times during childhood. Always he had entered wholeheartedly into the fun no matter what role she had assigned him. Now, she imagined he frowned for he did not answer immediately, and the moon continued to hide behind drifting clouds and no light came from the small dark waterfront shops. "So, what say you?" she prodded, the idea of confronting Caesar bothering her more than she liked to admit.

"Your Majesty, I am married and many know my wife."

Frowning, she said, "So we will have to change our story. We cannot be caught."

"We will not be intercepted. I have timed the Roman guards on their rounds. We will make it to the rug shop safely. As for my wife, she's a lovely lady, almost as beautiful as you, My Lady."

"Only you see beauty, Nicodemus." A bitterness edged into her voice, whose sweetness poets had immortalized. Its even tone had sudden snags and sharp corners, and she felt again the loneliness that had assailed her when she'd fled Alexandria. Others saw the prominence of her nose or grew frightened of her agile mind. But she'd always felt beautiful when she was around Iras, Charmion, and Nicodemus. Now, he belonged to someone, and she had never belonged to anyone.

She looked up the hill to where dark buildings shut out half the sky. Nicodemus was leading her rapidly down an alley. Cats yowled, one brushing her ankle in passing. Should she view it as an omen? She glanced away from the light filtering from a two-story building, her mind filled with thoughts of the past. "Are we there?"

"Two doors down," he whispered, pulling her closer to a wall. "Wait here. I'll make sure Apollodorus is alone."

She nodded, her equilibrium back. "Yes, go check on him, and if all is well and you signal to me, I will join you. If not, I will return to the boat."

A few minutes later she stood inside the building among piles of carpets, rugs of all colors and weave stacked nearly to the ceiling, a dry dusty smell permeating the room, the corners dark in shadow.

"You are sure you will be able to get into the palace?" Nicodemus asked the man who closed the door behind them.

Apollodorus was older than Cleopatra had anticipated, a swarthy, muscular man, taller than Nicodemus and towering over her. She watched closely as his expression became confidential, and his gaze, frankly curious, went from Nicodemus to her. As instructed, Nicodemus had not identified her.

"The Roman was here just a few days ago, looking through the carpets. 'I want something warm under my feet when I get up at night,' he said. 'But I cannot tarry today. Another time.' Yes, I am sure he will let me in."

Nicodemus handed the man a bag full of gold while Cleopatra smoothed out a rug with a bright red weave. "This one should do," she said shucking off her outer garment and standing in the middle of the carpet.

Apollodorus, muttered, "You must lie down, woman."

She hid the shock the words brought her, and stretching out on the carpet, she adjusted her sheer, pleated Grecian gown. "Ready."

As the Sicilian's eyes roved over her in a way few men dared do, she wanted to cry out, "Desist! Your gaze offends the Queen of Egypt." Pretending to be an ordinary woman wearing fake jewelry worked with the story Nicodemus had given him: she was a gift paying off a bet. But who knew where the Sicilian's loyalties lay? He could hold her, ransom her, or sell her to the highest bidder.

Apollodorus chuckled and touched an elbow to Nicodemus' side. "You picked a fine gift for the Roman. They say he is partial to ladies. But it is good she is small and I am strong, for I shall have to carry her up the hill."

Closing her eyes, she shut the merchant from sight. If the gossips were right, and if she had judged things properly, Caesar would be amused, perhaps enthralled with her. In her mind, she ticked off facts. On his victorious return from Gaul, he had fought Pompey for control of Italy and triumphed. So would she. The gods, Isis be praised, would tell her what to do. Her brother had an army; her sister had an army, Caesar was Caesar, and they were all against her. She had to prevail.

Apollodorus wrapped her in the rug, lifted the bundle and tossed it over his shoulder like she was a true woman of the night. *Isis, be with me*, she prayed.

"Be careful," Nicodemus warned. "If there is the least bit of trouble, come straight back with her. Neither you nor I need trouble with the Romans."

Cleopatra shouted, "No! No matter what, leave me at the palace," but her words, muffled by the wool, were an incoherent babble. What if her brother got there first? In his latest attack he said he wanted to belittle her. Now thirteen years old, Ptolemy fought alongside his soldiers, making, she was sure, a ridiculous figure, tall and gawky, hardly in the mold of Alexander the Great. Her brother had helped chase her from Alexandria, made her feel like tying the final wrap around his eventual mummy. "Leave me at the palace," she shouted again.

"Tell the *hetaera* to shut up or we won't get by the guards," Apollodorus warned.

How dare he! But of course he could. Comforted by the thought of Nicodemus trotting along beside her, murmuring encouragement through the open end of the rolled carpet, she tried to stop the thoughts galloping through her mind. But too soon his footsteps and voice disappeared, and only the rough movement continued, and the clear, cool air of the Alexandrian night.

What if Caesar indulged in sarcasm, cut her down in words and actions like Cato The Minor had done with her father in Rhodes? With him, she had waited in an anteroom while Cato conversed with them through a doorway as he sat on a marble toilet. She had never forgotten the insult or her dislike of Rome. The narrow streets, the dirt, the filth, so few buildings worthy of such a vast power, had disgusted her, as had the differences between Egyptian and Roman culture. Although the Romans imitated the Greeks, the Ptolemys *were* Greek, their ancestry pure, elevated to the Egyptian throne by Alexander the Great himself.

After a while, guards called out, and as Apollodorus paused to explain his mission, she tried to determine where they were, but the turns and twists confused her and the steep climb disoriented her. Several men spoke. Laughter followed rough talk. A door opened, and footsteps echoed over solid floor. Weapons clanked. Another door. Walls. The air grew still and close, and she surmised she was inside the palace. Impatient, she tried to kick loose, but the rug was wound tight like a cocoon.

A faint fragrance of incense and fresh flowers became stronger, and she sensed the space around her opening. Surrounded by a vast chamber, she knew instinctively it was the throne room. Determined not to tremble, she repeated recent history to herself. Pompey, the Roman on the run from Caesar, had landed in Egypt with shoulders slumped, eyes bloodshot from lack of sleep, and her brother's men had killed him. Stupid fools. Pompey and his troops could have kept Caesar busy when his flagship, warships and men docked in Alexandria's Harbor of Heavenly Return. Instead, Caesar had practically walked into the palace and taken it over.

Apollodorus's forward movement suddenly stopped, and she stiffened, ready to leap to her feet.

"For what is this intrusion?" Well-modulated diction echoed from the other end of the hall, the international Greek language classical and smooth. "You say you have a rug for me. How curious to deliver it tonight." The voice grew closer, and she knew Caesar must have moved swiftly. "It is almost midnight. Is this the way Alexandrians conduct business?" This was a man used to being obeyed. His voice challenged in a way that couldn't be ignored.

Intrigued despite her resolve to remain aloof, Cleopatra cocked an ear.

Apollodorus' voice had the smoothness of a salesman. "It is a gift, Sir. From one Nicodemus."

"Nicodemus? I know of no such one." His voice held an edge of suspicion.

"He knew of your desire to own a fine carpet."

"That is true, and it is obvious that you have brought one that demands my attention."

She was certain he was feeling the carpet for he muttered something about the thick nap before his voice rang like a summons. "He has picked well. The colors do not shy from the light, but reach out and grab it. Merchant, unroll this rug, and I shall see if it is a gift worthy of receiving. If not bring me this Nicodemus, for an insult must be returned to the giver in person."

Apollodorus lowered the carpet. When it touched the floor Cleopatra braced, and as the rug was unrolled, she leapt to her feet.

"By the Gods, what is it?" Caesar cried, his feet wide, the stance of a conqueror ready to do combat if necessary.

As she caught her balance, she saw him wave away the sentries who came running, drawing their swords. She saw the palace she had ruled after her father died. She saw the marble columns, the tiled floor, and her throne. Standing confidently, she brushed stray bits of wool from her bosom, straightened her jeweled collar as she studied the man facing her. As if he didn't have the power to hurt her, she stared. Julius Caesar looked very much like the image she had admired in Pompey's garden those months she and her father stayed in Rome, but more attractive than she had imagined. A man past his prime, with no ounce of fat, no blemish of feature, no wrinkled flesh, was surely unique.

Beyond him servants and slaves, caught in a moment of surprise, mouths open, eyes wide, paused to watch. Apollodorus, a look of dawning comprehension on his face, shook his head. It was clear that his carrying her to the palace would be a tale he would repeat in the market place for years.

Caesar, his mouth a slash of speculation slowly changing to amusement, strode around the perimeter of the carpet, examining her from every angle.

Swiveling her head slowly, Cleopatra kept him in sight as the silence built. Her neck stiff with tension, she glanced toward the shadows at the end of the hall.

Charmion, who had been as close to her as Iras and Nicodemus, moved into the light and went to her knees chanting, "Praise be to Osiris and gentle Isis, the gift of heaven has returned."

Caesar frowned and looked from one woman to the other. To Cleopatra, he said, "Tell me, madam, who are you?" His brusque manner showed his irritation at the unseemly interruption, but also heralded his interest. Beyond him scrolls were spread across a table, and an oil lamp made a puddle of light. Cleopatra's chair, with the lion's paw legs and ivory claws, had been shoved back from the table as if he'd risen in a hurry.

"Bow in the presence of Her Majesty Queen Cleopatra VII," Charmion chanted in a loud voice. "Queen of all Egyptian lands, Divine Lady, Beloved of her Father, Benefactor of all peoples, may she reign forever."

Immediately, slaves prostrated themselves, servants went to their knees, and Caesar, showing neither surprise nor disbelief, smiled and moved closer. "By all that's holy, is this true, Madam?"

"A Queen is a Queen whether she is delivered in a golden chariot or a Sicilian carpet," she said in lilting tones as if she recited a sacred poem. Going past him, she walked with all the grace and the confidence she could muster, never showing that she, a Ptolemy Queen, had a stomach lurching and the chill of night running like water up her spine. "You may rise," she said to Charmion. "And get someone to light the lamps in the hall. We must not hide our return beneath Roman darkness but let the world know we are here." She smiled at Charmion before turning back to Caesar. "What say you to that, Julius Caesar?" Walking slowly, the nervous tension dissipating, knowing that even in the dim light the sheer dress showed her curves, and that the Roman, whose people were much more conservative about such things, undoubtedly noticed. Did he also notice that her steps were firm as she climbed the dais to her throne? This was her home, and strength lay in its familiar marble and alabaster.

Caesar's toga rested upon her royal chair. Holding it out to him, she noted that he was not dressed as a soldier but wore a chiton with the purple stripe of a senator.

Frowning slightly, he took the toga.

She sat, her head high, her eyes sweeping the room before coming back to rest upon him. "So you're Julius Caesar." She knew she looked every inch the queen she was – shapely, muscular, and virginal, the last hardly evident. She'd seen her younger sister dally with this man and that. With each encounter, respect for Arsinoe's royal personage plummeted, the men using her to cement their power. Determined to give herself only to a man of royal birth or substance, she had watched slaves copulating in the kitchen gardens; read all the literature about coupling in Alexandria's great library and became knowledgeable if inexperienced.

"So you're Cleopatra." He lifted the chair with the lion's paw legs and put it on the dais in line with her throne. "They told me you had turned tail and run like a scared rabbit."

She leaned back until the throne's carving bit into her spine. "Do I look like I am running? Or afraid?" Up close he was not nearly as forbidding as her imagination had painted him.

"You look like you are ready to do battle. I am not sure its form." He sat, moving the chair so close his feet would touch hers if she shifted slightly.

"I am in hopes no battle is necessary. Accommodation is always easier and much more pleasant." How wonderful that he looked so vital, his legs well-muscled to match his arms, his brow almost smooth. When he smiled even the lines around his mouth disappeared. Her father had never been as fit.

"Accommodation you say? You are your father's daughter, and I grow weary of combat."

"I am the daughter mentioned in my father's will." Stating the fact plainly, she crossed her legs, careful not to touch him, but noting with amusement that his gaze followed her every move.

"Yes, but your father had another daughter as well as sons."

"But they are not here. I am, and I am the one he chose." She let her gaze touch his in an imperial way before she softened the look in her eyes. She longed to roam through the palace, seek out the places dear to her. But she was no mere girl coming home, but a queen trying to regain her throne. "Speaking of families, I knew your daughter, Julia, in Rome." She spoke conversationally to show him she was seeking friendship as well as restoration of the crown. As his eyes shadowed, she let her voice show the natural sympathy she felt for his loss. "She was my friend; Pompey was not."

He shrugged. "Pompey was not my friend either. Everyone knows that. Prove yourself, little one who sneaks into Caesar's presence in the night." He relaxed his posture, tipping his head to the side and studying her with a knowing eye. "Tell me of my daughter. She wrote nothing of you, except that you were in Rome, at her domicile."

She lowered her voice so that it became an intimate whisper, soft and alluring. "She was fairer than me, as fair as her father. Asparagus was her favorite vegetable and mead her favorite drink."

He nodded.

"She was not fond of gladiatorial combat but liked the theater. Once we went together and saw a play by Euripides."

"Yes, that sounds like her."

"She liked to discuss all things at the baths, but her favorite topic of conversation was her father."

His cheeks lifted slightly.

"She said much about your competence, your kindness, your abilities. She portrayed you in a very noble way." She got up and moved around the dais, taking a taper and lighting the lamps that remained unlit, knowing her voice, her body, her mind were among her greatest assets. "She made me aware of you even though you were in Gaul and I longed to be in Alexandria." She glanced at him through a fringe of lashes, confident her eyes were incomparable when elongated as they were with paint, the lashes colored. She willed her taut muscles to relax. This was no callow youth but a man appreciative of subtlety and charm.

Caesar said, "When she was born, like all men, I hoped for a son, an heir. But I never hesitated when they held her out to me, but claimed her immediately. The resemblance you mentioned was apparent even then."

Cleopatra put out the taper and stepped closer, her eyes glistening with unshed tears, the emotion of the night adding to their luster. "I grieved when I heard of Julia's death. Her demise was my loss. She was my friend."

Standing, Caesar studied Cleopatra for some time without speaking, and she waited patiently, knowing it was important.

At last he smiled. "By a simple matter of deduction, that should make you my friend."

She looked up at him, "Yes, Julius Caesar, conqueror of the world, I am your friend." Her voice ringing softly like a temple bell, she added, "But are you mine?"

Again looking amused, he said in an even tone, "I could choose you, or your sister, or your brother, or put a Roman on the throne. Tell me why I should choose you."

"Because I am most fitted. My brother is too young, my sister too flighty, and a Roman on an Egyptian throne...." She shrugged.

"But I...." Smiling, she circled him, not offering herself but not holding back the thought of it either. Her gaze was direct, with only a hint of flirtation, but she knew he saw it.

He shook his head and reaching out he took her hands and led her back to the throne. "Sit."

She sat.

"The throne is rightfully yours."

Letting time spin out, she waited, before saying, "It always has been, but I need the guarantee of Julius Caesar, my friend." As her gaze mixed with his, she slowly lifted her head.

He nodded. "Your sister, Arsinoe, fled the palace when I arrived. She had neither the courage nor the grace to face me. Your brother vacillates, challenging me one minute, and whining the next." His hand described an arc even as his knee bent slightly, "You are the only true Ptolemy I have seen, Egypt's rightful queen."

She let her gaze dwell in his, saw his admiration and interest. "Then I admit you are my very good friend," she said softly and flushed, for he did not look away during all this time like a younger man would have done, or like a commoner in the presence of royalty, but seemingly drank in her features, looking from her eyes to her mouth, not dwelling on her nose, but passing on to the curve of her neck and then back to her eyes.

Because she was sure Caesar would think it charming, and because she longed to speak again to her dear friend and companion, she jumped up, left the dais and went to Charmion. "I've missed you," she whispered, words seeming puny things when compared with the affection within her. Over Charmion's shoulder she glimpsed Caesar standing, elbow in hand, the other hand cradling his chin as if he were trying to figure out exactly what he would do with her. She could not leave it to chance.

"See to my rooms," she whispered to Charmion. "Flowers, incense, a freshly made bed." As a girl, along with Charmion and Iras, she had spied on a slave pair pleasuring one another, the man's love stick prominent. Afterward, her curiosity great she'd ordered him into her presence. As he trembled, she demanded he take off his kirtle and display himself. But his love-stick looked pitiful until she reached out and touched it. Quickly, she had pulled her hand back, and ordered him out of her sight. The remembrance was unsettling. Louder, she said, "Have the cooks prepare a midnight supper, and serve it here, in this chamber that has served royalty for more time than we all have lived. Pheasant, pigeon, freshly baked bread." She waved grandly as she moved away from Charmion. "Have olive oil for dipping and honey for sweetening. And beer," she added enthusiastically as she approached Caesar again, her gaze on his, "the golden draughts from the best vats, and pour it in goblets of pure design, only the mark of the house of Ptolemy upon them. For we honor tonight, the great Caesar." And before she joined him, she nodded her head slightly as tribute to his prowess.

Later, she watched as Rome's most eminent citizen ate with enjoyment, his table etiquette exquisite, his murmured appreciation of the food proper, his handling of napkin and fingers delicate. As she nibbled, too excited to eat much, he questioned her in a smooth and practiced way, his voice low, as if the questions were not momentous, merely conversation, he nodding encouragingly when she answered. Soon, he found out which countries helped her during her exile, knew exactly how many troops she had at her disposal, and how many Egyptians she could count on to help her.

He is clever, she thought as he told her, in flawless Greek, tales of Gaul, pointing out always what lessons he had learned. His voice had a cultured quality, soft at times, but it could ring with authority sending shivers up her back like the Nile rising at flood tide. She was glad she had told him the truth.

"You knew my father," she said when he paused to lift the linen napkin to his mouth and wipe away a minute spot of fat clinging to his lips.

For a while he talked softly of Auletes, and it was almost as if her father were there, alive, with her again. Especially as Caesar continued as if he were a teacher and she a student, telling about his campaign in Italy, shoving dishes around on the table as he explained the battles; an urn designated Caesar, a fluted vase became Pompey. "Toward the end, it was a rout." He shoved the vase aside, letting it tilt toward the floor.

Her eyes grew big. Silver, so scarce in Egypt, was highly prized. Inhaling quickly, she held out her hands, but he brushed them aside and caught the vase before it touched the floor, and then with a smile tossed the vase lightly from one hand to the other before replacing it on the table.

He shrugged. "Sometimes I think I let Pompey escape so I could pursue him again." He motioned for a bowl of water, washed his hands and wiped them on a clean napkin. Lifting his glass, he leaned back, regarding the liquid sloshing dangerously close to the edge before he sipped.

She wondered if he were reliving the civil war in his mind or perhaps fighting again in Gaul. "I have been told you are a formidable swordsmen, putting all to shame."

"A leader must be an example for his men."

"We have an ancient text that gives all the reasons <u>not</u> to be a soldier. He is rousted early from bed, driven hard, is hungry, his body exhausted. Dead while yet alive." She paused. "Women aren't mentioned. Are you an example for them, too?"

He chuckled. "I agree, a soldier's life is a hard one, but at times I find politics as challenging. But enough of war and men. Literature, theater, and women are much more interesting, not necessarily in that order." His eyes teased with her. "Your name has become legend."

"No more than yours, Julius Caesar. What do they say about me in Rome?"

"They speak of your wit." He nodded in tribute.

She lay her napkin down, folded her hands and faced him squarely, glad that he had not said beauty. "And?"

"They say your rule was just."

She inclined her head slightly.

"That you were beleaguered from within."

"At least they have that right. Arsinoe and Ptolemy." The names sounded like excrement on her tongue.

"Your sister's troops still engage my men, but Ptolemy and I have come to a fragile agreement." Caesar leaned his arms on the table and regarded her. "You are far more interesting. I have heard you have written several books. When I'm not soldiering or writing dispatches, I write, too."

"Your memoirs?"

He chuckled again. "You tweak the vanity of an old campaigner. I have lived long enough for several volumes, but I fear my books tell only about campaigns and war, not my personal life."

"My personal life is a quiet one."

"Quiet is often a metaphor for lonely."

"You are perceptive for a general. A triumvir could, I suppose be likened to a queen. And the same adjectives apply."

"Leaders speak to other leaders."

He spoke softly, and she knew without doubt that he was flirting with her in an elegant way. "I have never had a confidante, other than my ladies-in-waiting." She leaned toward the light she saw shining in his eyes, a light that reminded her of her father. Yet Caesar was nothing like Auletes, but like a man who wanted to kiss her. She not only saw it but also heard it in the slightly honeyed tone of his voice. A silence followed, and she tried to look away from his gaze but couldn't.

He asked, "So, what does Queen Cleopatra want to talk about, poetry perhaps?"

"You read poetry?"

"Often, and when I read something I like, I memorize it"

"As do I. I've even read your Roman poets."

"Some critics claim they are the best." He shrugged and leaned even closer to her.

A scent, unfamiliar, but unmistakably his tickled her nose pleasantly. Like sandalwood, it reminded her of warm baths and languid moments or had the beer she had drunk made her giddy with desires she had long denied? If she must submit to a Roman, at least it was the foremost one. "And you? What do you think?"

"I find that Egyptian poetry is bright with images that stir the heart." He closed his eyes a second and opening them recited, his voice a gentle murmur, husky with emotion, "Come through the garden, Love, to me. My love is like each flower that blows."

She finished the stanza, "Tall and straight as a young palm tree, and in each cheek a sweet blush rose."

Without taking his gaze from hers, he moved his chair closer and continued, "Black are her tresses as the blackness of the night."

In a lilting whisper she recited the next stanza, and he took turns with her, his voice rich as it caressed the strong rhythms and the sensuous words. With the poem shimmering between them and the knowledge of shared tastes running like wine through her veins, she fought back fear as he took her hands in his, holding them lightly, and completed the last stanza himself. "When in all her beauty before his throne she stands. Sweet of love is the daughter of the King!"

She could not look away.

Slowly, he lifted her hands to his lips before presenting them back to her like a gift.

A pleasant tingling sensation surged through her, and she wanted to sing out her joy and shout in exultation about the ease of it all. She was Queen again; and he wanted her. She tried not to compare this awareness, this capitulation to feelings she'd had in the past. When she was much younger, a fever had spread through her composed of adulation for Marc Anthony so strong she wondered now if it had been real. But that was long ago, and Anthony had hardly noticed her. But Caesar had restored her to the throne. Pushing away memories of the man who had nudged her into man-woman awareness, she said, "My Lord," giving Caesar a title.

He nodded acceptance of the tribute and looked around the spacious throne room, its brightly painted walls showing Egyptian triumphs. "This is not a setting for poetry's sweet sounds. Words echo when they should strike the ear like a sweet temple bell, like the soothing sounds of Queen Cleopatra."

"My palace has many rooms, my lord."

"I assume your chambers hold sound instead of echoing it."

"It contains sound like a temple contains grace, my lord."

"Lead on, little Egyptian Queen. For once Julius Caesar chooses to follow."

* * *

Washing himself in an adjacent room, he came to her chamber wearing an Egyptian kilt and moved around her room like a long-absent owner. Incense burned in silver urns, oil lamps shed soft light, and the cool breeze of the night came in the partially opened shutters, chasing aside the warmth of day. Examining chests, wall hangings, murals, and the bed with its golden headboard, he settled finally in a gilded chair and gestured to her. "Prepare for the night, little one."

Unable to slow the thump-thump of her heart, she stood quietly as her handmaidens undressed her, she turning like a dancer as they took away the gauzy gown, perfumed her body and rubbed it with unguents. She sat while they freed her hair from the ribbons and jewels and combed her long black locks until they shone with the sheen of midnight and fell in a shower nearly reaching her waist. Fire raced through her veins as Caesar's eyes narrowed and a small smile settled on his lips.

So, she thought as he remained seated. Waving imperiously, her head high, she sent the servants away and let her eyes meet his.

His smile of satisfaction slowly grew.

She didn't move.

Murmuring, "You cast a spell," he threw the kilt aside and scooping her up, carried her to the royal bed, its expanse so padded with cushions it provided a secret bower.

Practiced, sophisticated but gentle, he drew from her all the emotions and feelings she had dreamed about, and she knew it was good she had not squandered the feelings of a queen on a lesser being. A conflagration of passion ignited within her. Her body burned. Her spirits soared. She moved at once like a siren and an innocent girl, exulting in each movement, each progression into womanly experience. Coming together with Caesar was like rising to the heights of a pyramid, trembling on the brink of the sky and spilling over like the waters of the Nile. She laughed in glee, knowing triumph as well as submission, the latter a new feeling.

Leaning over her, he shook his head, delight showing in his crinkly-eyed, smiling face. "I caught a moth and made it a butterfly. Madam, you amaze me."

"A moth must wait for the right moment to test its wings and become a butterfly," she whispered touching his face with her fingertips, fondness for the Roman surprising her with its insistence.

"And this moment was worthy of a queen?"

"It was worth waiting for, My Lord."

"Ah, my little Queen. You are all and more than they say."

"And what else do they say?" Cleopatra asked, getting up and walking around the room, knowing he watched her, liking the sexual feelings that were still romping through her like a revel gone wild. Bringing back to the bed a bowl of figs, she offered him one.

He took but a bite before putting it on the table next to the bed. "Untrue words I realize now. But in the future Caesar will say Queen Cleopatra is purity and virtue, and she and Egypt are one."

Sitting cross-legged she paused before answering, acknowledging deep within her a feeling that had grown since childhood. She shook her head. "Egypt is more. Always more." It was Alexander the Great, it was the first Ptolemy, and it was the Egyptian dynasties preceding the Greek ascension. Egypt prevailed long before the Romans, and she would perpetuate its greatness. Caesar merely raised his eyebrows.

Sorting through the fruit, she selected the best to offer to him, but again he shook his head. It was clear he didn't share her feelings, but his not speaking against her passionate words was his way to declare the warmth of his feelings for her. Immediately the thought came: he has a wife! But she could not, must not dwell on such thoughts. Pushing retrospection aside, she kissed his cheek and then nuzzled his neck and pressed again his side.

"I have not appeased your hunger?"

"I fear I am learning about appetites." She set the bowl of figs aside and ran her fingers up his leg. "You are right, the fruit did not satisfy. Are you hungry now, my Lord?"

"The gods have been good to me this night. I am more than hungry, Cleopatra, I thirst."

"A poem as prelude?" Her head on his shoulder, she recited from an Egyptian poet, "My beloved is on yonder bank; dark with crocodiles the water...but his love protects me from slaughter." She looked up at him a question in her eyes.

"I will protect you, little one."

"You have given me appetizer and entrée, yet, I confess I am a woman who has eaten fowl and still yearns for honey."

He laughed. "For me, you are the honey. But then sleep. We must be up early for a meeting with your brother. When Ptolemy arrives, he must see you at my side."

She shook her head. "No, you at mine. I am the queen."

His eyes lost their smile. "On the throne because I decree it."

Well, she thought settling back. Then Caesar chuckled, and she knew, as long as she amused him, all would be safe.

* * *

In the morning Cleopatra felt rested despite her lack of substantive sleep. In the throne room Caesar, sitting on the dais next to her, cut off their conversation when Ptolemy XIII entered. Her brother had changed, his slender figure yet taller, his narrow shoulders showing the suggestion of maturity to come. For a moment he reminded her of mutual family ties. Still, he would dash her authority against the breakwaters of battle if possible. Gripping Caesar's hand she waited, an ache in her chest taking hold.

Ptolemy stopped mid-way to the throne. "So the rumor was true. My sister is back."

Not letting go of Caesar's hand, Cleopatra smiled. "How perceptive of you. I congratulate you on your excellent vision." Her voice had the superior sound Ptolemy always hated.

"Stop it!" he cried, stamping his foot. "First you wage war on me, and now this." He pointed to her hand linked with Caesar's. "You are *my* wife! How can you be so blatantly disobedient?"

"Dear, benighted brother, I am your wife in name only, because it is an Egyptian tradition and for me, nothing more. Do not make a further fool of yourself."

Scowling, her brother said, "My prime minister, Pothinus, and the other leaders of the city back me. And if you listen well, you will hear. Our people cry out for you to go."

Even as Ptolemy spoke people shouted for Caesar to leave, but shaking his head slightly, Caesar indicated he would handle it. Rising, he spoke soothingly to Ptolemy, his arm around the boy's shoulders, his voice confidential, as if it were between them only.

Not loosening his grip on Ptolemy, he added, "Such things mean little between friends who have broken bread together."

Ptolemy shook his head. "I'm not *her* friend." He pointed to Cleopatra. "The people would back *me*," he cried. "Not her."

"Quit your caterwauling," Cleopatra cried, but Caesar frowned at her, lowered his voice and spoke in a murmur only Ptolemy could hear. She imagined Caesar playing on Ptolemy's pride for Ptolemy nodded as the two walked toward the far exit, Caesar speaking earnestly, Ptolemy nodding or saying nothing.

She hurried to catch up, conscious as she had never been before of her muscles coordinating, one with the other, her body a thing of grace and feeling. Caesar had brought her alive in ways she hadn't anticipated, and now he must placate her people.

"Perhaps, My Lord," she said gaining his attention, "if we go outside, address the people, they will stop these demonstrations."

"Of course, the three of us." Caesar said, his arm still around Ptolemy's shoulders. "We will give them a show of solidarity."

She had not thought to include Ptolemy, but Caesar was right. Her brother/husband, whom she'd been forced to wed, must be at her side. Most people realized the marriage had been a sham from the first, he a child, she eight years older.

Within minutes, they stood on the palace steps, Caesar's voice, stroking egos, saying things in Greek meant to conciliate. The barely risen sun only just reached ornamental trees and flowers, but outlined Caesar's men nearby, the Egyptians below appearing as one. As Caesar bowed to her, she realized he had publicly acknowledged her sovereignty to the people, and speaking Egyptian, she repeated her love for the land and for the people, her words a hymn to the gods, and as she paused, a voice rose, and a spontaneous cheer followed, subdued but passionate.

Caesar raised a hand. "You are correct to cheer your Queen, and as a leader of the Roman people, I can not continue to hold property rightfully belonging under Ptolemy rule. Therefore, I give back to Egypt, the island of Cyprus, the jewel of the Mediterranean." As Cleopatra translated the speech, the cheering grew. Smiling, she walked back to the palace and wouldn't have noticed Rome's Master of the Horse if Caesar hadn't stopped to speak to him. Marc Anthony had a powerful figure, and his gaze brought back for a moment the time seven years before when she had first seen him. Startled, she glanced away and hurried inside.

Pothinus, who had schemed to send inferior grain to Rome, waited in the throne room. During the night, Cleopatra had relayed his plans to Caesar and watched with satisfaction now as he ignored Pothinus and went to his desk. "I must sign these papers giving Cyprus back to the Egyptian people." He spoke matter-of-factly before turning to

Pothinus and saying, "Ah, yes, Ptolemy's man. You have my permission to leave," and immediately turned away.

The powerful eunuch blinked before backing away and leaving the room, a puzzled Ptolemy following.

Seeing the snub as further endorsement of herself, Cleopatra circled the table, conscious that the room glowed with color, with richness, and now with warmth. "I can't wait to see Cypress again."

Caesar turned to her, a serious expression on his face. "But I intend to give Cyprus to your sister and your youngest brother. Arsinoe needs appeasing, not you. Her soldiers still fight me. As for your little brother, no doubt he has people in the palace backing him. I can't take any chances." Sitting down, he waved to an aide who ran forward. "Get me a scribe. I have letters to dictate."

Cleopatra hesitated a moment only. "Arsinoe is not mature enough to rule Cyprus at this time. And Ptolemy XIV is too young."

"Arsinoe's only a year younger than you, but I'll see that she doesn't get to Cyprus for years." He glanced up briefly, an amused look in his eyes. "Never fear, I shall make everyone responsible to Queen Cleopatra VII. Now, leave me; I have work to do."

He had dismissed her like a palace servant! Now that her sacred self was bedding the Roman, she must make sure he didn't take her for granted. With Caesar nothing would be easy, but she had no alternative. Walking off, she kept her head high.

Chapter II

48 – 47 BCE

Two days later a letter came from Arsinoe. Reading it out loud, Cleopatra paced rapidly and mimicked Arsinoe's fury. "Thank you for playing with my future. I would have been content ruling Cyprus. As it is, you once again treated me as if I wasn't our father's daughter. I can no longer accept such treatment. My Lord, Pretares backs me, and a most noble senior officer, Achillas, volunteers his military leadership. Tell the Roman, Julius Caesar, we have him and you boxed in and will not be content until he is begging for mercy and you are begging to rule Cyprus in my name. Queen Arsinoe IV"

Cleopatra ran to where Caesar inspected the ebony double-sided Senet board, with the game Tjau on the reverse side, a game she'd promised to teach him. "Prophetic," she muttered pointing to the game, "Tjau means robbers and Arsinoe would rob me of my rightful heritage. She's always hated me."

Raising his eyebrows, he sat, the calf of one leg resting on the knee of the other. "How far will she carry that hate?"

How could he remain so calm? Even after they made love, he could within seconds deal with other issues. "She's always been jealous of me. She'll go as far as possible."

He pushed the game board away. "Her man Achillas is a good officer. I must plan an offensive." He called for maps and when aides came running with them, he spread them upon the floor and moved from one to the other as he explained strategies. As she stood wondering what role she should play in all this, he looked up, saw her and said, "Oh, you're still here." Miffed, she left.

At first he was with her in the palace much of each day. Mornings she watched him at his toilet, picking his teeth, scrubbing his face, arranging the strands of his hair, and every night she knew his embrace. She answered his probing questions truthfully and felt amazed and exceedingly young each time he tricked her in conversation. His knowledge was vast, and when she spoke authoritatively but in ignorance, he corrected her. "You're very intelligent and capable, but you have much to learn."

Her face flamed, and feeling diminished by his words, resolution hardened within her. She would show him. No one had so challenged her since her father died. She hovered at the edges of his policy meetings, observed as he berated, cajoled, and condemned those under him. He was tough and brilliant, and when she quivered from his caresses, she was sure of the future. But when he acted as if she were not there, when he shut down the warmth of his gaze, it going as cold as the top of Mt. Olympus, she felt apprehension. He dallied with her because she pleased him, but he didn't need her, she needed him.

As savage street fighting raged, she lived safe in the palace but unable to go beyond the surrounding gardens. Shouts and cries were interrupted by ominous silence, but no one intruded on the large complex of palace buildings and grounds. Every day Caesar left at dawn, returned at dusk. It was almost as if war wasn't raging.Evenings, after briefing his officers, he talked literature, philosophy, astronomy, and military tactics to her. He enjoyed explaining and brooked no inattention. But when she spewed back his words, giving them a twist of her own, he smiled and nodded. It was a signal to her to press on. Reminding him of Egypt's glorious past, she spoke of the Ptolemys three hundred year rule, and the pharaohs who had reigned for thousands. Listening carefully, Caesar watched her as a lover watches the woman he desires. She knew exactly when he would stop all talk. A silent lover, he said little until he was sated, always taking the lead. Once he said, "You please me," and she repeated the words to herself.

Still, days were filled with shoring up her faltering government; she had little time to worry. Each morning she met with her ministers; each afternoon she studied. As the heat of day became oppressive, she conferred with kitchen staff, having cooks prepare dishes to tempt Caesar's slightly finicky appetite. Afterward, she spent hours at her toilet. She had never looked better, a slight glow permeating her skin, and when she moved, she glided effortlessly, her movements a blend of youth and sexuality.

One day, several weeks into the war, from an upstairs corridor, she detected a mass movement of fighting men between the palace and the Pharos lighthouse. Flinging the shutters wide, she leaned on the windowsill to watch. Achillas, leading Arsinoe's troops, attempting to conquer the mole, the strip of land leading to the lighthouse, attacked overland. Whoever controlled the lighthouse controlled the harbor, and for the first time since her liaison with Caesar, she knew real fear. Until now he had seemed invincible, and she had viewed the battles as delaying tactics, Achillas a mouse flirting with danger. Now, she knew the battle could go either way. With the Romans controlling the harbor, she could leave at any time. Caesar could send for reinforcements, draw on the thousands and thousands of men ready to do his bidding. But without the harbor he would be trapped.

The sun shone, no breeze fluttered the Romans' banners, but occasional commands, clinging to summer heat waves, carried to her. She cocked her head the better to hear. Brisk words, angry words, frightening words battered her complacence. Although tiny in her sight, the soldiers moved, not like toys, but like men in battle.

Caesar's men were sealing off the spot where the mole joined the mainland, and she identified a standard bearer, heard a trumpeter, and recognized a centurion waving his cohorts into position. Achillas would be massacred if he stormed the barricade Caesar's men were erecting. They moved vast quantities of wood and stone and piled them higher than a man on horseback and reinforced the wall with stone catapults and swordsmen at the ready. She nodded in admiration, her heart pounding in time with the frantic activity.

For his army to cross the Rhine, Caesar had built a bridge in ten days and surmounted insurmountable obstacles. She had assumed he would hold back Arsinoe's men and send them running in terror, but the size of Achillas' army astonished her. Thousands of troops spread in a long line toward the Nile in one direction and to the mole in the other. With difficulty she located Caesar.

A thrill raced through her, much like when he returned to the palace each evening. He wore a helmet and armor over a short military tunic, but his legs were bare from the knee down, sandals laced over his calves. She motioned for Charmion to join her. When this was over she'd send for Iras, bring her home, too. "Look how he moves with such assurance, but I fear for him," she whispered squeezing Charmion's arm.

"He is a great man, My Lady."

"Yes, but…" Part of Achillas' army had rowed toward the lighthouse. Landing on the mole behind Caesar, they would soon bear down on him. A cry of warning escaping her lips, she watched with horror as Achillas' men roared down behind the Roman lines, Overrun, the Romans dashed for the warships docked nearby. Only Caesar, sword in hand, stood fighting, his blade flashing cutting his enemies into pieces. But slowly, he was forced back. Plunging into the water, he swam toward safety while a hail of stones and arrows churned the water around him and burning torches catapulted after him, sputtered. Suddenly, Caesar dove beneath the surface and came up far from land.

Cleopatra gripped Charmion's arm. "He's safe," she cried as two hundred yards from shore, his men pulled him unto a ship.

"The gods be praised," Charmion murmured.

As Cleopatra nodded, Ptolemy XII pushed between her and Charmion and pointed to the beach. "Your noble Caesar had to flee like an ordinary soldier, leaving his purple cloak behind. It will make a magnificent trophy for the enemy." He stuck his lower lip out. "Can't you see, sister, dear, we're done. All because of your desire to sleep with the Roman. I should have stayed with Arsinoe. I always liked her better anyway."

Frustration, fear, all the insults she'd taken through the years combined, and she slammed her hand against his cheek, the sound reverberating like the crack of a whip.

Putting his hand to his cheek, and looking at her with injured eyes, Ptolemy muttered, "Poor, frightened sister."

Gripping his arm, she forced him around. "Who has whom running?"

He followed her gaze. "Holy pharaoh, Caesar's ships have closed with Achillas' boat!" Ptolemy's voice rose in surprise. "The Romans are beating them back."

Cleopatra loosened her hold. Once again, Caesar had forged success from failure, routed a superior force, sent a vast Egyptian navy running, its ships in ruin. Achillas' forces, desiccated in hand-to-hand fighting, the Romans swarmed over the Egyptian vessels like cats devouring mice. "Caesar swam to victory in full armor. Do you think you could do that, brother, dear?" Her voice purred like temple cats after a sacrifice.

Ptolemy frowned. "What do you want me to say? I was wrong? I admit it." He banged his fist against the windowsill.

"At times I can almost like you." She patted his arm. "You're clever, if misguided."

Ptolemy rolled his eyes. "You liking me is a condition I doubt I could tolerate."

She laughed, and he grinned before he left. For a moment, he paused on the threshold as if wanting to say something more. She waited, squinting her eyes to better see the similarities with their father. He had Auletes' mouth, and there was something about his jaw.... But he said nothing more, and her good feelings about him subsided.

Hurrying, she rushed to ready herself for Caesar's return. Already the sun dipped into the Mediterranean, and from all around she heard soldiers returning. Usually she waited for Caesar, incense burning, fresh flowers in vases, lamps lit. Now, she ran down to the garden to greet him, ready to throw herself into his arms.

He shook his head. "I reek of the Harbor."

"I don't care." She moved closer, touched the rents in his tunic. "You were magnificent." She proclaimed the words, wanting the whole world to hear.

"I did what was necessary. Anthony's troops landing at the Lighthouse while Achillas was busy fighting me aboard ship deserve some praise."

"You are too modest." She took his arm.

He shook her off. "Have patience. The dirt of battle was not washed off in the water of the Harbor, and the blood of many men stains my hands. I must bathe."

"I see nothing but the blood of traitors. I shall make a wreath for your head, and wield the stirgil myself, scraping the dirt from your skin, My Most Noble Lord."

"You have elevated me. Yesterday it was only, My Lord." He raised an eyebrow at her as they walked together into the palace.

"After all, I am a queen." She wanted to dance, celebrate.

He smiled. "Does that then make me a king?"

Thoughtfully, she looked around at the carved and painted columns, the bright murals, the gold and malachite doors, the gilded furnishings and answered, "If I married a man, he would be king."

"But I am married." He lengthened his stride. "A point everyone understands. I doubt you are different."

"I know. " And of course she knew he wanted to bathe before touching her. But Roman law was one thing, Egyptian another, and under Egyptian law, a ruler had few restrictions.

"Anyway, you are married to Ptolemy." He lowered his voice. "Send him out to fight, not to lead at a distance, and you accomplish two things with one stroke. He might not survive arm-to-arm combat. As for a liaison with you, it profits us both. But speak no more of marriage."

She regarded Caesar for a moment, imagining time standing still as it seemed to do whenever she watched a sundial.

Bending down, but not touching her pale blue gown, he pressed his lips to hers. He tasted of wind and weather and, she suspected, of death. As he headed toward his bath, his stride quick and even, it was clear the fighting had exhilarated him.

That night Ptolemy, saying he'd not give her a chance to bully him anymore, left the palace to join Arsinoe and Achillas. At the same time, troops from Syria arrived to bolster Caesar's forces.

For months, warring factions clashed. Each day Caesar regained more of the city and surrounding territory, mowing down Achillas' troops like a scythe harvesting wheat. Dispatching Achillas himself, Caesar had lesser leaders beheaded or imprisoned and put Arsinoe under house arrest. The day the war ended, Ptolemy was seen running toward the Nile.

Cleopatra approached Caesar as he wrote in his journal and spoke slowly, carefully, not sure of the feelings that ripped through her even though the sun turned her city to gold. "Did Ptolemy get away?" All her life she had sought to mollify him by honoring her father's wishes and Egyptian tradition, and he'd abandoned her.

Caesar didn't look up. "Poor misguided soul, he ran to the Nile and into a boat so full of men, it sank. No one was saved."

My brother drowned in the Nile, Cleopatra thought moving away from the table. Stepping around a column that ended in a carved lotus on top, she trailed her hand against the granite. *People came and went, the palace remained.* Ptolemy had thrown his blessings away as if they were wheat sown to the wind.

Caesar glanced toward her. "There's talk that he has risen again, that he was seen near the shore where he fished as a child. Some say he is a god." He turned back to his writing.

Eyes wide, Cleopatra shook her head. Her father was a god, and she'd known since childhood she was the living incarnation of the goddess, Isis. Her brother was a mere mortal. She frowned, pushing her thoughts from hurt to anger and raised her voice so Caesar would have no doubts she was addressing him. "Divers must locate the body of this boy who fought against me, the Queen of Egypt." Fighting back regret and sorrow, snapping her fingers in time with her thoughts, her words rang. "A Ptolemy does not rot on the bottom of a river. And, furthermore, I want the person starting these *god* rumors punished for spreading such lies." She turned away, anger at herself exploding. Her father had expected her to take care of Ptolemy, watch out for him, and she had failed. "I shall have the Nile dredged until we locate his body."

The next day she went to the apartments of her remaining brother, twelve-year-old Ptolemy, XIV. Three months since she'd seen him, and in her present mood, she felt shame.

She found him sitting on the floor playing with a pet monkey. A tray of half-eaten food sat on one side of him, a mechanical pull toy in the shape of a cat sat on the other. A table held potsherds and writing supplies, and a tutor was spreading out a papyrus.

"Stand up, the Queen is here," the tutor hissed, his gaze going to the door, his rolls of fat jiggling.

The boy scrambled to his feet, stuffing the remainder of a piece of bread into his mouth. His tunic was stained, and crumbs remained on his mouth. "H, h, hello." He tried to pry the monkey loose.

"Help him," Cleopatra said to the tutor.

Breathing hard, the man took the monkey while her youngest brother stared at her slack-jawed.

"Do you understand the customs and rules of Egyptian ascension?" she asked, her voice gentle.

He brushed at his mouth. "I know that you are the Queen and my brother is dead."

"The first you must never forget." She eyed the pear-shaped eunuch tutor and gave him permission to leave.

Ptolemy XIV said, "Every day they tell me you're queen." He frowned. "I remember."

"Good." She picked up the mechanical cat, set it on a table. "Tell me, will you miss your brother?"

"No. He called me fatty."

"Then I tell you now that because he is dead, you will be my new husband and colleague. Do you know what that means?" She moved toward the large carved double doors.

"That I will be the king and share the throne."

"No!" She bit out the words, anxious to be away from this place that seemed cloying and dead, incense not covering up the smell of linen damp with urine. "It means your name will be linked with mine, but I will be Queen, and you will still be my little brother. Do you understand?"

"I think it means I will do as you say."

"Good. In some ways you sound wiser than your brother. He would fight me." She hurried to the door. "The ceremony will be held at sunset. Be sure you are clean and wear a fresh tunic." She hurried out. He was not as bright as his brother, who had proved a worthy opponent, but Ptolemy XIV was probably easier to handle.

Three days later Ptolemy XIII was lifted to the surface of the lake, water-weeds clinging to his still form.

"If it were my brother who betrayed me, I'd display his body for all to see," Caesar said. "Criers would tell of his treachery, singers would chant, and prisoners would fight to the death."

She snapped. "We don't have gladiatorial combat in Egypt." She may not have loved her brother, but he was a Ptolemy, couldn't Caesar understand that? "I will not allow his body to be stared at by anyone," she whispered. "But, his golden armor will be carried through the streets on a litter and exhibited in the city."

Caesar shrugged. "Politically, it's a wise decision, but are you being timid, my little Queen? You sting when you could bite."

She had dreamed of her father during the night. Egypt must not be lost in the Roman embrace. The sun was wielding its brightest rays, the sluggish breezes carrying sand and grit. She lowered her voice, moved closer to Caesar. "Come with me on the mother of waters and I will show you Egypt as few people know it." Where they worshipped her as a queen and goddess. Where she would prove she was more than an innocent girl.

He stretched out his legs and rubbed his fingers over his mouth. "It would be wisest not to tarry, but a week or so more might not matter." He sipped watered wine before nodding. "I have long had a desire to see the mother of waters. How many ships shall we take down your river?" He was smiling now, watching as the sun painted her palace and her with light.

"Oh, a large expedition. I must prove to all those who supported Arsinoe that I am the true Queen. Three, four hundred, and they should bristle with troops. And you and I will lead the way on my barge." Reaching up, she loosed her hair, until it fell from its restricting bands in a waterfall that tickled the side of his face as she leaned down. It would not be easy to persuade him he needed her always, but maybe the secret she would share on the trip would help.

Chapter III

47 BCE

THE MORNING THEY left Alexandria, brilliant sun burst over the horizon turning the feathery papyrus and reeds of the delta to gold so suddenly Cleopatra gasped. A soft gentle warmth began to touch the land, driving away the chill of the desert night. As the large fleet cast off, one after the other, wildfowl took to the sky with a great flapping of wings, defying the quiet of the night just past. A few shallow-water papyrus boats, floating among the reeds along shore, made way. Silently, except for the splash and dip of oars, the armada slipped into the Nile proper and began the voyage to Upper Egypt. They were early enough to withstand the summer heat, but not so late the river would flood. The cargo ships carried gifts of wine from the vineyards in the delta for village elders and temple priests, gold and jewels for subjects needing to be placated and to reward those who had never shifted their allegiance to Arsinoe.

On deck, Cleopatra watched the rowers fight against the current, Caesar beside her, he pointing out, "The mouth of the river is as wide as a good day's march."

So the mighty Roman could be impressed. In either direction, she counted Egyptian and Roman vessels, but the royal barge made of cedar and cypress and as long as ten ordinary ships, moved with regal beauty, rising high above the water. As she enumerated the barge's amenities, including sleeping chambers, Caesar rubbed a hand along the gold trimmed, cedar railing.

"It is well My Lord has simple tastes," she murmured and was pleased when he laughed.

As Alexandria disappeared and the banks of the river became visible on both sides, she spoke about Ramses place in Egyptian history. Caesar listened respectfully and asked the right questions. His position as ruler, general, conqueror, and politician gave him an arrogance she understood, but sometimes he acted as if Egypt and Egyptians were beneath Roman attention, and at those times her antipathy for things Roman surfaced. But now he was a sponge, soaking up the knowledge she fed him as lush banks slid by, vegetable gardens crowding the lowlands, vineyards climbing the slopes, balsam trees bending gracefully.

At midmorning, three pyramids dominated the horizon, rising like huge creamy-white jewels against the cobalt of the sky. Caesar shook his head in amazement.

Pleased to impress him, she ordered the sails unfurled, and as they caught the North wind and swelled, she watched proudly as her ships' speed increased. "I have something special to show you."

"I look forward to it." Caesar unfolded his famous gold stool and sat, a subtle change in his expression taking hold as the fleet glided by the limestone quarried for the pyramids.

In late afternoon the ships tied up for the night. "The sandbars make night travel dangerous," she explained as servants rushed around setting a table on the poop deck. She and Caesar toasted one another with Egyptian beer until a serving girl carried in a roasted duck, boiled onions, raw radishes, and freshly baked bread, the bread bought from a village nearby and served on snowy linen.

As the sun made its precipitous dip into the west, a bed was prepared on deck. A cool breeze stirred the banners waving from the ships, and high above a glitter of stars Marked the sky as Cleopatra settled against pads and blankets. "The ancients believed the dead walked the sky on paths of beauty until the sun god, Re, rose again," she whispered until Caesar's snoring said he was already sleeping.

In the morning after Caesar's personal barber shaved him, the barge glided past temples and small villages, as well as ancient palaces where present day Egyptians, exploring or sight-seeing, were seen climbing over crumbling walls. He asked abruptly, "How much farther? My men want to go home."

"Soon," she promised as the sun climbed rapidly, morning shadows long. "It will be worth your wait. I promise." She sent runners ahead. The townspeople of Beni Hassam had to be properly prepared and Caesar placated.

Six days south of Memphis, the royal standard snapping smartly in the breeze, the large settlement showing ahead, Caesar smiled as his men called out to the women on shore.

The town grew up along the river's east bank, but the line of ships dropping anchor, extended far beyond the city. People poured from spacious villas and small country homes to see. Priests hurried from temples, artisans stepped from shops, and farmers came in from the fields. Women with flower wreaths, men playing music, dancers swaying to the rhythms, all ran to the docks with words of praise for the Queen. Sacrificial goats bleated, and chickens and ducks set up a racket competing with the music. Caesar's men, lining the railings, smiled and gestured to the Egyptians below.

Out of sight, Cleopatra prepared, and with the double crown of Egypt on her head, she stood where she could be seen, scarab rings and serpent bracelets flashing in a shimmer of sunlight. From her head to her gem-encrusted slippers she was Egypt's Pharaoh. Catching sight of her, the people of the city fell to their knees.

The breeze had stopped, the sun licking brutally at the sandy shore. Leaving the barge, Cleopatra motioned Caesar to join her. "Come with me, I want them to see Rome is Egypt's friend" *that we are one.* Caesar must see her as a god as well as a queen.

"Make way for her Serene Royal Majesty, Queen Cleopatra VII, the Goddess Isis, ruler and deliverer of the people of the city, Pharaoh of upper and lower Egypt, beloved and beneficent Lady Devine, " shouted the chamberlain.

"May sweet Hathor bless your most gracious and divine majesty and spread her smiles upon you," cried a woman, kissing the hem of Cleopatra's gown. It was an omen. The goddess Hathor, had smiled upon her.

When the flotilla was on its way again, sailors and legionaries sated after a night carousing through the city, she looked ahead. During the ceremonies on shore, Caesar had recognized her hold upon the people. She gestured. "I am their living incarnation of the past. In the cliff behind the city ancient tombs are their everyday link. The gods reward those who reward the gods."

The next day the cliffs fell back revealing a fertile strip of land running inland, and she explained the people raised emmer wheat like they had in ancient days. He appeared impressed by the broad fields and his men, excited by the sight of more riches and villages where women offered favors, joked and teased.

Later, where the cliffs formed a sheer wall down into the water, the oars were manned. From countless holes in the rocks where they nested, birds emerged, darkening the sky, and screaming in indignation as the ships passed. Wind gusts swooped down from the cliffs and whirled the flotilla toward sandbars in the frothy water. At a shouted command, the oarsmen dug in, and the boats swung away from the cliffs and kept from being grounded. All day they fought the narrows. Spray wet Cleopatra's face and, dampened her hair, but she wouldn't go below. The crew needed to see her standing near the prow, urging them on.

The next day date palms, sycamore, and pomegranate alternated with fields of flax and wheat. The armada passed boats going in both directions, some seaworthy as the Roman vessels, coming from as far away as Syria. The sailors and soldiers called back and forth, and emissaries sent Cleopatra messages, and an envoy pleaded for an audience. Wearing her crown, holding the flail and crook, she saw him with Caesar watching and impressed both.

But as the ships went almost due east for over a day before turning back around a great bend, Roman grumbles came once more. She told Caesar. "You must see Dendera. Humor me in this, please. Going home the current will carry us rapidly. The temple was built during the 18th Dynasty. My father expanded it, and I plan to add to it." She paused as he shrugged as if to say, so what. Lifting her head high, she stared at him with a stubborn gaze. "Even if you turn back, I will go on to Dendera, Roman."

"Roman, is it?" He shook his head. "You have courage, little one. Caesar decides where we go, not his men or you. But if Dendera means that much to you, I will humor you, but take heed, I am not usually this patient." His expression hard, he turned away and at Dendera he hurried toward the brightly painted temple.

She hurried to catch up, his soldiers and her attendants flanking them. "Even though you make light of Egyptian gods, Julius Caesar, surely you realize why we build on sites already sanctified by shrines when the first Ptolemy arrived."

"So stopping here is a political move on your part?"

She shook her head. "No, it's private and concerns the goddess Hathor who has little appeal to warriors. But this shrine should concern you." When he didn't answer she felt a foreboding and put her hand to her chest. "I believe you Romans call Isis Aphrodite. But Hathor is only Hathor, and of special importance to women. Look!" She pointed to a great, square, cobalt blue and gold building ahead. Sparkling in the desert sun, six giant columns rose above a wall, and at the top of each column Hathor's exquisitely benign face looked out, peaceful and loving.

Caesar's scowl slowly eroded. "She is indeed beautiful and her serenity is apparent."

Through the pylons she led him to the outer courtyard where giant double columns, wider than a man's height and higher than ten men, and as big around as a dozen men, formed a path. Every inch of the pedestals and columns, colored in contrasting shades, were carved with reliefs and hieroglyphics.

Caesar cut a glance her way. "Can you read this?"

"I learned all the ways of writing and speaking Egyptian so I could communicate with the people as well as the leaders." The rhythmic sound of ceremonial chants carried from inside the temple, and away from it, across wide patches of sand she glimpsed the sacred lake shaded by palm trees creating an oasis for the other buildings. "Come, around to the back. Hear that? The priests sing a hymn of praise before removing Hathor's robe and crown. They dress her each morning, let her rest each night." She took Caesar's hand. "I have something special to show you. Whatever reason you came with me, this is the reason for my trip up the Nile." She paused, her gaze direct. "Tell your men to wait."

He scowled but did as she directed. She hurried him around to the south wall of the temple. A feathering of palm trees showed a short walk from the building, and beyond them bare sandy land with occasional scrubby trees dominated, and then nothing showed but the awesome desert, hot, unrelieved, undulating.

"What is it?" Caesar demanded, looking back as if he were thinking of the trip to Alexandria.

"Here." She stepped closer to the temple, touching a wall that had few hieroglyphics.

A quizzical expression on his face, he didn't mask his impatience.

"I have instructed the engravers to carve a relief of me at this spot." She ran her hand along the stone. "It will rise five, six times higher than my head, much higher even than yours, and you are tall, My Lord. And here," she touched the wall again, "a cartouche shall spell my name."

He nodded curtly. "To immortalize yourself is wise. I have statues of myself in many places. But why tell me? Such things are routine." He shrugged and looked away again. "Get on with it."

She cut him off with a wave of the hand, not with a look of annoyance but as if she vibrated with some inner knowledge she must share with him. "And here." She touched the pale blue wall several steps down the walkway. "Here they shall carve the figure of my son." Her hand caressed the stone. "And his name shall reign here for all time and eternity."

Caesar tilted his head to the side. "Did I hear you right?" His low-voiced question was as urgent as his penetrating gaze.

"My Lord, I cannot be responsible for your hearing." She smiled and moved along the perimeter of the building, "And here will be a parade of gods coming to revere this newest star in the firmament." She turned back toward Caesar and stated words she had agonized over in the night. "Everyone will worship our son."

Although his brows were knit, his eyes shone as if lit from inside. "Are you saying you are with child? You are carrying my child?"

She said proudly, "Not child, My Lord, a son."

"My god, can it be so?" He gripped her shoulders.

"Yes," she cried, "It can. I will give you a son, Julius Caesar. Egypt and Cleopatra will give you what no one else has given. We will give you a son, My Lord."

"My God, if only that could be. You're sure?"

"That your seed has taken root in me? Yes, oh, yes. I am with child, and he will be as strong and as wise as his father."

Caesar shook his head and looked out over the land. "These many nights we have lain together. Are you saying my son will spring from your loins?" He glanced at her narrow hips and then smiling paced up and down, half talking to himself, "A son to counsel, to teach, to wield the sword." He turned back to her. "My god, woman, don't play with me."

She lifted her head, and for a time it was as if she were looking down on him from a great height. "Here at Dendera the god Horus was born, Isis's son by Osiris. Here today stands Caesar, the mighty, and here today stands Cleopatra VII, Isis who gives you, not a hollow reed, but a son, a son to carry on for us both."

He nodded slowly. "I longed for a son ever since I was old enough to scatter seed."

"My Lord, it has been ordained. Before you, there were no others. Caesar plowed a fallow field, but the gods smiled, the sun has shone, and the rivers ran full. The crops will burst from the ground for Egypt is fertile again. Her goddess *will* bear a son."

Solemn eyed, he slowly smiled. "Yes, I believe it is so." He put his arms around her and held her tenderly, and as the priests intoned the hymns of evening, he touched her face and said, "I must hurry to Rome, my little one, before word gets there before me."

All the next day Cleopatra stayed beneath a canopy as two Nubian boys wielding large feather fans, stirred the air. The obelisks and pylons of Thebes showed red in the sunset. Banners fluttered in the breeze, and behind the temples of Ramses, Amenhotep III, and Queen Hatshepsut, weathered cliffs rose.

Her mind going twice as fast as the fans, she told Caesar about the cliffs and gullies beyond the river, about donkey caravans traversing the small canyons. "The size of the kingdom our son will inherit is vast," she stated, leaning forward companionably and smiling. "From Rome to here and beyond."

Caesar's mouth became a grim line. "Romans marry Romans. That's how it is. That's the law." He turned aside. "This cursed desert is like an oven. My men think only of Rome. They need to collect their pay, see their families. Some have been gone for years. We will return to Alexandria with no more delay."

He had seen the riches of Egypt, witnessed the power that was hers, a power her son would inherit. But was it enough? She pushed down panic.

Chapter IV

47 BCE

Her thoughts stung like wind-blown sand. From Thebes to Alexandria, Caesar's talk had none of the give and take, getting-to-know-you repartee Cleopatra had enjoyed with him. Egypt's laws were one thing, Rome's another, and she doubted Caesar would circumvent them. Unless he acknowledged his paternity, made some provision for him, her child would be a nothing in Rome.

Her barge, nudging the bustling dock at Alexandria, brought her back to the present. Slaves, hardly distinguishable from free men, rushed to secure the royal ship. A small contingent of Roman soldiers stood among them, Marc Anthony a few steps ahead of the troops. She viewed him with an objectivity that would have surprised her a few years before.

She'd been fourteen the year Anthony was billeted in Alexandria. Fresh from spying upon slaves pleasuring one another in the palace kitchen garden, hot blood surging through her, she'd gone riding, pushing her favorite mount to a gallop. Returning to the royal stables, her hair whipping behind her, she sizzled with unknown desires. Slipping off the stallion, erotic scenes played in her mind. She'd stared open-mouthed at Anthony. His skin, muscles and bones rippled in such perfect alignment, she couldn't look away but watched him dismount and rub down his horse. It was as if the gods had interceded, and a thought coursing through her like the Nile in flood, she'd wondered: what would it be like to have him touch her?

As if feeling her perusal, he had turned to face her. His eyes awash with curiosity and interest, he'd looked her over as if she were a common woman until Charmion commanded a slave, "Here worthless one, take care of the Princess's horse." Instantly, Anthony had adopted a look of respect and turned away.

But the look in his eyes had stuck in her mind like honey, and for weeks she sought ways to see him without anyone knowing. But except at a distance she seldom did. Finally, she heard he was called back to Rome. Now, she viewed his attractions through the experience of a woman, and he was only the Master of the Horse, second in command to Caesar.

Leaning against the rail, Caesar, called. "Your face is long, Marc Anthony, what message do you bring?"

Anthony moved closer to the barge. "A message that can wait until you are on firm ground, Sir."

Caesar hurried down the gangplank.

Cleopatra watched the two men clasp forearms and regard one another, Caesar her lover, Anthony a man in his prime.

Caesar's voice carried. "It is good to see you again, my right hand. Tell me the truth of the world for I tire of perfume and pampering. A float trip puts little metal in a soldier's arsenal." He laughed, his mouth stretched wide, only the etched lines in his brow remaining.

Perfume and pampering! She wanted to lash out, but Anthony's voice carried as easily as Caesar's. "King Pharnaces of Pontus defies us. As if we didn't have men billeted in his land!"

Caesar shrugged. "Pharnaces' jabs are like the sting of a gnat, bothersome but easily disposed of. What else?" His words were light, and he never looked back as the two men walked off, talking earnestly, Caesar's voice holding a hint of weariness.

Fighting a hollow spot in her chest, her face flaming with anger, Cleopatra rode back through the city with only Iras and her personal retinue with her.

Days later, she woke to the quiet of the city, only birds singing, the splash of water against the shore, the subdued sounds of the harbor. No clank of armor, no marching feet, no Roman soldiers, no Caesar. He and his men were gone, and she knew an ineffable sadness and drew into her lungs the cooling tang of the sea.

Throwing herself from bed, she hurried through her toilet, and calling for Nicodemus, ordered a magnificent building erected in Julius

Caesar's honor. A huge edifice on the waterfront, it would be the first thing he saw when he returned for she had no doubt he would, if only to plunder Egypt's riches. The building would meld Greek and Egyptian architecture, a symbol of their liaison and proclaim to the world that Cleopatra and Caesar were one. Undoubtedly word of the babe growing inside her had already spread. "Have you heard," she asked Charmion, "does my sister speak of my child?" Arsinoe could not help but be envious.

"My Lady, I thought you knew. The Romans took Arsinoe with them."

Cleopatra's hand shook. It was one thing to put Arsinoe under house arrest, one thing to joust with her for domination of Egypt, but for Caesar to parade any Ptolemy in Rome would be tantamount to parading her. Yet, for the good of Egypt, she must ignore this royal insult, and figure how best to please Caesar.

Summer had descended when the child came tearing at her body and, she bit her lips to keep back cries of pain. Near the Solstice, as Caesar roared through Asia Minor, the baby was born. When her attendants held up the red and wrinkled future ruler, she named him Ptolemy Caesar as a reminder of his importance, and called him Caesarion as a reminder of his heritage. She felt fiercely protective, the depth of her love surprising her. Hearty and well-favored, the baby brought her pride, and that night, in his honor she freed one hundred political prisoners and ordered sacrifices to the gods.

She sent Caesar an announcement. "A son and heir was born this day to Julius Caesar and Queen Cleopatra VII. Of lusty mien and intelligent eye, he awaits his father."

But no word came from Caesar.

She sent another announcement, this one to Tarentum. But when the messenger arrived at the seaside city, Caesar had already left to put down trouble in one of Rome's provinces in Africa.

Later in the summer, a trio of her couriers arrived back in Alexandria. From their travel-stained clothes, it was evident they had hurried. The two younger men seemed eager to speak, as if wanting to get it over with and rush off. The eldest leaned on a staff, his eyes downcast. Knowing that her every move would be reported to Caesar by some spy in her royal court, she played one man off against the others, questioned and re-questioned and listened carefully as all three eventually told things they'd normally not repeat. The mighty Caesar spent most of his time with Queen Eunoe, wife of King Bogud of Mauretania.

She wasn't surprised. Caesar hadn't hesitated bedding her no matter he had a young and attractive wife in Rome. Still the thought of him cavorting with another woman while she brought forth his son hurt. She gazed over the heads of the couriers to the open window where her ships sat in the harbor. She had entered into a dangerous game, her country and crown for her love shield. But now she had a son, and the stakes were higher, her own feelings and frustrations of minor importance in a wager she could not lose. Court gossip said Queen Eunoe had grace and beauty. Although her heart beat furiously, she spoke dispassionately. "I understand she is pleasing in voice and manner." She spoke in a throw-away fashion, her voice sweet as a vine-ripened berry, its taste still on the tongue.

Immediately all three spoke at once. The Queen of Egypt's voice made the Queen of Mauretania's sound like a screeching owl, a howling monkey.

"I also heard she is with child."

"No, Your Divine Majesty, that she is not."

Neither was his wife. Feeling an immense relief, she poured gold coins into their hands, coins showing her suckling a child in the manner of Isis with Horus. "Give Julius Caesar one of the coins and keep the rest yourselves. Now, go."

Within weeks they returned with word from Caesar, a scroll placed within a sealed box carved with Caesar's initials. She waited until she was alone before she unrolled the papyrus and read: "Ptolemy Caesar, I send this message in care of your mother, the esteemed and noble queen of Egypt. I salute you, and thank the gods you are well and fit. Julius Caesar."

Shaking, Cleopatra put the letter down and paced the room. Not a word acknowledging that the child was his! No special word for her! As if she had not spent months with him in passion and tenderness, day and night, talking philosophy, literature, art, politics, and war. And acting as if the personal liaison would go on forever!

During the time when her belly had been big and she clumsy, she had thought of one thing: her son ruling the world. The child was Caesar's heir, and in some way she'd get him to acknowledge the relationship. He had called her an esteemed and noble queen.

No, she'd never let Caesar know her anxiety; She'd ignore his dalliance with Eunoe and other women. She'd be polite but distant to his wife, and by the very force of her own personality she'd insure her own position. Caesar ruled Rome. His word, his nod, his desires made things happen, but only a son could take his name into the future.

Formalizing diplomatic appointments in writing, she sought a new treaty similar to the one her father had made years earlier and with her brother and son set sail for Rome.

46 BCE

She arrived at the docks in Ostia, the seaport near Rome, with her fleet outnumbering all the others in the harbor. Her flagship, a fast cutter, escorted large cargo-carriers loaded with wheat. Oared vessels, ordinarily used for war, were filled with gold, precious jewels and costly cinnamon, tokens of Egypt's affection for Rome. Caesar might have power, but she had wealth.

Looking past the jostling crowd of roustabouts, slaves, freemen, dock tenders, traders, sailors, and a sprinkling of aristocrats overseeing bills of lading for cargo arriving from Africa and the world, she searched for Caesar. He was nowhere in sight. Neither did she hear his attendants shouting at the riff-raff to make way for his litter. Only the cacophony of many languages blended in a hum she couldn't shut out as the familiar fishy smells of the piers rose.

She fought back disappointment as Marc Anthony, leading a diplomatic contingent to escort her to Rome, many wearing togas bearing the stripe of a senator, strode into view. Some of the men she had received in Alexandria, others had helped elevate Caesar to his position. But it was Anthony, striding like a man pleased with himself and his place in the world she watched with dispassionate interest. Since Caesarion's birth, she thought only of Caesar.

Anthony stood in front of the welcoming contingent. "Divine one, pharaoh of Egypt, Isis Incarnate, Julius Caesar would return the gracious hospitality your majesty showed Rome and bade me accompany you into the city." He bowed, his eyes downcast.

Amused by his show—raw strength seemed to press against the restraints of his uniform——she raised her chin to give the allusion of looking down at him. "And My Lord Caesar?"

"He is busy making plans to celebrate his triumphant return to Rome from battle against four enemy states, but he puts one of his domiciles at your disposal, Your Majesty."

Great Pharaoh, she should have delayed her trip; Egypt was one of the vanquished countries. Careful not to let her feelings show, she acknowledged the dignitaries with Anthony and surveyed the outriders, criers, bearers, priests, and soldiers beating back the crowd. At least she had been accorded the welcome of a head of state. Caesar's own palanquin waited for her to enter, it's gold and mahogany trimmed poles resting on the shoulders of slaves named after generals he had defeated.

As the sun began to slide beneath the sky, she passed through the congested streets of Rome, the common people, from shoe-makers to barbers, stopping work to gawk. Her turbaned eunuchs from Parthia, the black men from Nubia, the bejeweled women of her court, stared back as the city unfolded.

New houses, many of fine brick, and graceful public buildings of marble and granite with windows of alabaster, had been built since she'd visited as a child. But mostly the parade of litters wound past bakeries where donkeys trod in circles grinding wheat, where wine shops and food bars proliferated, where mosaic made attractive stone counters. The squares, where teachers and pupils gathered early in the day for schooling, held statues to the gods, to the ancients, to Caesar.

It was impossible to avoid narrow streets where apartment houses went seven stories high, and people leaned on windowsills and gawked. Staring from doorways, some called words that made passersby laugh, others called her Caesar's Egyptian whore. A bucket of slops, dumped from an upper story, barely missed her. Not bothering to hide her disgust, she said, "So this is mighty Rome."

Alexandria's sewers were citywide; Rome had open cesspits at the end of a block. Only the rich had running water. Alexandria's superiority didn't need stressing, and she was relieved when the bearers left the common sections of the city behind. Soon, the ride grew smoother as the bearers trotted along paved boulevards and up and down hills where handsome villas sprawled.

Finally, her litter stopped near the southeastern corner of the Janiculum Hill at the entrance to the estate Caesar put at her disposal. With a spurt of joy, she saw Caesar's personal guards and knew he had to be within the mansion.

Taking Caesarion from his nurse, she walked slowly and regally to the broad front door, glad that the day was fair, her hair in place, her face paint emphasizing her splendid eyes. Her gown swished around her legs, soft as the down on a duck's breast, her jewels flashed as brightly as its forest-green tail feathers, and soon her jewel-trimmed sandals touched the stones of the entry. Inside, Julius Caesar was advancing toward her, away from servants and slaves who hovered silently in the background.

"My Lord," she said, back straight, lips in a pleasant smile, eyes sparkling with only a hint of flirtation. She held out the pillow upon which two-month-old Caesarion slept. "I predicted our child would be a son, and gentle Isis concurred." Her voice was clear and musical, royal as she.

Caesar stepped closer, his stride firm, his body relaxed yet full of unleashed power. "The gift of foresight is never to be taken lightly." He glanced over the vast retinue trailing her, but his voice softened when he looked back at her. "My little Egyptian Queen, I trust you had a good trip."

She inclined her head slightly. "It was no better or worse than any other sea voyage."

Ptolemy XIV shook his head, and pushing to the front, whined, "How anyone wants to cross the waters is beyond me. We were tossed about until I couldn't hold anything on my stomach. And then that wretched trip from Ostia." His face was rounder than ever, his body slack, rolls of fat showing at his waist.

As always, she had almost forgotten him. "You remember my brother, the new king?"

"How could I forget?" Caesar smiled politely at the boy. "Your rooms are ready, Ptolemy. No doubt you would like to rest after your long journey and the trip from the port of Ostia."

"Actually, I would like a bite to eat. Do you have figs or dates, something familiar? As we came through the city I bought some local bread, but it was too heavy for my liking."

"I am sure we can find something." Caesar snapped his fingers and slaves rushed forward to confer with Cleopatra's major-domo. Soon Iras led slaves, servants and Ptolemy toward upstairs quarters, stairs beginning at the end of the hall.

When they were out of sight, Cleopatra held out the pillow again. In Rome, if a man turned away from his child, did not accept him, the baby could be put out to die. If Caesar didn't acknowledge Caesarion, her hopes for solidifying Egypt's place in the world would plummet. Although Egyptian children weren't abandoned on dung heaps, set out like garbage, her dreams of empire for her son would vanish.

Caesar cocked his head and regarded the baby. "He has all his parts?"

A note of defiance invaded her voice. "Do you need to ask?"

Caesar's mouth curved into a smile.

Hers became warmer than sun at the summit of its daily travels. Up close the lines delineating Caesar's mouth had deepened, but nothing else showed the passage of age for his gaze was piercing, his figure as trim as ever. "Look closely, mighty Caesar. Is he not beyond compare?" Her heart beating like drums in her ears, she turned back the blanket swaddling Caesarion, exposing Caesar's sturdy, handsome child.

Caesar put out a finger, and immediately Caesarion wrapped his own around it.

Shaking his head as if overcome, he said softly. "So at last."

Cleopatra strained to hear.

With great solemnity he took the pillow with his son from her.

She had gambled and won! Tears stung her eyes. Overcome with emotion, she cried, "Thanks be to Osiris and Isis."

"And to all that is holy for he is most favorable," Caesar muttered, cradling the child in his arms, his hands trembling as he gently touched the baby's face.

Murmuring words she could not distinguish, Caesar's gaze stayed on the child. Shaking his head, a look of wonder and awe in his eyes, his face turned pale so swiftly Cleopatra heard herself crying out, "My Lord, are you all right?"

He said, his voice rich but fraught with emotion, "Yes, of course." He shrugged slightly as if to denigrate his own reactions. "Julius Caesar walked this earth for more than half a century, and now, having conquered the world and tasted its riches he's over-whelmed by a child." Shaking his head, he smiled. "The gods, indeed, be praised."

As he looked toward her, Cleopatra felt a deep contentment. But then his eyes glazed over and became distant, and she realized, he didn't see her at all. His body grew rigid and his hands loosened their hold upon Caesarion. Pillow and baby slipped from his grasp.

Moving swiftly, Cleopatra grabbed Caesarion before he landed on the floor like his father who slammed down like a dead weight against the ceramic tiles, his eyes rolling back. Only the white showed as a line of spittle appeared on his lips.

"It is the falling sickness," Charmion whispered.

Cleopatra had never witnessed it before. She felt her stomach lurch, felt it like a message from an angry god. "Do something," she cried, hugging Caesarion close in her arms, her gaze on Charmion who was pulling her back from the man who thrashed on the floor. When she glanced over her shoulder his people were securing his head, holding him still. Sweat poured from his body.

She turned away again. Was this the mighty Caesar? When she glanced back, color was returning to his face and recognition to his eyes. Servants were sponging him with cold water, wrapping him in a fresh robe.

Reviving completely, he growled, "Leave me," to those holding him. Getting up, brushing at his clean tunic, he scowled at Cleopatra. "Now you have seen." His voice was harsh.

Intuiting immediately that his anger was at himself, not her, she cried, "Out," to the clutch of Egyptians still lingering in the hall. As they backed off, Charmion took charge and they were soon scrambling out of sight.

Caesar stabbed Cleopatra with a look. "Does it frighten you, these spells that come over me?" He wiped his face with a linen square, his imperious manner in place again.

She whispered, "Some say a demon possesses you."

"Nonsense. The sickness is brought on by excitement." He shook his head. "Only in combat am I safe from it."

"My coming here with Caesarion bothers you?"

"I am bothered by the future of a boy who is only part Roman." His piercing eyes stabbed her.

Comparing his spells to a future for Caesarion, Caesar's falling-down-sickness was not the issue. She lifted her head high. "Ptolemy is an honorable and great name. The onus clings to those who suggest otherwise." She spoke with some aspersion.

"By Jupiter, do you think I would chose this path for my son?" Speaking hoarsely, he grabbed her by the arm and pulled her down the hall decorated with glowing murals in teal and green.

"Do you not want people to hear you admit he is yours?" she hissed, his servants lingering nearby.

"I admit nothing." He shook his head, pausing to regard her silently before asking, "Why are you arguing with me? Surely you heard of these spells. I'm sorry you had to witness one. Now come, put the babe to rest."

She faced him squarely, saw the Caesar she remembered: tall, his eyes proud, his back straight, a clean linen square in his hands, the soiled one tossed to a servant, his sweat-stained toga out of sight. "At this stage Caesarion sleeps and eats, but I grant you it won't be long until he's talking and walking." The words came easier than the thoughts in her mind. What if Caesarion, too, had the falling sickness? Was it a message from the gods?

"I expect nothing less than the best from him." Caesar paused in front of a door, and looking directly at her, smiled before saying, "Cleopatra, you brought me joy."

"More joy than problems, My Lord?"

For answer he opened the door behind him and beckoned to the half dozen women who waited in the room. "These nurses will take care of the young master."

She glimpsed a child's room with a profusion of toys upon the tables, chests decorated with impish figures, walls painted with maps of the world. Remembering her lonely childhood, knowing the intrigues of Rome, she shook her head. "My child shall be with me at all times."

A flicker of admiration shone in Caesar's eyes. "Very well." He issued orders and ushered Cleopatra to a vast bedroom.

As servants made a bed for the baby, draping and swathing it with finest linens, she noted, "The mural with the maps showed Egypt as but a small part of the whole world. A mistake, no doubt?"

Caesar chuckled, "Now I remember why you intrigued me."

"I want my son to grow up with no misconceptions." She glided noiselessly around the room, jiggling a fretting Caesarion up and down as she inspected carved wooden chests and a bed with feet of ivory, the woodwork inlaid with tortoise shell and gold. Through a window a small garden beckoned, its flowers flaunting their final full blooming before the fall equinox.

She put Caesarion down. He cried, and a nurse rushed to offer him a bit of cloth soaked in honey. Soon, he was sucking contentedly.

"In truth I have missed you," Caesar said as the baby quieted, and the nurses departed. He faced Cleopatra across the sleeping form of their son. "Come here."

She put seduction into her walk. "A moment, My Lord," she said as his hands ran with familiarity over her body when she reached him. This time she would employ the sponge of Egyptian coupling. Another child would make competition for Caesarion, and until his future was secure, she would do what she could to insure she would have no other children.

* * *

Dark had entered the room when Caesar rose from bed. Stretching like a temple cat, she smiled into the night. Caesar had wielded his love stick like a fiery youth, and she glowed from his attentions. Once more he had recited poetry, and she wanted to laugh at the ease with which she had brought him back to her. Or had she? He was dressing, making sure his hair, so sparse, covered his scalp, doing all the things that made her realize he was going out.

Few Romans visited during the dark of night when runners bearing torches had to precede them, when guards ready to fight if necessary had to accompany them. Bearers and litters had to compete with wagons rumbling into the city with goods and foodstuffs. Only the richest residents, men like Caesar, hired night watchmen. She asked, "You have an appointment at this hour?"

Astonishment stamped Caesar's face. "Appointment? I merely return home."

To Calpurnia. Showing her naiveté angered her more than the look on his face. She felt grateful when Caesarion whimpered. Padding barefoot across the tiles, she gathered him up and held him against her shoulder. "I was thinking of our son."

Caesar began to pace the room, walking with the measured beat of a soldier, pausing long enough to say when near her. "Don't do this to us." His voice held no soft corners. "You forget, Madam, that I am not a boy who has lain with a Queen, but the ruler of Rome, nay all of Italy and its provinces. I have conquered lands and peoples, taken them from the hands of tyrants, lifted uncivilized tribes to positions of consequence, and you think I do not think of this child?" He scowled at her and taking Caesarion from her continued pacing.

She waited a beat and then countered, "If you refer to Roman law, I thought Caesar was the law. Surely you can change what doesn't please you, insure your son's inheritance."

"This is not a royal house, but a republic, Madam. Remember that." He kicked a table hard enough to make an oil lamp jiggle.

She strode to him, her arms outstretched, her voice ringing with the richness of the passion just shared on the bed near the window. "I have no doubt, My Lord, you will succeed at whatever you do. Now, kiss your son, and remember we await you. If I have sounded upset, it is the lateness of the hour and my concern for the child that betrays my happiness at being with you again."

His eyes narrowed. "You have a way about you, my little Queen." He handed her their no longer whimpering son.

"I have learned from the most noble man in Rome."

He nodded. "In the next two weeks Rome will celebrate my four triumphs. The Queen of Egypt must do as she pleases, but Caesar will take the applause of his countrymen. Tomorrow my centurions will march, and it will begin a parade of pageants." He put his hand on her face. "Take care, little one. You are so impetuous and unpredictable I know not what you will do." He shook his head and smiled ruefully. "But your Ptolemy impetuousness makes life interesting." He hurried to the door. "I will be back when I can."

"If I am not here, I am sure someone will tell you where to find me." She spoke lightly and was relieved when he laughed.

Sitting down on the bed, she suckled her babe, the warmth of the moment shutting out her anger that Egypt would in some way be held up to ridicule in the very celebrations that would add blossoms to Caesar's laurel wreath.

The next day the sound of a group of Caesar's military men marching through the city, voices lifted, drew her to the front gate, Caesarion clasped in her arms.

Wearing helmets, laced boots, and mail shirts, the soldiers shouted gleefully, and she prepared to go inside when their words arrested her. "Put away your wives, you men of Rome. We bring the baldhead lecher home." All soldiers had their ribald ditties. But suddenly, she heard, "The Egyptian Queen took him on her barge, and with a babe thinks she's in charge."

Hurrying to her rooms, she almost collided with a slave scattering sawdust over the floor. Another wielding a broom fell to her knees, others, dashing sponges against pillars and cornices, hastily lowered their heads, but she knew they had heard.

All day and the next night, she stayed in the villa, visiting with Charmion, playing games with Iras, anything to take her mind from what Caesar and the Roman people were doing.

She received a note from a woman saying,

"My esteemed friend, Julius Caesar, tells me you are in the city. I am entertaining a few friends and family members and would deem it an especial honor if the Divine Ruler of Egypt would grace my villa. My son, Brutus and his wife, Porcia, his friend Cassius, my half brother Cato, and his friend, Cicero will be with me. No doubt you remember some of them from your earlier visit to Rome when you were a child. Cato recalls you met him in Rhodes. They all look forward to seeing you again, and I to making your acquaintance. My dear friend Caesar does not wish you to spend these days alone." Your Roman friend, Servilia

Cleopatra directed Charmion to start a discrete investigation to find out if the message was authentic. If Servilia really existed, who was she?

That night Charmion reported Servilia, now a respected matron, had once been a great beauty Caesar almost married. But she had been married twice before, and at forty would probably not bear a son. He had wed eighteen-year-old Calpurnia instead. Even though Servilia's son, Brutus fought against Caesar at Pharsalus, because of his great affection for Servilia, Caesar forgave him. No word of gossip touched her, and she indeed knew and was friends or kin of the people listed in her note.

Cleopatra had no desire to see Cato again, and she was sure Cicero, who had snubbed her and her father, hadn't mellowed. But it would be worth her while to count Servilia a friend. Wetting her hands with lotus blossom scent, she slowly rubbed it into the flesh of her arms, her bosom and neck while making plans.

The next day with Charmion and Iras at her side, each dressed almost as sumptuously as she, a half dozen slaves walking ahead of their litter, a half dozen behind, and eight bearers toting the large covered chair, she set out for Servilia's. A fine breeze blew, and the day was balmy. Languidly, she watched as she passed big square houses and sprawling walled estates all with access to the viaduct carrying water to people of substance. The few windows faced inner courtyards.

Servilia's house was on the Via Sacra, past the next Intersection, but at the cross street, a crowd of people overflowed the four corners, making progress impossible. Their attention focused to the left of the intersection as a blare of trumpets sounded, and a line of musicians, followed by dozens of smartly clad Roman soldiers, armor gleaming, marched into view. The day's triumphal march had begun.

Cleopatra wagged a foot impatiently. The day's parade had started before the sun had reached its zenith, trapping her litter, chairs and people filling the street behind her, the procession blocking the way ahead. To announce her presence would not be wise; she'd have to wait it out. Ranks of victorious Roman legionnaires streamed by, their might showing in their victorious stance. She looked aside; she'd seen enough of Roman soldiers. With the breeze barely blowing now, the sun baked down.

A group of Egyptian prisoners was prodded past the cross road, their shoulders slumped, their faces lined with defeat. Pushed by Romans from behind, the once proud fighting men stared defiantly at the people who lined the street. A bystander tripped one of the men. Stumbling, he fell, was cuffed and kicked to his feet, spat upon, and yelled at by the crowd. Blood stained his soiled uniform, cuts and bruises blemished his body.

Humiliated and angry, she focused on a line of Roman slaves carrying a dozen huge framed pictures. In vivid color, the finely executed paintings displayed the deaths of Achillas and Pothinus, each picture a moment in the final battles for control of Egypt. As if presented with a feast, the Roman citizens shouted gleefully at pictures showing Alexandria burning and wasted, her wondrous city vanquished. Shopkeepers and farmers on holiday shouted their hatred of the enemy even as they cheered approval, respect and love for Caesar.

'I will not stay here," she snapped through clenched teeth. "Get me out of here." It was one thing to be among the Romans of the city, another to witness Egypt belittled.

"Please sit back, My Lady. There is no way out," Charmion whispered, putting down the side curtains.

Even as she implored Charmion to check again, see if they could push past the people behind, more Romans from the *domus* and *insulaes* nearby flooded the streets, leaned from balconies and apartment buildings and added their voices, their taunts and their shouts of approval. Young men, with recently acquired togas slung over their shoulders in a pleasing display of burgeoning manhood, chanted, "Caesar, Caesar, Caesar."

Trapped, Cleopatra stared stoically ahead. If she were recognized, anything could happen. Biting her lip, she kept her head lowered as donkey carts rumbled along the parade route and caged animals squealed, squawked, barked, and roared. Children, wielding sticks, prodded tawny lions pacing behind bars and shrieked in fear as the lions roared. The crowd laughed as the children sprinted back to the sidelines.

"It is not nearly as impressive as the Ptolemaia," Iras said in a placating tone.

As camels, pulled by a half-dozen slaves, balked, Cleopatra agreed. Egyptians were used to seeing wild animals and daylong celebrations without anyone being hurt. Now, a slave fell and was trampled before he could be pulled out of the way. The crowd throwing rocks at a camel, wagered *denarii* on whether the downed slave could continue the march. Backers nudged and prodded him until he got shakily to his feet, his dirty clothes torn, his skin bruised and cut, blood running.

A gaggle of captured foreigners, their chalked feet indicating they had been recently imported, the women bare breasted, the men naked, followed the camels. People from the grand houses nearby appraised them judgmentally. "That one looks like he'd wear out before you got your money's worth. That one has an ornery look, likely to be troublesome."

Cleopatra exchanged haughty glances with Charmion and Iras. Although slavery existed throughout Egypt, to belittle a slave during a public parade was discouraged. Such barbaric attitudes gave her strength, and she maintained a critical silence watching. A large wagon carried a giraffe secured by a dozen ropes. As the animal swiveled its long neck right and left, women screamed and men who initially laughed, jumped back, pushing crying children ahead of them.

Giraffes, a common sight in Alexandria's gigantic spectacles, had Iras giggling, Charmion smothering a laugh. Cleopatra smiled. All she had seen corroborated Alexandria's pre-eminence, Rome's secondary status. Strength and resolve raced through her. More Egyptian prisoners were shuffling by, their feet chained closely together. These weren't soldiers who expected death if they lost a battle, but men who had held diplomatic posts, learned intellectuals who had at times argued philosophy with her. They gazed from glazed eyes, their tortured expressions making clear their misery. She felt no pity for traitors who had turned on her, but these were non-combatants, friends loaded with chains, bowed down with shame. Tears pricked her eyes.

Then Pretares, the man behind Arsinoe's bid for the throne, the man who had swaggered through Alexandria's court, blinding her sister, seducing her into treachery, shuffled into view and a sudden spurt of energy sped through her. His blue eyes darted around like two round balls, and renewed anger at his betrayal rose like a waterspout drenching her with resolve and anger. His swagger reduced to a limp, his curly hair matted, his arms bruised, and his chains clanking at every step, he still appeared the epitome of arrogance, hatred glaring from his eyes. Cleopatra trembled. He had brought about this moment; caused her to be trapped like a gaffed fish unable to get back to the water. He needed to be punished, not by the Romans, but by her.

"Charmion, tell my guards to take care of him. May the gods smite the breath from the foul and loathsome traitor." Head high, not even attempting to stay hidden, she watched Charmion jump down from the litter and confer with the guard. Pushing their way through the crowd, Egyptian voices raised, knives flashing, the guards struck repeated blows. As Pretares slumped and fell, his body shoved to the side of the road, a wild and uproarious yelling erupted, and she barely managed not to recoil.

Uncertain how the uneducated minions would react, she sat still, but as people touched and patted her guards, congratulating them in a rough Roman way, laughing and pushing at them, they spotted her, her jewels gleaming in the sun.

A Roman soldier standing near her litter, his brow knit in thought, cried, "May the gods preserve us, it's the Queen of Egypt! Your majesty," he ended in accented Greek. But his words were drowned in a cry coming from down the block, and the crowd strained to see what wondrous sight approached, and Cleopatra knew the joy of relief. Their attention had been taken from her.

Caesar's chariot burst into view. Blonde manes drifting, a matched pair of horses pulled the golden chariot where Caesar stood, feet braced, head high, shouting to his steeds, to the crowd, to the gods. A ruler of the known world, a leader, a prophet, a statesman and a soldier, no longer gentle and unassuming or modest, he shouted with unabashed glee, a conqueror bringing home the spoils of war, and she understood his feelings for she had felt the same when Pretares had recognized his assailants. She started to cheer, but sound stuck in her throat. The bedraggled figure running behind the Roman chariot, bound by the wrists with a six foot length of chain fastened to the back of his chariot, was a woman alternately stumbling, regaining her feet and running again. Arsinoe! Arsinoe her enemy, Arsinoe her sometimes friend, Arsinoe her sister!

Chest aching, images from the past danced in front of her. Trembling with anger and humiliation, she saw a dirty and disheveled Arsinoe stumble and it was as if she, too, had been forced to run the torturous trail behind Caesar's chariot. Arsinoe's hair matted with dirt and dung, her bare feet bleeding, her once grand gown dusty and torn, she lurched, fell, was dragged along the stone roadway before she staggered to her feet again. Blood ran from her bruised and scraped arms. It poured from a wound on her lip, it welled slowly from her knees, bubbled from her lips. Tears ran from her swollen eyes. She looked broken and bowed, but young and brave, and Cleopatra knew sympathy and empathy. If she fought Caesar and lost, would she, too, be dragged through the streets like a common woman held up to scorn and ridicule? A tremor in her limbs would not recede.

The crowd grew silent, and those who had watched her guards take care of Pretares, had heard the Roman soldier identify her, remained mute. She felt as if a cold hand pressed relentlessly against her breast, and her breathing came harsh as punishment in which she had no say. Last night Caesar had claimed her with dignified gusto, and all the while a Ptolemy had lain in a prison cell like any prisoner, worse than a slave. And now the ruler of Rome and her sister were out of sight, and only she, Cleopatra VII, Queen of Egypt, divine reincarnation of Isis, remained to mourn their passing. She gave the signal to leave and with dull eyes watched the people retreat, move their litters and carts out of the way for the Queen of Egypt. No one cheered, but no one booed.

Late in the afternoon Caesar appeared at the mansion, his eyes glowing brightly, his laugh coming easily. He scooped her up and swung her around. "Hurry, get ready. Caesar is giving a party the likes of which have never been seen in the city."

She said nothing when he set her down, but he didn't seem to notice for he paced back and forth as he talked, his enthusiasm high. "A banquet in the park for everyone. Thousands will be there to sample what the butchers, bakers, and cooks have roasted and basted and whatever they do, and by God, I am hungry, for food and," he kissed her, "for you."

While the city waited, he made love to her like a conquering hero, lusty and boisterous. No poetry, no philosophy, and with no help from her. Again, he hardly seemed to notice. "Two triumphs down, two to go," he said rising from her bed.

She watched him move quickly around the room as he dressed, her mind a dither of contradictory thoughts. After the last triumph a garrote would be slipped around the prisoners' necks and in the

Roman way they'd be strangled, men, women, and perhaps children, too, although often the latter were taken into Roman homes and raised in the Roman way.

"So what happens after the city quiets down? What will you do to top this?" she asked as Caesar took a grape from a cluster and popped one into her mouth, the action unlike him. Anger welled up in her, anger that Egypt had been belittled and a Ptolemy displayed like any common creature. "Perhaps you could build a state library," she said swallowing the grape and reaching for another. "You could model it after the one in Alexandria." She spoke without passion but inside she churned with feeling, needing to show these Romans the superiority of Egyptian ways. "After all, there isn't any in Rome. So remiss of you, my lord, mighty Caesar."

He apparently didn't notice her emotionless response had a mocking close. "A good idea. A library for the people." He smiled at her, got up and strolled the room. "You'd better get up. So many people want to meet you. You don't want to be late."

She put one leg outside the covers. "In a minute. You haven't heard my next suggestion. Perhaps you should change your calendar. Your present system is archaic. To follow it would be to make anyone late." She looked at him without blinking. So many things she could say. No, better wait. *One thing at a time.* "The royal astronomer is part of my party. Perhaps you would like me to set up a meeting."

"Your suggestions as always are worthy of consideration." He went to the garden window. "Do you know it is still daylight? I feel as if a hundred days had passed in one. God, what a feeling!"

She pushed herself up in bed. "I have one more thing. Not a suggestion, but a request."

He turned, fixed his gaze upon her. "Ah, yes, you have that look in your eyes. What is it you want me to do? Get back in bed, scratch your back, bite your...." He laughed. "By the gods, I feel great."

She shot him a hard look. "I want you to spare my sister."

His eyebrows went up.

"Do not humiliate Egypt further." She turned away, not wanting him to see she had tears in her eyes at the thought of a Ptolemy in such a degrading position.

He pursed his lips slightly and then nodded. "Done. It's a good suggestion. The people grew quiet when they saw her. She has some of your bravery. I respect that. Anyway, this day I am pleased to do as you ask. Now get up before I am forced to come back to bed, and I cannot miss a party that is the biggest this city has ever known."

Not savoring the victory as much as she'd anticipated, she forced a smile, threw aside the cover and got up. She must send a note of apology to Servilia, plan an audience, let Rome know officially a queen had arrived.

Chapter V

46 BCE

WORD OF HER antipathy for Pretares had already spread, and sympathy for her sister, Arsinoe, grew. Romans who had looked at her with askance, now curried her favor, but she saw little of Caesar. Her diplomats had been conferring with their Roman counterparts ever since arriving in Rome. Cicero, in an elegant way, excoriated Egypt and belittled Cleopatra. He had opposed Caesar during the battles with Pompey, and now made clear he had no fondness for Egypt. In a speech he said, "Rome must not be seduced by the trappings of royalty. The question must be asked, is the Ptolemaic line truly that of the pharaohs?" But the treaty, along the lines her father had negotiated years before was renegotiated in her favor when Caesar gave it his approval long past the time of his Egyptian Triumph.

Still she saw little of him and was thrilled after the treaty was signed when he sent word he'd be with her soon. She sent home the Romans who looked for favors or who came to argue philosophy. Stripping herself of jewels and a gown that floated like air, she put on a simple white robe similar to those ordinary Roman women wore, and sat down on the floor with Caesarion in her arms. She would present to Caesar a woman as Republican as he, a mother with her child

She was laughing and playing with Caesarion as if she had not a care in the world when Caesar arrived. He stood watching for some time before he spoke, clearly enamored with the scene. She smiled at him but said nothing.

Coming to her, he held out his arms for Caesarion and dandled the baby for a minute or two, his face showing his satisfaction before he handed the babe to a nurse.

"Come," he held out a hand to Cleopatra., drawing her to her feet, embracing her. "I have something to show you, little one." His smile bubbled up as if from an artesian well, his pride clearly evident, his voice modulated, his eyes gleaming. He led her outside to his litter, and they were carried into the heart of the city.

Romans always amazed her. They swaggered through the world like they owned it, Cato patronizing her father, Caesar and Pompey using him, all of them acting as if the Egyptians were inferior. Still she was impressed with their power and during her growing years had imagined their city bigger and more magnificent than anything she had ever known, its temples and palaces more palatial, befitting a people who dominated the world. Now, she knew better, magnificence sat only blocks from squalor.

On top of the hill, she heard the litter bearers breathing, the wind riffling the trees, birds singing, but all of it drowned in racket once the bearers descended into the city proper. Everyday life roared and stomped, shouted and cried, and away from the hill with its grand villas, a stink, more rotten than the chicken entrails and the blood and sweat of gored oxen bleeding in sacrifice in Alexandria, assaulted her. Beneath the burning wood and cooking oil smells, the open cesspits and fecal mounds sent their foul odors like wind-driven plague. She covered her nose with her robe.

"We're going to the Forum Julium," Caesar explained, seemingly not noticing her discomfort or discomfited by the sounds and smells offending her. "Tomorrow's the official opening, but I wanted you to see it first. I ordered it done when you first arrived in Rome." He smiled at her, shrugged. "For one thing, the Forum Romanum has become too crowded, making it important to expand."

Where the road leveled off, shops opened directly onto the streets, and among the clatter and bang of commerce, the murmur of many voices, she glimpsed whole families living in lofts above tiny stores or coming or going from brick or clay apartments. Women, returning from the public fountains with water in jars on their heads, cheered as Caesar's palanquin passed, but catching sight of Cleopatra, they stared.

"Is it much farther?" She wasn't ready to take any more insults. Cicero had walked through her gardens, his nostrils flared as if he were looking for a scandal he could report. She should have had her bodyguards run him off, but a group of poets joined him, and she could do nothing. She had pretended he wasn't there.

Caesar shook his head. "It won't be long now."

People crowded the narrow walks fronting the streets, some hurried across on stepping stones before Caesar's bearers ordered them out of the way. A baker pulling bread from an oven proffered a loaf. Above his door hung a model of a cat with a huge human phallus. Men and women, young, old, dirty, clean, ragged or well-clothed, shouted Caesar's name, smiled and waved as they leaned from balconies and windows.

"They watch with a mixture of adulation and scorn," Cleopatra observed, as they approached a square. "Adulation for you, my lord, scorn for me."

"We've reversed roles, my little queen. The people of Egypt cast the evil eye when I set foot in Alexandria."

"So, we're even. What's that building ahead? It's lovely."

"It's the Temple of Venus, the Mother. It's what I wanted you to see."

Inside, her eyes adjusting to the semi-dark, she was drawn to an image of Venus, as lovely a depiction as she'd ever seen. Next to it stood a gilt-bronze statue of herself, all of her femininity, all of her royal presence shown. Drawing a quick breath, she whispered, "Praise be to Isis," and looking up at Caesar she added, "you do me honor."

"A token of my esteem. My family is descended from Venus, of course." His voice held the tenderness she'd heard when he made love to her with his words as well as his body.

Overwhelmed, she murmured, "Venus and Isis are one, Isis who wed Osiris, Osiris and Isis who bore Horus." Her voice held reverence, awe.

He put his hands on her shoulders. "I'm glad you're pleased." No foreign ruler had ever been so honored in Rome.

"Oh, my lord, I am speechless. The gods are truly with me."

"You have the gods and Caesar's esteem."

She met his eyes. "Then we are in agreement." As her heart danced, her mind whirled. With this public display of Caesar's protection, the people of Rome would not dare deride or in any way impede her or her people from now on. She, the living Isis, had been openly linked to Caesar in a Roman temple. The message was unmistakable. "Oh, my lord," she managed, tears in her eyes.

"You please me greatly, little one." His voice had a hushed quality, and he held her loosely.

"I've never been so happy." She put her head against his chest, a woman who saw the world within her grasp, a girl who was grateful. This surely meant her son would someday rule the world.

Two days later, turbaned eunuchs carrying her chair, Ptolemy next to her, on the way to the baths, a woman called, "Praise be to Isis," and along the street other women echoed the sentiment. A pedagogue and his pupils cheered, and near the forum, most men turned benign expressions upon her, a few nodded.

Her brother shook his head. "Because Caesar honored you with a statue, we're tolerated, but no matter what they say, they hate us."

"You find fault in everything." But doubt existed, although she'd never admit it to Ptolemy. Her bearers had to wait at a cross street while a wealthy Roman's chair passed, the woman inside not acknowledging her, and near the baths, several men stared at her with far from benevolent eyes.

Stuffing food into his mouth, Ptolemy countered, "Do they like us as much as at home?"

"Don't be ridiculous." Since the day, early in her reign, when she'd returned the Apis bull to them, the people of the Nile adored her. The sacred bull had died, and she'd taken a replacement as an offering from the gods. To insure her position in Rome she'd have to invite both Caesar and Calpurnia to a grand reception she'd been planning. Show that she hid nothing.

The night of the party, lilies floated the shallow waters of the *impluvium*, the pool in the house's entrance, open to the sky. Figs and dates filled bowls to the right and left of the pool, and guests entering the atrium were directed to a room with a row of alabaster windows and a long red and gold carpet leading to gold and ivory chairs where she and Ptolemy would receive.

Few Romans ignored or turned down her invitation, and she followed her father's pattern, sumptuous displays of food and drink, soft music, dancing girls scantily clad. Incense burned, oil lamps fluttered, and the great expanse of white ceiling, scrubbed down by slaves that day, would gradually grow sooty again. Now it gleamed almost as brightly as the gold coins in a bowl at the entrance to the salon, free for all to take. The coins bore her likeness, a not very subtle reminder of her royal blood and Egyptian riches.

A crowd had ssembled before she entered from a small door behind her chair. They're curious, she surmised, as the educated and powerful approached her, men and women who had not found their way to her salon earlier. She said little, letting the picture she presented speak for itself. Several layers of sheer gauze swirled around her legs, ruby, carnelian, amethyst, topaz, and pearl strings lay on her chest, silver earrings and bracelets of turquoise and mother-of-pearl dangled from her ears and circled her arms, studded with diamonds from the far reaches beyond Egypt, winking in the waning light of late afternoon. Nothing could dampen her spirits, even her fat pigeon of a brother who grew increasing irritable as the evening progressed, and guests queuing to speak to her, ignored him, as much as she did, he slumped in the chair next to her.

Listening quietly to often obsequious, sometimes fawning, comments by Rome's finest amused her. While outwardly deploring it, as her father had said often, Republicans were dazzled by royalty. Still they needed charming, and so at intervals she let her voice drift like a flute over the room and almost forgot that neither Caesar nor Calpurnia were in evidence.

Spotting Cato in line, standing, not like a supplicant as so many others, but superbly confident, chatting to those behind him and not once glancing her way, she wanted to run. How dare he have the nerve to approach her, his toga bunched over one arm, and flowing like a flag! The insult to her father and her years ago rose like a sandstorm in the desert. She stared down at him defiantly, contempt barely hidden.

Turning one of her coins in his hand, Cato studied it before he took the final step to her dais. His voice carrying the hauteur of their earlier encounter, he said, "So the little princess is now a queen." He looked from the coin to her. "Or is it a pharaoh? I get so confused with these Egyptian relationships. Brothers and sisters…" His look of disdain had grown, a sneering quality to his mouth and posture as well as his words.

How dare he hint that she and Ptolemy…! Looking down at him, she lifted a hand, and her major domo leaned forward. If she signaled, the guard would kill if necessary. Even her brother, hearing Cato's words, sat up straighter, only his eyes showing concern. Everyone in the room grew silent and watched covertly. She said, "But you have not changed a whit, Master Cato. Your tongue still follows the same paths."

Several women giggled, and the man behind him said, "She has you dead to rights, Cato."

The man's eyes were deep set and his expression had a scolding quality about it that she had always disliked. Before she could speak, he stepped up next to Cato, not even inclining his head toward her. "So Caesar's triumph brings us the Egyptian queen."

The man as rude as Cato was Cicero, the interloper in her garden, the man whose oratory, often lauded in Roman circles, attacked her. She spoke rapidly. "And Caesar's triumph brings you to me." Early in life she had vowed never to study the language of Rome. Speaking in the official language of the world, Greek, when he didn't answer immediately, she followed it with Armaic and Egyptian. "Surely you understand the languages of diplomatic exchange." Wanting to keep him off balance, she added, throwing in a pretty shrug, and a smile, "Introduce yourself, sir."

Cato laughed out loud, the sound approaching a guffaw. "It appears that not everyone recognizes our master orator."

A soft pink colored Cicero's cheeks, his eyes narrowed and he shrugged as if the exchange was of little consequence. To Cleopatra he said, his hands in flight. "When a strange bird flies into one's coop, a wise man inspects the plumage."

Neither smiling nor frowning, her voice a melody, she said, "And would this wise man watch in case the bird dropped a feather?"

"He would."

"And would he pick it up, or watch for an accumulation of plumage?"

"A wise man waits. The plumage is bright, but brightness can dull. Which makes me wonder how Caesar can top this triumph." His smile held a hint of sarcasm. "After bringing us three Ptolemys, anything else would be anticlimactic."

"No one *brings* this Ptolemy anywhere, sir. Cleopatra VII decides where Ptolemys travel. As for your republican leader, I am sure he can top any action he has presented so far."

Cicero shrugged. "A man's deeds speak for themselves, of course, and possibly a woman's words." He smirked and turned away as if it weren't necessary for her to dismiss him.

Inwardly fuming, Cleopatra turned to the next person in line, her smile, her poise impeccable, her voice sweeter then a lark's, while her heart beat a tattoo, and she wished she had not been so quick to get even. After a decent interval, she rose, left the room, and caused a general exodus. Casesar never appeared.

Still, visitors came from all over the city to ingratiate themselves with her. Charmion reported invitations to Cleopatra's salons were sought like prizes in a lottery. Two days after the reception, Servilia sent a note requesting an audience. The meeting nagging at her with its implications, Cleopatra didn't delay. At one time Caesar had almost married the lady, and it was rumored her son, Brutus, at times claimed Caesar as a father. She had seen neither. Now, the woman faced her.

"I am so sorry the crowd kept you from attending my small reception." Servilia bent her knee, approximating a bow as she approached where Cleopatra stood. "I so wanted to welcome your majesty to the city."

Although taller, Servilia was also old enough to be her mother; her face bearing lines, her walk the walk of an older woman, her appearance, while attractive, her face bearing remnants of a pretty youth, she looked older than Caesar. Perhaps she was. Cleopatra knew a moment of pure joy and extended her hands. "No, you must accept my apologies for not returning your kind invitation earlier. Come, I have had my people prepare a lunch for us. "

They sat in a room with murals covering the walls, the gods dallying with earthly maidens, the sky a radiant pink and soft blue, extending to the door through which she saw a patch of sky, a slice of greenery.

As they dined on fish served with *garum* sauce, asparagus, and bread soaked in milk, the excess liquid removed, the bread fried and served with honey, traditional Roman foods washed down with watered wine, Cleopatra discovered Servilia had a quick wit and a warm way that would serve them both well. It was evident the fires Caesar had once flared were banked; Servilia was truly his friend, more like a sister than a former lover. "We must make this a habit," she said as Servilia left, Cleopatra's parting gift, a flagon of Egyptian perfume in her hand, its fragrance the newest in Egyptian exports.

The meeting bought Servilia, her family and friends entree to Cleopatra's garden parties. Although she enjoyed exchanging literary quotations with poets and actors who appeared with Servilia, she never quite trusted the woman's family. Although she discounted Brutus's claim to be Caesar's son, she privately feared it. Anyone who was a threat to Caesarion was a threat to her. She merely tolerated him and his wife and actively snubbed Cicero and Cato, who sometimes followed in Servilia's wake.

But for the most part she dwelled on a high plane. With self-assurance blazing from her face, her body, her feelings, she attended the theater Caesar had built. The stage he'd designed had separate rotating parts, scenes changing rapidly, a feature she would surely implement in Alexandria. And one day, with her attendants, her guards, her banner flying above her litter, she resplendent in a gown of sunlight yellow complemented by amber and onyx jewelry, she saw Calpurnia for the first time. Caesar's Roman wife surely rivaled Helen of Troy, perfection in each feature and the whole so innocent-seeming a man would never forget it.

Cleopatra recalled little of the play afterward. What she remembered was Caesar being tender, solicitous, and courteous with Calpurnia. Hastily, she had looked away, but a roaring in her ears had persisted. Later she forced herself to think positively. She had bested Arsinoe; her sister who was even now on her way to Ephesus, alive because of her intercession. Calpurnia would not be half as difficult. She undoubtedly was soft, compliant, a woman who would never challenge

Caesar. She'd never suggest ideas he had not thought of first. She'd never titillate his mind as well as his body. No, she would not worry about Calpurnia.

Happily, she planned an intimate party, one with vast quantities of food, couches so they could lounge in the Roman way, and invited Servilia as well as Caesar and his Master of the Horse. But Calpurnia sent out invitations to a party for the same night. Regrets began to pour in, Calpurnia's invitation taking precedence. Caesar's lady fought in a lady-like way, but she fought.

Chapter VI

46 BCE

CLEOPATRA'S ANNOYANCE DEEPENED when Marc Anthony's wife, Fulvia, and the train of women who paraded in her shadow, openly snubbed her. Word was Fulvia had captivated Anthony with her beauty and kept him with her aggressiveness. She talked military strategy as if she was a general, and Cleopatra feared her more than she did Calpurnia. Conspiracies and intrigues were more convoluted in Rome than in Alexandria. People changed sides constantly; Cicero had supported and abandoned Caesar at times. So had many others.

Instead of competing with either lady, Cleopatra courted musicians and philosophers, poets and playwrights as well as disaffected politicians and patricians who lingered at her salons to partake of the rich life she made available. She knew her strengths and had learned to avoid events where she'd be lessened.

Caesar's fourth Triumph took place after she had been in Rome for a while. A scant hour before sunset that day, Cleopatra held court in the peristyle garden and listened as a youthful poet stood beneath a statue of Dionysus and recited an ode to her. Lemon-yellow light played shafts of gold along the edge of the fountain, highlighting the row of statues representing the gods. It presented a perfect time for Caesar to arrive, but only Cicero, Cato, and their entourage burst through the gate and passed between rows of Cypress and strode toward the assembled guests, Servilia among them.

Cicero raised his hand for attention, striking a pose at the end of the rectangular pool and spoke in a loud voice. "I have witnessed the final Triumph."

Strolling couples, guests seated on benches in the grape arbor, and groups of Stoics and Epicureans clustered together in conversation along the plaza, paused to listen.

Rising, Cleopatra fixed Cicero with a haughty stare. She could have him thrown out; his disdain for her was palpable, and he had no love for Caesar either, supporting Pompey in the civil struggles that had ended when Egypt ended Pompey's life. Now, he pretended not to see her until he had the attention of all assembled.

His voice penetrated to all corners of the garden. "This was a Triumphal celebration like no other. Truly different." He paused dramatically and turned a lazy gaze upon her.

"How was it different?" she demanded, her curiosity intense. By coming here was he reminding people Egypt had been defeated, too?

"How?" he repeated taking a stance beneath a life-size statue of Zeus. "If I must say so, this was Caesar's most masterful touch."

She shook her head. "Don't keep us in suspense, sir. A speaker cheats his audience by making them wait."

Several people smiled.

Flushing, he brought his hands together as if to emphasize a point. "Actually, it was rather brilliant. For weeks our noble Caesar dazzled us with spectacle and thrilled us with words, taking us to the heights of battle and rhetoric—a mock naval battle, parades, a theater presentation." At the last word he bowed toward Cleopatra and slowly let his arms drop to his sides. "This time he amazed us with a simplicity of words, as I shall do also." He paused, shrugged. "I wish I had thought of them first, although I think he stole them from the Greeks, which doesn't surprise me at all, knowing our beloved Caesar." He chuckled.

"Great Pharaoh, what did he say, Master Orator?" Cleopatra demanded, not bothering to hide her annoyance and drawing out the word, 'master,' as Cato settled in beside his sister, Servilia making room on the marble bench where she sat.

Cicero addressed Cleopatra directly, "Madam, you call me orator, a designation I do not accord myself. I am but a simple philosopher, not in a league with Aristotle whose discernments were not unlike a river of gold, but mine still bear a small degree of merit."

"You have outdone yourself with introduction. We await the body of your talk—which you assured us was to the point."

Cicero raised his head, and looked down his nose at her. "*Vine, vidi, vici.* I came, I saw, I conquered." He drew out the phrases dramatically.

Envisioning her father at a Ptolemaia, riding an elephant, preceded and followed by censor-bearing priests who threw money to the crowds, her father giving away a fortune in jewels, she wondered: was Cicero making fun of Auletes or mocking her or both? "That's all?" She spoke disparagingly.

Staring at her, he spoke slowly, enunciating each word carefully. "Surely you see the simplicity of the action. Following the extravagance of the three previous Triumphs, it was brilliant."

"Everyone knows simplicity can sometimes be dramatic," she snapped, but she hadn't, and she knew it. "Thank you for enlightening us with your little story, Master Cicero." She despised the man. Rising, she moved closer to the poet who had been reciting earlier. "Before Master Cicero enlightened us, you favored us with poetic expression most pleasing. Your poems were much appreciated, but I doubt you know this one." She gestured toward Cicero as if dedicating the poem to him. "The foul humors of conceit have fled, like Bedouins galloping in the night, while in their tent the people sleep, and peace and harmony fill the land."

"No, Your Majesty, I don't." the poet said, with some confusion for it was apparent she wasn't speaking to him.

"Of course, you couldn't. I just composed it." A thrill passed through her as both Cicero and Cato frowned and Servilia smiled. How could her friend be related to such men? In strictly poetic circles Cicero's poetry was not always regarded the same respect as his orations, although he had a following.

As the waning sun no longer lit the garden, and a cool wind rose, she sent for her musicians and directed them to play a rollicking tune from her childhood. Soon, Cicero's voice, disclaiming on the properties of minimalism, was drowned in music.

The day left a strange taste on her tongue. Hours later when Caesar arrived, her head swam from the words she'd mulled through her mind. The foul humors of conceit have fled, *I came, I saw, I conquered.* When Caesar reached for her, his eyes glittering with remembrance of his day, she murmured, "Not yet, My Lord." With deft touches she slowly divested a protesting Julius Caesar of his toga, his sandals, his laurel wreath, his tunic, and his shift before she fit herself into his arms. *I came, I saw, I conquered*, she thought.

* * *

With Caesar once more a frequent visitor to her house, others, who had stayed away, followed him to her salons. Literary figures argued with military men, pedagogues with businessmen, musicians with actors, and many sang her praises. Caesar, arriving during a far-reaching discussion about the mortal and immortal life, argued against immortality of the soul. "The only immortality Romans believe in is fame. Unless, of course, one becomes a god."

Everyone laughed, but Cleopatra, shocked at this further evidence of the gulf between Egypt and Rome, didn't. She couldn't properly greet the day until she heard the bells and knew the priests were sacrificing to the gods. And no day felt complete if she had not communed with Isis. Sometimes the dichotomy between queen and goddess disappeared, the two blended so completely she had to remind herself of her own mortality. That Romans could joke about such things appalled her.

But mostly the months passed without incident, her life a routine of entertaining lavishly, going to the baths, whispering with Iras and Charmion, gossiping with Servilia, and in an effort to cement Egypt's ties to the Roman people, distributing gifts to people who attended her soirees and bribes to those in power. When Caesar called her his little queen, and delighted in Caesarion's rapid growth, the boy going from babe to toddler, she knew contentment. Once hearing that Calpurnia didn't ride horseback, she suggested an outing including Caesarion. Caesar agreed.

At the stables, the light was dim, and she waited for her vision to clear before she walked all the way in, stepping lightly on the hay-strewn floor, and eyeing the horses in their stalls with a practiced eye. The buildings, while vast, were inferior to the cedar lined horse barn in Alexandria. She wrinkled her nose, and spotting Marc Anthony leading Caesar's horse, she paused. For a second, his eyes gleamed in a way she recalled seeing at the royal stables in Egypt so many years ago. She felt the power of the memory, and Anthony, undoubtedly remembered too, for he looked away immediately and sent an underling to ready a horse for her.

Arriving soon after, Caesar took Caesarion from Iras. "He will ride with me."

It was one of the happiest days of the year, Cleopatra confessed that night, the sight of her son with the ruler of Rome. The taste of the raw air of winter still in her lungs, the yellow leaves of fall became, not an omen, but a promise of better things to come.

But Pompey's sons, with the army Pompey had built with his riches and power, were sacking Southern Spain, and Caesar left to put them down, hardly saying goodbye, his eyes already on the coming battle.

Within days, homesickness assailed her. Rome without Caesar contained a lifelessness that roared past the forum and up the hill. Fewer people attended her afternoons at home, fewer women joined her coterie at the baths, her Nubians were jostled. But worst of all, rumors slithered back from Spain with the ease of a garden snake. King Bogud of Mauretania had allied himself with Caesar and was fighting at Caesar's side. With Bogud in Spain, so was Queen Eunoe. The beautiful one, Cleopatra mused, fearing the mistress more than she did Calpurnia who, in her soft acquiescence, seemed less and less a threat.

She paced the bedroom. From her arms he had gone to Queen Eunoe before. Now, he had done it again. The woman's name was whispered throughout Rome. At the entrance to the public baths Cicero laughed in her face. Steam rising from the rooms beyond the entry-way, a chorus of voices echoing from around the pools, Cicero's voice overrode them all as he spoke of Eunoe's beauty, his tone caressing the words. Cleopatra left before everyone noticed. She determined never to be belittled again.

Every day Caesarion grew more like his father, his fair hair and piercing eyes reminding her of his place in the world. To insure it, she wrote Caesar bulletins about their son's health and with satisfaction read and re-read the one letter he sent back. When he returned, would she be in Rome? Yes, she answered, anxious to go home but knowing she had no choice. The much smaller villa was less warm, less comfortable than the Alexandrian palace. Slaves belonging to Caesar, opened doors, cleared corridors and reminded her daily that Caesar was on loan to her as much as his house. In the kitchen meat turned on a spit, bread baked in an oven, but in the garden, Roman idols and house gods were carved in stone.

One day, both Charmion and Iras on errands, footsteps approached down the corridor, and Servilia rushed in from outside. Her hair was damp, and raindrops ran down her face.

"What brings you here in such a flurry?" Cleopatra asked as a cold draft attacked her.

Servilia put a hand to her heaving chest. "I am sorry to come without announcing my intentions. Excuse my bad manners, but I had to see you."

"What is it? You look as if you have news that bodes no one well." She directed the servants to bring refreshments into the main salon. Taking Servilia's arm, she led the way.

In a spate of words, Servilia said that Caesar's health had failed him in Spain.

Caesar sick? It did not seem possible. He out-worked, out-fought, out-thought men young enough to be his sons. She stared at the older woman. "How bad?"

"He's recovering, but getting to the southern reaches of Spain in twenty-seven days, averaging fifty or sixty miles a day must have taken something out of him." Servilia's face held a hint of pride. "You must admit it was quite a feat for a man of fifty-four." Not for the first time the matter of age hung suspended in Cleopatra's mind like a dangling corpse. A crippled, sick, debilitated Caesar was incomprehensible. While Servilia gossiped and laughed with her at the baths and at their respective villas, their friendship had its limits. They seldom mentioned Cato, Brutus, Cicero, or Caesar. Their talk concentrated on neutral subjects or they tossed barbs toward Calpurnia and Fulvia and their respective circle of friends. She wanted to pull the ribbon bow from Servilia's graying hair and shake her now.

Of an age with Caesar, Servilia remembered his early days, and now she seemed knowledgeable about what was happening to him in Spain and was damnably slow getting to the point. "War is difficult. But overcoming obstacles is something I expect from Julius Caesar." A frieze near the ceiling depicted Caesar's conquests, a brightly painted mural showed him with his family, his mother Aurelia with her hand on his arm, his father nearby. Could there be a conspiracy against him?

Was that what Servilia was getting at? Ptolemys had always lived amid intrigue, familial and otherwise. She motioned Servilia to a seat near her.

Within seconds a slave girl appeared with a tray bearing a pitcher of watered wine and a plate of honey cakes. "Taste it," Cleopatra ordered. The girl drank. When she neither gagged nor fainted nor clutched at her stomach, Cleopatra accepted glasses for Servilia and herself and repeated the procedure with the honey cakes.

"I'm surprised they don't grow fat." Servilia's voice held a note of irony, but her eyes showed she understood Cleopatra's show of power.

The charcoal braziers gave little warmth in the vast room, and Cleopatra leaned over the nearest one, images of Caesar wracked by seizures and fainting spells invading her mind. Her gaze on Servilia's gray eyes, she said, "So?"

Servilia set down her glass and sighed. "I don't quite know how to say this."

Cleopatra frowned. "Say what? Make yourself clear."

"Please, I infer nothing, but you know, certainly, that my brother and my son fought against Caesar in the war."

Except for Pompey's sons, she had not heard the names of others allied against Caesar. She set down her glass so rapidly the wine sloshed over. "Cato and Brutus fought against Caesar? Took arms against him?"

Servilia nodded. "My brother Cato and I never agreed entirely. He spoke very forcefully about his beliefs and had many followers, among them Pompey's sons. And of course, my son, although I'm sure Brutus didn't want to be involved; Caesar has always been so kind to him." She sighed again. "My dear friend faced three-to-one odds."

Cleopatra felt her face freeze. How could Servilia sit and talk so calmly about Caesar in the same breath with Cato and Brutus, men who were clearly traitors? She wanted to evict her, chase her from the house, but she also needed to find out all she could. "But Caesar won the war in Spain."

Servilia's smile was lop-sided. "Always he wins."

"Of course. Would you think otherwise?" And so would she. Her appetite gone, she pushed the plate of sweets away, seeing the lines in Servilia's face not as lines of compassion but of conspiracy. If Brutus were truly Caesar's son, as some gossip contended, wouldn't she have said so long ago? And wouldn't Caesar have found some way to claim his Roman son?

Eyes clouded, Servilia said softly. "In the past I prayed for Caesar to be victorious. This time I couldn't. At the end people killed themselves rather than be taken prisoner." She moved to the edge of her seat. "My brother was among those who took the honorable way out. He committed suicide." Her look had an expectant quality, as if she wanted to be asked for details.

Cleopatra got to her feet, wanting to get rid of this woman who stirred memories of Cato that stunk like a pile of dung. "In war it is customary for the vanquished to lose their lives, whether by their own doing or by their conquerors. I bore your brother no great affection, Madam, and I don't understand why you're here."

Servilia shook her head. "Because you and I have spent time together, and Caesar and I are close friends. I thought perhaps you would want to know about anything affecting him." She placed her hands together palms touching and leaned forward. "After dinner with his closest friends, my brother took his dagger and ripped open his stomach. A doctor tried to help, but when he left Cato reopened the wound. Do you need more description? More explanation?" Her voice, brittle but firm, rose even as her eyes closed down, became slits. "The next day they found him dead, one hand clutching his intestines, the other a copy of Plato."

What could Servilia possibly be thinking? Her long-lived antipathy toward Cato would certainly not dissipate like rain during drought. "You have told more than enough." She shook her head and rose. "I give you permission to leave."

Throwing on her mantle, Servilia said, "There is one bit more." She opened her eyes wide again. "From your mother's love, I ask you to speak to Caesar about my son. I pray for clemency."

She, too, would beg, would plead if it were Caesarion they were discussing. Looking away, she forced her mind to stay clear, not fog over with sympathy. If she let down her guard, sought details, it could not help but could possibly hinder. Nothing must mar her son's chances. "You dare ask such a thing," she whispered. "When my own sister fought against Caesar, I got him to spare her life, and now she plots against me. I will not speak for your son."

"A sister is not the same as a son. I thought you understood that. Sorry, I bothered you." Bowing slightly, Servilia went out.

Cleopatra fought back tears. She would miss the woman who had chatted with her about makeup, about jewelry, whose sense of life so resembled her own. They had laughed together as Caesarion fought to stay upright in a pell-mell rush from one woman's protective arms to the others. Yet, she could not speak up for Brutus to the possible detriment of her own son.

When word came that Caesar was back, staying at his estate at Lavicum, southeast of Rome, she planned a banquet in his honor, but days passed, and he didn't arrive. Whispers from all over the city informed her, he was not resting or womanizing, but depositing a will with the Vestal Virgins. The document made clear he had adopted his nephew, nineteen-year-old Octavian, that he had also named the boy his official heir. Octavian would inherit three-fourths of Caesar's vast estate, the rest of his wealth to be divided into various bequests, gifts, and charities.

A cold sweat broke out on her brow. Not even a mention of Caesarion in the will! Her son forgotten, her son a non-entity. As if a shaft had been driven into her heart, she stared unseeingly ahead, her mind speeding like a bird batting its wings against the wind's current. She made plans, discarded them, made others in a frenzy of thought. Common sense told her Caesar could not publicly acknowledge Caesarion. Because of Roman law, he had no alternative. The law forbade her son inheriting either his father's fortune or his mantle. But Caesar could have acknowledged him in writing, made clear the relationship.

At last, her mind slowing down, whole scenes floated like clouds before her eyes. Built years before her birth, the mansion's floors were without heat, and the chill of Rome penetrated to her bones. Was Caesar repudiating her indirectly? If so she must be prepared to leave, say nothing, act above it all. Whatever she did, she must maintain the position she had now and not let Caesarion's birthright slip through her fingers.

Three weeks later, her people reported Caesar appeared quiet and withdrawn, barely acknowledging citizens lining the route on his return. He went directly to Calpurnia and lingered for a day, but the next day, as shadows climbed the walls, Iras reported seeing his litter on the route to Janiculum Hill. When he made the turn into the villa, Cleopatra pulled Caesarion to her side, and, as if sensing her nervousness, he clung to her wool skirt. The warm Roman dress, would not immediately remind Caesar of Egypt.

As he entered the villa, a whiff of outdoors preceding him, she heard the twitter and self-conscious laughter of slaves and servants as they scurried out of his path and the shifting of feet and the welcome of those who didn't move quickly enough. He paused on the threshold of the room where she waited, and she said in her huskiest tones, "Welcome home, My Lord."

His head came around as if he had just spied her, and a smile eased the strain showing on his face. "So my little queen is still here." Gaunt, his face drawn, his voice sounded tired, weak.

She nudged Caesarion gently. "Say hello to your father." Her words seemed loud in the renewed silence of the house, only the splash of the fountain interrupting.

Caesar's high, laced shoes and sparkling toga had a look of freshness, but his eyes were distant, as if he were still dwelling in other places, or as if the present were past, and he didn't quite know what he wanted to do next. She read fatigue in his eyes, as if old age had caught up with him on the Spanish peninsula.

Turning his attention to Caesarion, his eyes widened.

Now a year old, the boy lifted his head and said, "Hello."

Cleopatra felt a resurgence of hope. "What else," she coached, looking from her son to Caesar.

"Father."

She hugged the child to her side. "My son and I greet you, Julius Caesar." Her smile had all the brilliance and warmth of Alexandria. Caesar's smile did not. At any moment she imagined it could turn into a frown.

"You have taught him well, and he speaks clearly for one so young. But you... I cannot so easily categorize you." He shrugged, his eyes finally coming to her. "The Queen of Egypt greets me and reminds me of my obligations in one fell swoop." He strode closer as she imagined he might close in on an adversary.

"Would you deny him, My Lord?" Surely he could see the resemblance, Caesarian so sturdy and yet so elegant in his bearing, the directness of his gaze and brightness of his eyes like his father's.

Caesar shook his head in a show of impatience. "If this is about my will, I cannot acknowledge him in writing. You know that." His sharp gaze rested upon her, and he tossed a hand in a dismissive gesture.

"But, surely..."

"There are no buts in Roman law." Unwinding his toga, he cast it upon a chair.

"You could change the law. I would." It shocked her when his compatriots castigated his rule, speaking guardedly even against Caesar. "Roman freedom is a misnomer, meant to protect everyone but the leader. How can you allow this?" As a frown raced across his forehead, she hesitated. Lately Roman poets composed witticisms against her that the proletariat repeated. Cicero made fun of her daily.

Caesar lifted a hand and shook his head. "Let us not go into that again. I am no king."

"You should be. I am sure many of your subjects would support you as supreme ruler."

"You think I don't take advantage of my position? Only an idiot would not garner what benefits were available. I have been involved in politics and running this state longer than you have lived. And think you not I don't see that lately it doesn't sit well?"

Although he smiled in the middle of the speech, making the words lose some of their weight, she realized he was serious. "I don't intend to argue it, my Lord. Instead the Queen of Egypt would welcome you as befits the most noble leader in the Western world." Her voice purred flute-like and she stepped toward him in one fluid movement, Caesarion keeping pace and sticking to her like honey. "Father," he said again, and held out the single daisy Cleopatra had plucked from a bouquet.

Caesar smiled, took the flower and tousled the few hairs on Caesarion's head. "I admit I am weary." He took Cleopatra into his arms. "Well, little one." He looked down at Caesarion. "So he talks now."

"My priests say he surpasses other children of his age."

"It is well." Caesar touched his lips to hers and ran his hands down her body. It was clear he had other things in mind.

Chapter VII

44 BCE

As Caesar spent more time at the villa, Cleopatra wondered aloud whether Egypt should remain neutral now in their dealings with Parthia.

Scowling, Caesar turned from the table where he'd been working, papyrus spread out before him. "By the god Zeus, are you mad, woman?" He got up and began pacing back and forth, listing Parthia's perfidious actions through the years, stabbing a finger toward her at the end of each recitation.

Careful to speak calmly, she murmured sympathetically, "How dreadful. In truth, they have never been particularly friendly to Egypt. Certainly we'll help you in whatever way we can." She strolled the room, picking up toys Caesarion had left on the floor.

He nodded thoughtfully. "Are you suggesting I launch a campaign against them?"

"My Lord, I would never presume to tell Caesar what the whole world has always expected."

He lifted an eyebrow before nodding again. "I admit Parthia's comeuppance is long past due. My men whetted their appetite on Spain and long for heartier fare, bigger rewards. Perhaps it's time." Resuming his seat, he pushed the chair back from the table and regarded her. "You jog me into my duty. If I do this thing, what can Egypt offer Rome?"

As if he didn't know. Again he was testing her, but the light in his eyes reflected the warmth she felt as he regarded her. She spoke carefully, reminding him again of Egypt's riches. "A successful invasion necessitates much preparation. Egypt can make a strategic launching site. Your legions would not have far to go, and our fertile lands would ensure that Caesar's army is not without sustenance. " She shrugged. "That's if Caesar is of a mind for another conquest, although I wonder why. You already control much of the world. You hardly need it all." She piled the toys she'd collected on the edge of the table where he'd been working.

"Egypt provides a superior place to launch an invasion, and you have delineated its advantages well. But it's only one country I've considered using in the past."

As he sat quietly, brow knit, she suggested, "If you like, I'll put my map-makers and geographers at your disposal immediately."

"Yes, of course," he muttered.

His shoulders were no longer slumped and a far-away look brightened his eyes. It was clear he was already making plans to command an army the likes of which the world had never seen. Caesar's ancient enemy would be vanquished, and she, with Caesarion at her side, would be waiting for her triumphant lover.

During the following days she poured over maps of Egypt with him, the peculiar lemon-light of Rome sliding across their battle table like a benediction. She loved listening while her Egyptian mapmakers explained the location of waterholes, of ground cover and natural rock formations. Caesar listened respectfully and asked pertinent questions. He also conferred often with Marc Anthony and Lepidus, who had become Master of the Horse, Anthony's old position. The three leaders and others in the inner circle came often to the villa at the top of the hill.

As preparations for the campaign grew, Cleopatra suspended her own plans while Caesar tightened his hold on the Roman people Using the prerogatives of power, he gradually assumed the trappings of royalty, and she did nothing to discourage him. Monarchy was what she knew, what she believed in. An undercurrent of hostility arose from those who had once idolized him. Cicero led cries of "tyrant" in the Senate, cries that were refuted by others, but his tirades against Cleopatra went unchecked.

Once she urged Caesar to arrest him, not thinking before she uttered the words.

Caesar whirled on her. "You forget, Madam, this is not Egypt." His eyes bore the steel of the battlefield.

Knowing better than to protest, she said softly, "I only worry about you, My Lord."

In the following days she watched with interest as Caesar quieted his opponents with flattery and concessions, and when that didn't work by threats and iron control. Few members of the proletariat complained for he had instituted changes that helped the poor and gave more freedom to slaves and servants, an action she had trouble understanding. His frequent and exotic spectacles – once three hundred gladiators contested at one time – were events furthering peace in the province. His plans for a canal system, similar to one in Egypt, brought much praise, even though Cassius and his clique shouted, "The Republic is drowning in Caesar's plans." He ignored them or made their speeches in the Forum look silly. He had the people on his side.

He was with Cleopatra often now, spending a whole week one time, and finally making his headquarters with her. When he appointed himself dictator for life, she gave fervent thanks to the gods. She could see nothing but benefit for her and Caesarion if Caesar ruled Rome in perpetuity. Her son's three or four words had now grown to a dozen,

One morning Cleopatra put him in bed between her and Caesar, and Caesar tickled and played with Caesarion until all three were laughing, and as the boy approached his third birthday, no one could miss Caesar's increased delight in the child. He took him in his chariot to the senate, on horseback to the fields, and had him sit by his side when friends came to discuss matters of importance. One day as rain splashed steadily into the *impluvium*, he ate early and called for a plate for Caesarion. As they ate, Caesar quizzed him as if he were an older boy, making him count and explain words, and listen while he talked military strategy. Caesar seemed smilingly satisfied with Caesarion's answers and attention, holding him on his knee afterward and whispering words Cleopatra couldn't hear.

She almost wept with joy when she heard the rumors being passed on in the markets and wine shops. They said, Caesar was going to change Roman law so he could marry the Egyptian queen. She knew better, but in Alexandria everyone would honor her liaison with him. There, Caesar would be acknowledged as her husband, Caesarion as his child. She couldn't lose, no matter that Cicero and his followers dubbed her "The whore of the Nile."

Ignoring the gossip, she watched with a loving eye as Caesarion garnered his father's affections. Several times she caught the boy running into Caesar's office. Caesar would look up from the desk where he wrote his Commentaries, scrolls of blank papyrus waiting for the final word, space in the wall niches waiting for the final scroll. Or he'd be meeting with Marc Anthony, the two bent over maps. But Caesar would smile at Caesarion, put down his pen and hold out an arm. Caesarion would catch hold and swing on it. The sight invariably thrilled her.

One day Caesar announced, "We leave for Alexandria the seventeenth of March."

Elated, she had Iras and Charmion begin the preparations. Although she had kept abreast of what was happening at home, she missed the sounds and sights of the city. She longed for the wide streets, the great buildings, the hustle and bustle at the docks, yearned to hear languages from the four corners of the earth. She missed seeing the light from Pharos brightening the night, missed the cinnamon smells of the royal kitchens, and the tastes she had taken into herself with her gruel as a child. She'd grown up in the palace, but in those early years, without luxury. Her father had wanted her to know what it was like to eat from plain plate, to write on pot-sherds, to wear plain clothes. But grandeur surrounded her.

Memories grew strong as the departure date drew near. After Caesar conquered Parthia, she would remind him of India, giving him the title her father had conjured up years before. To keep him in her part of the world she must always be one step ahead, never forgetting Caesar's power, but skillfully reminding him of her own. Perhaps one morning when dawn came with a fanfare of color, the sun making flamboyant the laurel, myrtle and narcissus beneath her window, or one night when a full moon shone and the whole city was washed with silver, she'd bear him another child. The prospect of having him with her away from Rome, churned like milk, not going sour, but fermenting into something tasty.

Three days before they were to leave, Caesar returned to Calpurnia, but Cleopatra expected nothing else. It was there he met with clients, gave familial orders, discussed the affairs of Rome. Only the campaign against Parthia took place in the villa on the hill.

Still, restless, unable to sleep, wondering if he'd seek his wife's bed, twice she got up to check on Caesarion. Each time she found him sleeping peacefully.

The next night, when mist was occluding the sky and the dampness of night stuck in her nose like a bad odor, she rose early, not liking the dreams that had disrupted her sleep, leaving her tingling with anger. A strange feeling, of death and destruction that only the sweetness, goodness, and compassion of Isis could assuage, gripped her. Throwing a cloak around her shoulders, she strolled in the garden where Isis came to her, and she lost herself in the moment. Sitting on a stone bench, she raised her face to the sky, not wanting to hide her unease from the gods. She never heard or noticed Charmion until her auburn-haired friend stood next to her. She listened as Charmion related the gossip originating in the scullery and back rooms of Calpurnia's house. Caesar's wife had also risen early, distraught, crying and carrying on about a dream that had so frightened her she had begged Caesar not to go to the senate on March 17.

A cold chill gripped Cleopatra. "What did he do?"

"He paid no attention to her, of course," Charmion said with alacrity, apparently pleased that she could bring this evidence of his waning sense of loyalty to Calpurnia.

Cleopatra shook her head, seeing past the fog to something basic and true, the chill solidifying, becoming block-like and hard as granite. "He should have," she whispered. In her dreams the shadow of death had loomed, omens existed. A cock had crowed in the middle of the night, and earlier, while she focused on Isis, a star shot across the sky, so fast it had blurred her vision. Heart pounding, she rushed into the house, but Caesarion slept soundly, and only the slaves getting up competed with the sounds warring in her head.

Chapter VIII

46 BCE - 43 BCE

Hours later, Charmion brought the word: Caesar was dead. Brought down in the senate. Brought down by those he'd known, brought down by those to whom he'd given preferential treatment, brought down by those he'd considered friends.

Sitting with Caesarion on her lap, Cleopatra flinched, not in surprise, for the omens had been too strong, but in shock. Caesar had epitomized strength and power, but in the end he couldn't save himself. All the ideas he'd presented so forcefully, all the dreams she had floated would never be achieved. Her child was sleeping and safe, but his father was no more. His people had thrust knife blade after knife blade into him until at last, bleeding, falling to the floor, he had covered his head with his toga so no one could see him die. She had given herself to him, had cast Caesarion's future with him, and he was dead.

An emptiness filled her, as if all she had been had drained away with Caesar's blood. The light of Rome flickering like a candle ready to go out, she listened to Charmion's terse account, to Iras's emotional one, to the words of the servants who beat their breasts in sympathy. Cassius, Brutus and others had killed him. She heard from people who seemed to enjoy recounting details, she did not hear from others who had worshiped at Caesar's feet, and through the hearing and the non-hearing, she did not cry. Finally she heard from Marc Anthony.

Standing in the doorway, clutching a piece of bloody cloth, he looked as wretched as she felt, his clothes filthy, his face streaked and tear-stained. Why did he think he had to come to her looking so pitiful? She had no sympathy to give him, her heart was bleeding for

Caesarion and herself, and for the mighty Caesar. A man so proud, so strong should not be humbled, but should die gloriously in battle, victorious to the end. In the weak, watery light leaking in the shuttered courtyard windows, Anthony became a blur, an intrusion she couldn't pretend didn't exist.

Didn't Anthony realize it was the Romans who had robbed her, and he was one, moving with the same lazy arrogance, his powerful legs covered with the slime of the mob? All of them had partaken of her largesse, hung on to hers and Caesar's words and then turned on him, murdering him. How was Anthony any different? She lifted her head, giving him, not permission to speak but to leave. Yet, she could not lift her arm no matter how hard she tried.

"His toga," he said gesturing with the piece of cloth. " I thought… perhaps…" His gaze on his feet, he slowly looked up. "I loved him," he added, the words hanging like sludge in the gloom of the room.

How could he speak of love to her! Was this not Caesar's child she held, had she not known the mighty Caesar's embraces?

"He was like a father to me." His voice hung like a cobweb in the room.

Hollow-eyed she looked past him. Like a father? Caesar had been Caesarian's father. Her son's father. The only man she had known intimately, the only man to offer her a future, and those lowly, grubbing Romans had ended it for her.

"He was my teacher."

She tried to shake her head. Had Caesar not taught her, even as she had taught him? Who could know better than she? She scowled at Anthony.

"He was my friend."

"Friend!" She spat the word like spitting venom from her mouth. The sound ricocheted from the walls, and Anthony took a step backward. "What do you know of friendship?" Caesar had been her friend from the moment he realized she was Egypt's rightful ruler. More than a lover, he was her mentor, her companion, her strong arm, her intellectual equal. Wanting to slice Anthony's conceit into pieces, she lifted her head and looked straight at him. Dejection showed in every line of his body and face, his misery like an extension of her own. Quickly, she glanced aside. Caesarion, disturbed by the emotional charges ratcheting through her, woke. She nodded at Charmion who took him from the room. Without her son in her arms, she wanted to submit to howling grief, but she would not break down in front of a Roman.

Anthony's voice caught, balanced on the brink of cracking. "He looked out for me on the battlefield; I for him. I loved him as a brother."

"He was my friend, too. My father's friend, a friend to Egypt." She glanced at Anthony. "There is nothing you can tell me about Julius Caesar, Marc Anthony." Her voice rose and fell like a professional mourner's, like those who had stood in the shadows of her father's bed when his stomach pain erupted into death.

Anthony cleared his voice. "He loved us both."

Love? Neither she nor Caesar had ever said the word, but now Anthony had mentioned it twice, and all the times she had laughed with Caesar, all the times he had reached out to her with his mind, his body, his intellect and his power came back to her in an all encompassing rush. His poetry echoed in her ears, his voice speaking to Caesarion, resounded in the room, the memories plunging her into sorrow as quickly as death had come to him. Twenty-three times they had stabbed him until he quietly succumbed.

She fought back the great hard mass in her chest. If they could kill Caesar, they would not hesitate to kill her, too. The need, to be away, throbbed violently within her. Through the lump in her throat, she said, "Thank you for coming. Now, I must hurry home."

He nodded and set down the scrap of cloth he had folded and refolded. "For the boy."

As he started to leave, a thought caught her, rocked her with its significance. "Know you Octavian?" The boy Caesar had adopted, who would gain from Caesar's will.

Marc Anthony turned back, and she imagined a change in his posture, a stiffening of his spine. "Caesar's nephew. A sickly youth." He shrugged as if Octavian were of little consequence.

She watched him turn away, and impulsively she called, "But you are not."

He paused, and again she noted the pain, the fatigue and hurt that had driven him since Caesar's death. She'd heard he had swayed the crowd, turned them against the traitors with his rhetoric.

"No, I am not," he said.

And neither am I, she thought, pushing aside the need to wail and shout, to mourn in the Egyptian way. Caesar was no more, but for Caesarion, she must be strong. She had to get him back to Egypt, to Alexandria where she'd make things right again.

"I will see you get to your ship safely," Anthony said "Be ready to leave in the sunset hour."

***

At home, acting with a rapidity that astounded consuls and officials who had shirked their duties while she was gone, she banished some, imprisoned others, and ordered others slain. Her dreams had bled out on the floor of the Roman senate, but each day, surrounded by a now loyal court, the air reminded her she was home. Soft as down, it caressed her, whispering, *your son is safe.* Priests and populace, men, women, and children looked at Caesarion with reverence, respect, and love. She would feed the Romans their dirty tribute and all the time build up the Egyptian military so she could forget the rest of the world. Let them come into her ports to trade, but she would stay aloof. She wanted nothing but peace.

For a time she knew a depression of spirit that all the gods could not assuage. But as time passed and she strolled through her gardens or walked among the scholars at the museum and library, she knew a joy that couldn't be squelched. Caesarion was alive and healthy, and showed no signs of the falling sickness. Already his curiosity thrilled her. She wanted him to be a scholar in the mold of his father as well as a soldier. At the Museum, when he paused to listen to a roving philosopher and question his statements, she knew deep pride. In the city, escorted by guards and the court, he walked with her past small shops and through the bazaar, and while she dallied, choosing perfumes, fine ivory or silks, he watched mimes, musicians and tricksters, wide-eyed with delight but always learning. At the waterfront he pestered shipwrights and other workers, asked them about their jobs and declared one day he'd captain the growing Egyptian armada. She swelled with pride.

He shared her love of the theater and chariot racing. Often she had him with her in the royal box at the Hippodrome. Sorrow slipped away, and she abandoned regret, feeling renewed excitement at being alive. Caesar had awakened her as a woman, but his city had been harsh, and eventually bloody and revolting. No, in Egypt she would forge a better life for her son.

When Caesarion was four, no tutor suited her, so she taught him herself. He was a quick study, and the morning hours seated with him in the nursery were her favorite times. At noon when the sun began to reach into the corners of the room, he went with her into the garden and sat beneath a grape arbor or under an acacia tree to eat their bread, fruit, and cake. He prattled, jumping from one subject to another, or trotted out riddles in an attempt to stump her. He announced them with a sidewise look and a tiny smile that slowly grew until he was laughing uproariously as she pretended to consider his questions seriously. "How many oarsman does it take to row a royal barge?" he asked one day, and when she hesitated, he cried, "As many as you want. If you don't have enough, you just make someone else row, too." Already he had grasped the idea of royal privilege. Still, she allowed no foolishness, making him work for pats on the head and kisses she dropped on the back of his neck.

After lunch, while he napped, she listened while her ministers reported on the affairs of the world. Her envoy to Rome, her people in Greece, the Egyptian delegation in Syria all repeated similar tales about Rome: Anthony and Octavian had joined forces with Lepidus, and the three were fighting Caesar's assassins

As long as Rome left her alone, she could relax. Cicero, who had only spread spoken lies about her while Caesar was alive, now belittled her in print. Sneering openly, he outdid himself tarnishing her image. He called her an adulterer buying friendships with gold, a witch with portfolio, not really royal, Greek not Egyptian, a fraud and charlatan.

She itched to retaliate, but Roman legions still remained in Egypt, and Cassius, who had been one of the first to stick his blade into Caesar's flesh, demanded ships and money, as did Anthony and Octavian. For Egypt to survive, she had to play the Roman game. She finally cast her lot with Anthony and Octavian, but her ships, caught in a storm, were unable to deliver the help Marc Anthony demanded. Had she thrown her support to the other side, he asked in a communiqué? "Damn the Romans! Damn Marc Anthony!" she cried, her remaining ships returning home.

At the same time the advisers and officials surrounding Ptolemy XIV boycotted her audiences, held secret meetings and lied to her. When she confronted them with the truth, they dared her to do something about it.

Cold reality washed over her, harsher than the winter months in Rome or the salt spray of the Mediterranean. Striding down halls and up staircases until she found Ptolemy cowering in his old nursery, she spat out, "Tell me."

His jowls jiggling, his lips trembling, he managed, "What?"

"You know. What you and your advisers have been up to."

He flushed and stammered, and when she pressed him about the secret meetings, he thrust out his bottom lip. "You don't let me be a real king. I should sign papers and give orders."

He was still nothing more than a fat boy whom others manipulated. How could she save him? "So you want to become a "real" king?" She spoke softly, her pity almost palpable.

"Yes."

"And when you are a real king, will you let me be a real queen?"

His fat fingers slid over one another as he attempted to snap them as his brother had done so easily. Giving up trying, he said, "I'll let you do as much as you let me do."

They had coached him well. She turned to the window where the breeze coming from the harbor was salt tinged. Only yesterday she had walked there with Caesarion. "And my son, your nephew?"

"That Roman boy?" Ptolemy said, clearly puzzled. Discovering a pull toy among the dusty remnants of his childhood, he grinned. "I remember this!" He blew off the dust and kneeled to pull the tiny chariot along the floor.

"That Roman boy as you put it is my son!"

Ptolemy shrugged and glanced briefly at her while pulling the toy in a circle. "Let me see. Although there was nothing I liked about it, you did take me with you to Rome." His face brightened. "If I should travel, I will include your boy among my people."

His naiveté was as dangerous as a temple cat she had tried to tame as a child. She rushed away before her mind would soften. His men spoke against her everywhere, lurked in the corridors of her private quarters, and tried to keep Caesarion's depiction from Egypt's coins. A frisson of fear invaded her. "Do whatever you have to do to protect Caesarion," she told her people.

Two weeks later Ptolemy XIV, Cleopatra's half brother and husband in name, was found dead, apparently of food poisoning. His backers were blamed and executed, and she and the court grieved publicly. Privately she berated herself and spent hours begging Isis and Osiris for comfort. When they did not answer immediately, she understood. News from Rome said Julius Caesar had been declared a god and Octavian was calling himself the son of Julius the god. The words appeared on his coins. The gods had no time to deal with her lesser affairs.

To protect Caesarion, when he turned six she placed him on the throne as her fellow monarch and broadcast his new titles. Henceforth he would be Ptolemy XV Caesar, Theos Philopator Philometor, the God who loves his father and mother. The message to the world couldn't be denied. Caesarion was an Egyptian pharaoh, but also a Roman.

She had learned men add to his knowledge, bringing the Greek geographer, Strabo to the Museum. Mornings Caesarion studied with him, learning political and geographical boundaries, the trade routes of the world. In addition, he began the study of languages, learning grammar and syntax. He had the same facility for learning she had. Each night he brought a new maxim he had memorized, and they discussed it while studying the stars that swirled over the city, he sitting in the circle of her arm, or getting up to stride like his father while he recited, astronomy another of his new subjects. "Love is the oldest of all the gods" became a vehicle she used to recall again the glories of Caesar.

Life was pleasant, and she solidified her hold on her people's loyalty by relaxing strict laws. She had Caesarion's inscription added to the temple at Dendera. For eons Egyptians would sing her son's praises as they sang hers now.

Learning Anthony had avenged Caesar by killing both Brutus and Cassius, she sighed with relief. Anthony, Octavian and Lepidus had carved up the Roman Empire. Claiming the eastern provinces, Anthony's popularity insured allegiances, but Egypt's temporary reprieve ended when Anthony again requested her help.

Cleopatra ignored one and then two requests for assistance, hoping he would merely shrug off her avoidance. He didn't. Demanding, he sent dispatches and envoys backed up by troops. Roman warriors were suddenly everywhere in Alexandria, causing consternation in the public square as well as in diplomatic circles. Each day a Roman envoy, accompanied by a contingent of warriors, came to the palace and politely waited for her answer.

Caesar had said, barring himself, Anthony was the best general the world had ever seen, and he had backed her into a corner. No matter how loyal the Egyptian people, Egypt was not a fortress. The Romans would not hesitate to decimate her land, slaughter everyone in the royal palace, including her and Caesarion.

Money, supplies and, treaties could be negotiated, but to keep Egypt safe from complete Roman domination would take more. No longer the young girl bedazzled by a strong calf, she understood what she had to do. A week later she dispatched a letter of state accompanied by all the pomp of her office—advance troops, litter bearers, scribes, and an ambassador of good will, who with much ceremony would speak for Egypt. Anthony would be reminded she was not a female who would bend to his every demand as Calpurnia had acceded to Caesar's demands. Neither was she an ersatz Fulvia ready to wield a sword like a man. He would feel her power and know she was not only a queen but also a woman, for when he unrolled the Egyptian letters her scent would anoint the room.

Chapter IX

41 BCE

CLEOPATRA SAT AT her alabaster dressing table planning. Lately Romans agitated for action, wanting revenge for past aggressions by Parthia, and in this Anthony needed her assistance. In a short time, with lightening attacks Marc Anthony had put down recalcitrant provinces and countries, awing the multitudes as much as Caesar had. Rome had deified Caesar, and Anthony had taken Caesar's earthly place. People poured money into his coffers, convinced he was a god, and Anthony, claiming descent from Dionysus, did nothing to deny it. This interested her greatly.

The people of the great city Ephesus erected statues and monuments dedicated to him. When he extended the rights of asylum to the temple at Ephesus, ignoring Arsinoe who had taken sanctuary in the city, Ephesians stated he was a proper consort for Cleopatra who was Isis incarnate. Words whispered on the wind, shouted in marketplaces, said slyly in wine shops, and repeated at home, paired her with him in Tarsus.

When she accepted as proper his divinity, word of her capitulation spread rapidly, talk about the rendezvous abounding. Caesar had barely acknowledged her status as Isis, seldom referring to it, but Anthony apparently worshiped her as Isis's earthly incarnation. She had to appear absolutely ravishing. She had to appear strong but vulnerable, a woman a Roman god would desire. A man in his prime, Anthony was a true symbol of a god on earth, and she must be imbued with grace and glamour as well as strength. It was an added bonus that he was more of an age with her.

She looked out to where her fleet lay at anchor, a symbol to Rome of her strength as well as her riches. She'd been naïve with Caesar, and she'd had to flee Rome like an enemy they had defeated. Now she must defeat them, not in impossible battles, but diplomatically and with her person *That* long ago day in the stables, Anthony's eyes had flared with appreciation before he'd realized who she was. The coming meeting could well prove the future of Egypt. She tried but could recall little of that dark night he had helped her escape Rome, now he'd made clear his position by demanding her presence at Tarsus. She had no out.

She sat still as Iras outlined her eyes with kohl. If Caesar was a lover of women, Anthony was more so, and his long list of conquests wore beauty like a gift. His third wife, Fulvia, had drawn second glances and people hinted her ambition pushed Anthony to success. Cicero said Fulvia ruled the Anthony household. Anthony shrugged off the insult as a joke, his easy-going attitude putting him in good stead with Rome's legionnaires. They had revered Caesar but loved Anthony who drank, whored, and gambled with them.

She inspected herself. Pleased that her skin showed smooth, no lines anywhere, and her eyes, her best feature, sparkled, she studied her mouth. It was not too spare or too large, and when she emphasized both, few noticed her nose. It was no longer than many others, certainly not as long as Anthony's, but it was wider than usual, a Macedonian nose. In Rome, some had made sport of her, Cicero calling her nose a proboscis, even Servilia smiling. Caesar's liaisons grew out of political need; were Anthony's only the same?

Or was there a chance he wanted more? With Caesar she had learned the art of love; with Anthony she would perfect it.

And so she left Alexandria leading a large contingent of ships, determined to arrive looking lovely but in charge. As her armada approached Tarsus, she lolled on a purple couch, her cedar and gold ship gliding over the water like a swan. The rail embedded with precious stones glittered, and with pearls wound through her hair, her arms and neck and ankles circled with a wealth of jewels, her breasts bare, the nipples rouged, showing beneath a shimmer of diaphanous material, her golden skin complementing her violet eyes, she glittered, too.

She lay quietly as her ship entered the lagoon, her attendants fanning her with ostrich feathers, and swinging perfumed censors, the fragrance wafting in the afternoon breeze. Iras and Charmion strew flowers shoreward, and she watched the blossoms float on the now serene waters. A blend of flutes, castanets, pipes, and tambourines , music sweet as birdsong mingled with the scent of sandalwood and jasmine in a spicy-sweet aroma. Along the shore people pushed and shoved to get a glimpse of her. They waved from banks, or watched from small boats rising and falling on the swells of her ship's passing, its purple sails fluttering, its golden poop deck gleaming. They hurried to the docks awe showing on their faces and gaped at a living goddess in grand human form.

She wished she were taller, but her curves complimented one another, and her gown drifted like downy clouds, her dress appearing now amber, now gold, the color taking on the hue of the flowers banked around her, the blue of the sky, her eyes. A shifting and changing dancing radiance of light appeared to bathe her, and people gawking bowed their heads and fell to their knees in adoration. Iras released doves from golden cages, and for a moment, bird wings beat the air and a murmur coming from shore lifted like a benediction.

At the docks, a lookout shouted, "The Queen of Egypt, the goddess Isis is here!" and soon the rattle of wagons and carts and the thud of countless feet sounded as countless people rushed to see.

Her somnolence exploding in a tingling excitement, she wondered. What changes had the years brought to Anthony, or was he, like Caesar, ageless? Would he dazzle her as he had thirteen years before? While Caesar's heir, Octavian, claimed to be the son of a god, in the rich and exotic East, Anthony *was* a god.

She tried to glimpse him. Leaning on an elbow, she peered shoreward as her floating palace came to anchor. Costumed as the graces, Iras, Charmion and the lesser ladies of the court lined the rails and waved merrily as befitted those attending a goddess who had come to see a god. But where was he? A crowd had followed her progress from the mouth of the river. Now all manner of people jostled for position, rich, poor, clean, dirty, important and not, but none of them was Anthony. She frowned. Was all this preparation for naught? Making her wait like a serving maid, was he getting even for her delay in answering his previous summons? How should she retaliate for this humiliation?

A young man pushed his way through the crowd on the docks. "Let me through, I have a letter from My Lord Anthony."

Although her heart pounded fiercely, she showed nothing of her feelings as she read the message twice before calling for a scribe. Anthony invited her to dine on shore with him. So he would have her go yet another distance to see him! Seething with indignation, she made her voice hum sweetly while dictating a reply. "Your very kind invitation is deeply appreciated, but it is most appropriate for My Lord Anthony to dine with me. I offer Egyptian hospitality, and I assure you your appetite(s) will not go unfulfilled. Cleopatra VII, divine ruler of both Upper and Lower Egypt awaits your decision as if it were her own."

Before the hour ended, Anthony sent his acceptance and soon after arrived amid a flurry of common foot soldiers and officers, he laughing and joking with them before he broke away and moved toward the barge, his officers close behind. She met him at the top of the gangplank. His gaze swept over the ship before he brought it back to her with the force of Caesar and more. An elemental earthiness shone in the slight upturn of his lips, the crinkle in his eyes. Her peevishness disappeared as swiftly as dust in a rainstorm.

Returning his look, she saw him not as an adjunct of Caesar, but as the new leader of the world, a tall, powerfully built man, handsome in a rough way that was most attractive, as appealing as when she had seen him so many years before in the stables in Alexandria. An element of swagger lingered, but it was tempered by his new station and age. His eyes showed his understanding of the roles they were playing and his liking for her as a woman.

Holding out a henna-painted hand, she moved toward him, her gown a breath of air, floating about her legs. Her dangling earrings tinkled musically, her jeweled collar flashed and glittered, one drawing attention to her large almond-shaped eyes and the other to her firm, shapely bosom. The world said Isis had come to revel with Dionysus for Asia's sake, and now it would take little effort, she admitted to herself aware of the affect she had on him and his effect on her.

"Egypt and her Queen welcome you, my Lord." She moved carefully, aware that her body caught the light from lamps placed throughout the ship in groups, and the enticing illumination turned the night to phosphorescence and was reflected in the water like an otherworldly dream.

"By the gods," he said, his voice rough but straight forward and filled with emotion. "In all ways you have brought splendor." His eyes paid tribute to her before he gestured toward the garlanded statues and beyond to the series of small tables where Iras and Charmion were seating his officers. "You are kind to a rough soldier, surrounding him with beauty."

"A token of the affection long celebrated between our two countries, My Lord."

He looked around boldly, inspecting the bower on the deck. One table stood a little removed from the half dozen others; hidden behind cloth-of-gold draperies it had been set with service plates of gold, as were all the place settings. Touching the curtains blowing like willow-the-wisps in the sweet-scented breeze, he said, "Call me Marc Anthony. I'm not used to titles."

"But I've heard you've earned them."

He lifted an eyebrow. "I fought like a bull if that is what you mean."

"Everyone sings your praises. But pray be seated, Marc Anthony." She glided past him in a movement as fluid as one of her royal dancers and indicated a chair set on feet of gold and replete with lapis lazuli, garnet, and agate insets.

He shook his head. "Romans don't sit on thrones."

Was he hinting that although Caesar had named himself dictator for life, a king although not in name, that what suited one didn't necessarily suit the other? "It was my father's," she said simply. Despite his words, she was sure Anthony was impressed with luxury.

"This will serve me fine." He indicated a plain chair carved from mahogany.

She motioned to a servant who took Auletes' chair away and put the other in its place.

A slave attempted to place a wreath of blue lotus flowers around his neck. Anthony waved her off. "I may have adopted many of your customs, but not that one. I'm not adverse to Egyptian wine though." He accepted a glass, the jewel-encrusted goblet disappearing in his hand and the wine down his throat.

The sky had paled; pewter evening would soon become purple night. A lute player strummed in time with the quiet splash of the river against the dock. Cleopatra refilled Anthony's glass herself, watched as he tossed it down, too. He grinned at her, his look somehow boyish and yet challenging, too, a man who knew he was appealing to women, but a man who also understood he was a force to be reckoned with.

"Wine to whet my appetite, or should I make that plural?"

His quick wit and intelligence appealed to her. But with Caesar drinking had never been a problem for after a glass or two he merely tasted the fresh glasses of beer and wine that accompanied each course. Would it be a problem with Anthony? He often caroused with his men until dawn. Now, his gaze baiting her to keep up with him, he filled her glass with wine.

She lifted it. "May the gods look with favor upon our meeting." She signaled, and serving girls lingering near the richly embroidered tapestry, its threads of shimmering gold and silver insuring privacy, brought a platter of dormice stuffed with groat. Anthony ate with relish and without comment, licked his fingers after finishing. Immediately, two girls appeared, one with a bowl of warm water, another with a soft cloth.

"You spoil me." He smiled at Cleopatra. "Would you treat Octavian the same?"

Settling back in her chair, she said with scorn, "He is but a child."

He chuckled and named the third member of the ruling Roman triumvirate. "What of Lepidus?"

She shrugged. "I hear he is not very capable."

His eyes narrowed. "And me?"

She waited a moment. The flickering light danced along the bridge of Anthony's nose and made mysterious the column of his neck. A gold medallion presented to him by the Ephesians shone rich against his chest. "That you are a man worthy of wearing Caesar's mantle." She spoke in her softest voice, caressing the words as if caressing him.

He tipped his head to the side. "Already Parthia is marching west. So, how much will Egypt help me?"

"Egypt lies between Parthia and Rome. We, too, have needs." Her voice came softly, ingratiatingly.

He shrugged his massive shoulders slightly. "Your needs are Rome's needs."

She spoke with amusement. "People told me you were blunt, but I didn't believe them."

Anthony laughed, first with her and then again as his dirty plate was whisked away and replaced with a fresh one also of gold. "By Jupiter, a man can get used to such indulgence." He helped himself to the fish fillets being offered. "I should be angry. I asked for your aid a year or so ago, but you didn't bring it. Then I heard you were assisting my enemies."

"Assisting traitors? That is a blatant lie." Her gaze was as direct as his. "But why talk about what is history? Egypt is here now." Smiling, she reached across the table and put a helping of cabbage cooked with sesame seeds on his plate. "Try that, Anthony. Egyptian hospitality properly seasoned cannot be equaled."

He looked from the plate to her and slowly took a bite, his eyes holding hers. "I admit my information may have been flawed."

"Undoubtedly," she said as the servants again replaced dirty dishes with fresh ones for the baked pheasant, the goat studded with garlic, the asparagus.

"And you know well how to satisfy a man's appetite…for food." For a while he didn't allow her to look away. Then with a grin, he winked and concentrated on his meal.

She followed suit. She would let him lead, or at least let him think he led.

"A woman who fills a man's stomach, and his eyes, deserves knowing it," he said, dipping his hands in a fresh bowl of water, again grinning, his wolfish eyes taking her in deliberately, as if relishing what he saw, not denigrating it.

She met his flattering look long enough to feel a thrill run up her spine.

"So," he said, "now that our countries have established a report, shall I rout your troublesome sister, make her answer for her perfidy, or do you harbor lingering familial devotion?"

His swift change of subject, his harsh sounding voice startled her. Arsinoe's countenance floated up in front of her, and she clenched her teeth to keep from crying out. Torchlight reflected in the river, shimmering like ideas too delicate to broach. Hadn't her father taught her the right way to deal with traitors? With measured tone, she said, "I have not seen my sister for years."

"Still, she maintains she is the rightful sovereign, not you."

"Maintaining and being are different things, Marc Anthony." She shrugged. "I leave the disposition of my half-sister up to you." How could she put Arsinoe above Caesarion? Needing to bury the troubling thought, she motioned, and dates and honey cake were set before Anthony.

He ate more slowly now, smiling at her between bites. When a bowl of walnuts replaced the dates, he shook his head, leaned back in his chair and said, "Even Marc Anthony has his limits. I pledge the same or better tomorrow. My major domo has made arrangements for a banquet where your people may eat with mine." He wiped his lips on the edge of his robe. "You gave me a feast, Cleopatra." He used her name without a title.

She forced herself not to react.

He gestured. "But you took from me my duty as host as if it was yours to usurp."

"I take only what will please you, my lord."

His eyes narrowed slightly. "Everyone deserves a feast, but not the aftermath. The day after a banquet for all, you will dine with me." He put his forearms on the table and leaning toward her caught her in the orbit of his eyes. "Alone."

There was no mistaking his intent. She met his look without a hint of artifice, one ruler speaking to another. "I look forward, my Lord to sampling Roman fare."

He laughed. "By the gods, Marc Anthony, soldier and Roman, cannot wait."

His smile was as warm as hers with Caesarion, more intimate than anything she had seen in years. Shook, she motioned toward the moon, its fullness prophesied by her astronomers. "But the gods have not walked across the night sky yet. You must have patience, Marc Anthony."

"God's truth, I must, and it was never my best attribute, Madam."

She felt a pleasant loosening of her limbs and following a scripted evening, her musicians produced a fanfare on schedule. Temple dancers emerged from behind a filigreed screen; girls barely past puberty, gilded with gold, glided sensuously.

"By all that's holy," Anthony cried, "you know how to entertain."

He moved his chair closer to hers, and, as the evening progressed, let his hand fall on the arm of her chair. His legs, like mighty oars, dipped into the rhythm, keeping time with the music. His feet were large, not long and elegant as Caesar's but strong and wide, and the hairs on his calves were as black as those glimpsed on his chest. Warmth, better than a charcoal brazier, invaded her body and moved faster than fermented drink into her mind.

When the dancers disappeared behind the screen, he said soberly, "Tell me of your son. Is he well?"

Was he always this unpredictable? His eyes bore the interest of a friend, one who really cared. "He's very much like his father," she said swiftly, "intelligent, curious, eager to learn." Then pushing caution aside, she said, "But he needs a man's guiding hand."

Anthony's smile reached his eyes. "And you? Have you no one to... massage your neck when you've been leaning over papyri all day."

Did he imagine she had a lover? She shook her head. "No one."

His smile teased. "I give a good...massage."

She rose. He had promised much and nothing, as had she. Soon his officers would hope to learn what he had or had not accomplished for Rome. "It is late. Until tomorrow, Marc Anthony."

He jumped to his feet"Tomorrow," he said, and would have gone down the gangplank, except she stopped him, her voice gentle and sweet as a pigeon cooing. "A token of Egypt's affection, My Lord."

Charmion handed him the plates of gold upon which he had eaten his meal, and serving girls handed the same to his men.

He scowled. "A rough soldier cannot hope to equal this." Hefting the plates, he grinned.

"Equality comes in many guises," Cleopatra whispered in a deep, throaty way, and for a moment held his gaze fully before he left, his men following.

The next day Anthony led her to the head table on the shore, its prominence backed by tapestries depicting the forum in Rome. The message was not lost upon her, but as long as she was willing to bankroll his legions, he would give and grant her much. Only once did he override her, his voice brooking no interference. She had come prepared to pay heavily, and so did not argue the point.

The following night, she arrived at Anthony's residence on the appointed hour. She had expected him to have the best house in the ancient city, but he'd expropriated a petty official's headquarters. The modest two-story edifice had the advantage of being on the harbor. No one could enter Tarsus by water without his knowledge. He had to have known she'd arrived. She scowled, but smiled sweetly when she spied him. He wore a simple, short tunic and high-laced sandals and was pacing along the road when she appeared. His men standing along the wall outside the house, and from positions in the garden, looked up, their gazes respectful. She could hardly accuse him now.

"Welcome to this Roman outpost," he said ushering her through the atrium and past a pleasant terrace, the canopy supported by simple Doric columns. "It's not exactly a palace, but I trust you will be comfortable."

"The Queen of Egypt doesn't require opulence," she replied, hoping he'd linger outside. Pots of flowers and two Greek statues faced her in an arrangement pleasing to the eye, but Anthony strode to an arched doorway and gestured she enter, and stopped her attendants from following. "If your mistress needs you, we will send for you." He led her to an inside room where the air was close and the light dim, and where a table had been set. "Last night we were surrounded by advisers. Tonight it will be me," he touched his chest, "and you."

The room had no hangings, no murals, no decoration of any kind. Was he testing her?

"At one time I'd hoped to dazzle you with a great feast. Now, I'm determined to provide you a simple meal, but I swear you won't go away hungry." He pulled a chair from the table and seated her, his hands touching her shoulders briefly. The stone floor was cold, and she hugged herself. Great slabs of bread stacked on a plate and bowls of pickles resting in brine sat on the table.

Anthony seated himself as a servant girl appeared with platters of meat she set on the table between them. "A simple repast, but plentiful."

"Enough for an army, "she said as the woman bustled from the kitchen with huge bowls of chick peas, beans, and melon until there was no place for the final dish.

Shrugging, Anthony removed one of the lamps so she could set down the final platter of ham and chicken. "The plates are far from gold, but you're dining with a simple soldier."

" I'm not complaining."

"I am. You were supposed to be overwhelmed by my superior meal and my most noble bearing." Smiling, he poured her glass full of wine. "If the food isn't edible, you can wash it down. I can vouch for the wine."

She sipped. "It has a noble taste, and your bearing, my lord, is not affected by the food."

"Then all is not lost." He grinned. "Marc Anthony."

"Marc Anthony." She picked at overripe melon and nibbled coarse bread. As he had done before, he ate with gusto, glancing up now and then to ask if she wanted some more "stringy" ham or "dry" chicken.

Pleased that he could make fun of himself, she laughed and didn't protest when he refilled her glass.

After a while, he wiped his greasy hands and mouth on a cloth and regarded her with a gentle smile as he tossed the cloth aside. "You know, the day before yesterday I thought you and your courtiers would come ashore and present themselves to me." He chuckled ruefully. "There I was, seated at the public tribunal in the market place, and you were on your barge, and I didn't know you'd arrived until too late."

Relieved, she smiled. "So we were both mistaken. I thought you were deliberately reminding me of my client status." She shrugged. "But then I hardly know you, Marc Anthony."

"I'm sure you've heard the worst about me."

"There's been some gossip."

"Such as?" His voice was gruff.

Hers came in a soft rush, her mouth moving around the words as if hurrying them out. "You favor actresses."

He made a brushing motion with his hands as if to say it was of little consequence.

"Denial, sir? Or only deference to the sensibilities of a Queen?"

"You confuse a simple man."

"Marc Anthony simple? I beg to disagree."

He laughed. "By the gods, you are real. As real as my noble birth. I grew up with a good name, but my family was poor. My grandfather was a famous orator, my father a commander." He gestured. "And I became a soldier with a soldier's foibles and fortunes." Settling back in his seat, he said, "What do you want to talk about?"

"I've heard Marc Anthony is exceedingly brave."

"Exaggeration, naturally."

She smiled as he took the bait and told increasingly outrageous stories of battle, anecdotes that became slightly off-color, possibly meant to titillate.

Unlike Caesar, he would not enjoy poetry or too much subtlety. When he paused, she countered his tales with short verses that impinged on the bawdy, verses she, Charmion and Iras had whispered as children, not quite understanding. Raising her voice, she gestured and mimicked an actor on stage, her voice a song, emphasizing words and phrases, hurrying in places, slowing down in others, the tempo and tone as well as the words pulling in everyone who ever listened to her. Caesar would have thought the stories beneath him, but Anthony laughed and nodded, his eyes bright, and offered a ditty of his own. When she could remember no more rhymes, she composed a new one, liking that Anthony's eyes shone with appreciation, and he came around the table on the pretext of pouring her another glass of wine. His fingers touched hers, and awareness of him shot through her like an arrow dipped in honey. Mindful of the hairs curling on his arm and the muscles bunching his legs, she pushed slightly back from the table.

He pulled his chair next to hers and sat with his head level with hers. She saw the fine lines at the corners of his eyes and felt the raw sexual energy pouring from him and reminded herself not to lose track of who and what he was. He'd demonstrated his intelligence many times in the past. If tonight he had tried to duplicate the banquet she'd given, he would have failed miserably, but this night, with its intimacy and lack of servants and soldiers, demonstrated his perception. He was quick and clever and the evening was different enough to enchant her.

His gaze played over her face. "You know what I want don't you?" His voice was low, intimate.

She picked up her glass of wine and drank. A suffocating feeling filled her chest, blood rushed to her head, the years since Caesar died had been sterile and lacking, her body warm with longing. Despite the gossip, she'd known no other man, although she never failed to notice those well favored and at times had flirted with the idea of taking one to her bedchamber. She never had. Marc Anthony, despite his marriage to Fulvia, could have, often did have, any woman he wanted. He was tremendously male, his movements sensual as well as arrogant. But a liaison with Anthony carried more than appeared on the surface. Although his words were blunt they were also sharp with meaning, going far deeper than a romantic connection. Taking a deep breath she met his gaze, expelled the air in a breathy explosive, "You want Egypt."

His face registered surprise, and he shook his head. "No, only Egypt's help."

Relief flooded her. He was far less ambitious than her spies had indicated. "That's all?" Her worries for Caesarion, never far from the surface, lessened.

Anthony pushed the plates aside, leaned his arms on the table, and regarded her as if seeing her for the first time. "It depends upon a certain queen's cooperation." He held his hand palm up. "I have no interest in using force except in battle." His eyes narrowed.

She spoke softly. "So, Cleopatra will learn what makes Marc Anthony a soldier–and a man." She shifted slightly. "And a god?"

"They say that I am."

She let her gaze meet his fully. "When a goddess is with a god, she's a woman and a queen," she said softly, her voice running like liquid through the room, washing against him.

A smile transformed his face, taking it from rough to gentle, the harsh lines softening, so that she wanted to touch his face, feel it beneath her fingers.

He chuckled, filled her wine cup again and said in a low voice, "I've waited for you for a long time. Since you were a girl flaunting your girlish charms around Alexandria."

Reading the amusement and the desire in his eyes, and seeing the sudden arrogant lift to his head, she said, "I've waited, too, but no more wine or the room will spin, and the Queen may forget she's a Queen."

"Maybe I want the Queen to forget." He pressed the cup into her hand. "Is the Queen of Egypt afraid to take a chance?"

"The Queen of Egypt is afraid of nothing." She lifted the cup to her lips and drank slowly but steadily until no wine remained.

He laughed, and rising, pushed back his chair so quickly it went over backwards. Shouting, he bid the servant woman to get out of his house and stay away all night. And then before Cleopatra could get out of her chair, he lifted her up in his mighty arms and held her, and when she pushed away, this sudden onslaught taking from her the control she craved, he tightened his embrace, laced his fingers through her hair and pulled her head back and kissed her thoroughly, his mouth taking hers, his tongue forcing her lips open.

She fought to come up for air, and then she fought to be kissed again for his big hands were feeling, caressing, holding, and she was turning to liquid. "Damned Roman," she cried, her hands playing over his neck and shoulders and then grabbing his ears to bring his mouth down over hers again.

His rollicking laughter caught her in between kisses, and he muttered, "Egyptian sorceress," his voice caressing her with words lesser men would be punished for. But his kisses grew soft and gentle as he carried her across the room. "All the time you sat with Caesar, you looked at me with those big eyes, and I wanted to take you then, scoop you up and carry you off." With her in his arms, he kicked the door open to the next room and carried her inside. She spied a rough bed, several chests and lamp-stands, and a desk where he undoubtedly worked. Maps as well as drawings of women in poses meant to rouse the senses covered the walls. She thought he might dump her unceremoniously upon the bed, but he put her down gently and quickly divested himself of his tunic. Not to be outdone, she began to take off her clothing, but he stopped her, insisting he would do it. As her gown's many tucks outwitted him, the smile left his face, and before she realized what was happening, he had hooked his fingers in the bodice of her gown and ripped it away. Her necklace followed. As he forced her back against the blankets with kisses, she heard pearls and rubies rolling across the floor. A barbarian, she thought, but when she murmured, "Not so fast," he slowed down, like Caesar, but better, taking her places she had never been before. His sweet words touched her with such reverence, she knew this was not a simple man, but one infinitely more complex than she'd realized.

Later, when she moved outside the boundaries that Caesar had dictated, intuiting that Anthony would not be repulsed if she at times took the lead, he grinned and made riotous love to her in a wild assault on both their senses, making her laugh as much as he.

Later, as they lay arms around one another, Anthony, feathering kisses over her neck and shoulders, her cheeks, and eyelids, muttered, "My love,"

She sat up. "Love, my lord?"

He frowned. "Would it be out of line for me to love you?"

"No, not at all," she cried and let him pull her down into his embrace. Caesar had never expressed such a sentiment. She had never been so satisfied, her body so fine-tuned, so receptive, Anthony was tender and yet boisterous, and she wanted to shout. Toward dawn she did.

Egypt and Rome were united, but where it would lead was a puzzle to which she had no answer.

Chapter X

Winter, 41-40 BCE

Cleopatra revisited in memory the idyll at Tarsus daily. Despite its many magical moments, Anthony hadn't gone back to Alexandria with her, saying he had issues to attend to first. Despite their growing raport, was he reliably on her side? Visions of the handsome Fulvia sneaked snakelike into her mind, and word came from many sources, Arsinoe still connived to take the Egyptian throne. Would there never be a time when she could let her guard down and relax? Then word arrived: Arsinoe had been executed. Anthony had cemented Cleopatra's place in Egypt and with him.

A montage of images like a spear-point to the gut raced through her: she and Arsinoe as children at Auletes' dinner party for visiting Romans, the Romans disparaging their father, laughing at Egyptian customs, belittling Aluetes in voices meant to be overheard. She and Arsinoe had clutched one another. Like a wound to the gut, she saw again Arsinoe being dragged behind Caesar's chariot, and a lump gathered in her throat.

She looked out from the palace to the docks where a constant flow of ships and people were coming or going, slaves and freedmen, friends and foes. Life continually rushed at her so fast it left little time to assess what had happened. In the other direction, away from the sea, cats roamed the streets in vast numbers, the felines so sacred no one dared molest them. A Roman visitor who'd forgotten had been put to death. As queen she must protect and defend Egypt. She could not fault Anthony for doing what he could to protect her from an attempted coup. Yet, the interval at Tarsus must not keep her from being alert. Anthony had put Herod and his brother on the thrones of Jerusalem and Galilee, and her father had constantly reminded her Judaea by right belonged to Egypt. She would say nothing now, but the knowledge might be useful later on. In all else, Anthony pleased her even more than Caesar.

As weeks passed, daily she scanned the sea hoping to see Anthony arriving. In the early morning sun, the mirrors of the Pharos lighthouse shot blinding rays, and thick black smoke rose from the fire extinguished at daybreak. Beyond Pharos the sea became one blue gray band, but nearer shore turquoise, azure and ultramarine faded into the white ruffled edges of the rolling surf.

One day as she listened to the gulls swooping and dipping, Caesarion came to stand with her and gaze down on the city coming to life. Priests and their retinues slowly crossed Canopic Way. Later in the day, chariots and litters would move four abreast down the wide street. Now street vendors were setting up sidewalk shops, and sailors at the wharves were sluicing down ships' decks, students were heading for the museum, some to the library. Everywhere there was motion. "Do you remember your father?"

Caesarion glanced at her. "Of course, you always talk to me about him."

"But do you remember?" she persisted.

He shrugged. "I don't know. I remember what you told me. I remember he used to let me play in the room where he worked on his books. Once he said it was a shame I wasn't a Roman."

Cleopatra shook her head vehemently. "You are part Roman, and I want you to promise never to forget your heritage. But soon you will meet the man who took his place, a man as important in his way as your father was."

Caesarion tipped his head to the side. "Is it Octavian?"

Cleopatra wrinkled her nose as if a foul smell had entered the room and taking his arm she made him face her. "Understand one thing. It will never be Octavian. *Never*." She dropped his arm but held his attention with her voice. Caesarion, looking so much like his father, gave her pause. He had the same sculpted features, the same high cheekbones and deep-set eyes as Caesar. "No, the new Roman leader, is our friend Marc Anthony."

"Is he the man you saw in Tarsus?"

As if he didn't know. "Yes, and he is coming here soon, the gods be willing. I hope you will like him."

"As much as my father?"

His sharp gaze reminded her of Caesar's. "No, but very much."

"I suppose I will like him, but maybe not." He grinned.

Realizing he had teased her in a particularly adult way, she delighted at this further evidence of a mind much like her own.

When Anthony finally arrived, not as a head of state surrounded by his troops, but as an ordinary citizen with a small retinue of retainers, the breeze off the Mediterranean was cooler than it had been. Throughout the city, people hailed him as a friend, and Cleopatra watched his progress from the palace. Often stopped by dealers selling wares, people who wanted to talk, laugh, or share a joke, they jostled for position near him, and he spoke to them

Determined to outdo him in simplicity, she donned a simple dress and no jewels and hurried to the palace steps to await him.

From a distance his gaze encompassed her, and when in range, he bowed, adding a sweeping gesture of his sword arm, underscoring her importance but not denigrating his. In the brightness of the sun, his hair held the sheen of night, but his eyes reflected the lightness of the day, sending messages his powerful body shouted with each step. Swept away by the sight of him, she buried recurrent doubts about Rome, and fighting back a broad smile, she forced a haughty expression.

Mouthing polite phrases, he bowed formally as she bid him welcome. Attendants, friends, eunuchs, and government officials added their voices, and Anthony, flashing his famous smile, had words for everyone.

She indicated Caesarion. "You remember my son, heir to the mantle of Julius Caesar and to the Egyptian throne."

Anthony's eyes showed surprise before it was replaced with an inscrutable expression. "I remember a child, but now I see a young man." Inclining his head slightly, and relaxing his knees, Anthony touched his hand to his heart.

Caesarion, glanced at his mother before saying in a loud, clear voice, "Welcome to Alexandria, sir."

Later, alone with Anthony in the palace, she watched as he walked around her apartment, taking note of everything, shaking his head at times, but smiling throughout his inspection. Speaking with humor of the spectacle she, he and Caesarion had staged on the palace steps, she waited for his response. His smile increased. It was as if the world had turned in her favor, and life would never be difficult again. While Anthony spoke of himself as a simple warrior, he seemed enamored with the luxury in her rooms, studying the incense burners hanging from jewel-encrusted tripods. Sniffing the fragrances, he grinned at her afterward. The floors were covered with glowing tiles or carpets of thick nap and rich color. Alabaster benches filled niches, chairs of burnished gold took his weight with no difficulty, and the walls, bright with painted murals depicting the gods— Osiris, Isis, their son Horus, Serapis and Anubis—attracted him. Pausing before a tapestry of gold thread gleaming behind a couch piled high with cushions, he held out his arms. She knew she had him. Anthony was hers.

She'd never been so happy. If she slept late she'd find that Anthony and Caesarion had gone off together, Anthony teaching Caesarion to defend himself, to use his fists as well as his sword. Sometimes she went with them riding, fishing or picnicking as a family, and these were such special times she found her eyes misting with the beauty of it. She gave lavish banquets and entertainments for Anthony, and let Caesarion sometimes join the festivities as her father had done with her. If he were to be the future ruler of Egypt, nay the world, he must absorb much information.

Wine flowing, beer a staple, Anthony said she spoiled a simple soldier with exotic foods and erotic dancing girls, but she only laughed, knowing he liked the luxury as much as he liked to romp with her. Once he drank too much and when the company at table talked about a ship from Parthia docked in Alexandria, he grabbed a bottle of wine from the table and led Cleopatra and a bevy of attendants in a walk that took them to the wharf. Dusk nibbled at the edges of the city, the Pharos light was being lit, and foreign sailors, on the ships creaking at anchor, watched silently.

Anthony walked up and down studying the *gauloi* from Parthia, the last in a long line of ships docked in the harbor. "She's a cargo carrier," he declared, throwing his head back and bellowing a laugh. "A tub, and the men sailing her are weak as lap dogs." He shook his head, and his friends laughed with him, all of them slapping one another's back, hanging on to one another until the sailors on board glowered and offered insults in their own language.

It took all of Cleopatra's powers of persuasion to turn Anthony and the others back to the palace.

In the future she learned to satisfy Anthony's need to hobnob with people of the city, to roister and fight—and to laugh—at nonsensical things. She started a club whose main object was to have fun. But before it could begin, she realized her flow was late.

"Anthony," she said one morning as he lay in bed and watched her dress, she attempting to do what a half-dozen maids usually did for her. She pushed her feet into sandals and opened the drawers of a jewelry chest. "What think you of my legs?" she asked holding them out one at a time.

He pretended to come to a decision, and then winking and smiling lasciviously said, "They are beautifully shaped, my love, but I like them better wrapped around me."

Sorting through imposing jeweled collars inherited from other Ptolemy queens, she continued, "And my hips and waist, are they not in proper proportion?" Hands on hips, she posed saucily.

"I have seen..." he paused and winked at her again, "none better." His words matched his ebullient mood. The plans for the campaign into Parthia were taking definite form.

Choosing her words carefully, Cleopatra asked in a bored sounding voice, "And when I'm large and ungainly, what then? "

"You large? Never. You are a perfect little woman. You are, my dear, incomparable."

Sensing his impatience with her, she smiled, knowing that if she laughed so would he, his mood ready to swing into light-heartedness, but this was serious. "I am with child," she whispered.

His eyebrows shot together and he pushed himself up on one elbow, dislodging several pillows. "You're carrying my child? Is that what this is all about?"

She nodded, a self-satisfied, smug look on her face. He grinned and shook his head. "You're sure?"

"Yes!" she cried. "As the gods know, I'm having your child."

"Of course!" he shouted, jumped up, picked her up, swung her around and pressed kisses to the top of her head.

"You're happy?"

"Of course." He set her down. "But how about Caesarion? Will he be all right with this?"

Her heart swelled with happiness that the question had come to him, and with utter sweetness, she said, "Yes, he will be fine."

The following days she rode a wave of euphoria, and in a magnanimous gesture announced clemency for prisoners, gave alms to the poor, and instituted sweeping reforms that would help government officials who said she had tied their hands. She gave thanks to Isis daily, had sacrifices made in the temple, and bound Anthony closer to her with sweetness and luxury. Life became utterly valuable, and the thought of the future sweetly divine.

Too soon, a message came for Anthony. Fulvia had raised an army against Octavian and was fighting him in Italy. His shaky relationship with Octavian had been compromised by her actions. "I determine when and where to confront Octavian. Fulvia's a damned spitfire, and this time she's overstepped her bounds." He slammed his hand against the wall. "By the gods, this is too much. I must return to Rome, give Fulvia a bill of divorcement and strip her of everything. And then I'll wipe that smirk from Octavian's face."

He merely glanced at Cleopatra, but a thrill rode through her like the Mediterranean sweeping against the shore when he left. As his ships were lost in the blue haze of ocean and sky, and the ripples in the water had subsided, she went home.

In the weeks to come, his condemnation and censure of Fulvia appeared a moot point, for within weeks she died of a long-standing illness, and five months later Cleopatra gave birth to healthy, handsome twins. She dictated a letter to Anthony, sure that, learning the news, he would return soon.

What came was a note. "By the gods, lady, twins, is it? Isis and Osiris be praised. I am on my way to Brundusium to meet with Octavian, but I extend you felicitations and good health. Yours, Marc Anthony." Months passed, and no other word came. Finally, she named the babies for Alexander The Great and for herself – her son, Alexander Helios, her daughter, Cleopatra Selene, together the sun and the moon.

Chapter XI

39 BCE

A YEAR LATER, Cleopatra reminded herself, no matter how much she needed Anthony at her side, she was queen of Egypt and he was simply a Roman. She must—she would—insure Egypt's future. Sitting in the garden adjacent to the throne room, she waited for Laknefer to arrive. In his guise as an astrologer, he moved freely between Anthony's and Octavian's headquarters, neither suspecting that he was in her employ, and now that Anthony ignored her, she was glad she'd taken such a measure.

As a shadow fell on the scroll she was reading, she glanced up in time to see Laknefer make his obeisance. Setting aside dispatches, she waved the sharp-faced astrologer to the stone bench across from her, and looking down the broad terraces to the sparkling sea, she murmured. "Have you any news?"

Lowering his voice and eyelids appropriately, he pursed his mouth as if considering, and she almost expected him to get out his charts and consult the stars. The reliability of his astrological pronouncements was phenomenal, although she doubted the science would catch on universally. People were used to the whimsical character of the gods, not omens charted through celestial bodies. She craved details, reasoning, overheard confidences, wary glances and secrets exchanged at midnight meetings. "Yes, get on with it."

Laknefer adjusted the folds of his gown, his hands shaking as he looked into the distance, down steps leading to lower terraces.

"Why are you hesitating? Speak up."

"Octavian is no soldier. He needs Anthony to fight the Parthians." He stroked his beard. "And something to show Anthony will honor the bargain."

She looked to where currant, peach, and pomegranate trees shaded the side of the building. Bright sun beat against an arbor bursting with roses and slanted toward herb gardens where sweet marjoram and laurel grew. Often, she had strolled there with Anthony. What was Laknafer holding back? If he weren't so useful, she'd send him to Upper Egypt. "Tell me what you mean."

Laknefer's foot began to twitch. "The Triumvirate has been extended, each of the three—Octavian, Lepidus, and Anthony—to maintain their spheres of influence. Anthony got land for his men."

"Holy Pharaoh, speak up man. What did Octavian get?"

Laknefer cleared his throat and croaked, "He got that which binds My Lord Anthony to Octavian in a way nothing else can."

She raised a hand. "May the gods smite you dead if you don't speak soon. Out with it man."

Looking as if he would rather die, the astrologer whispered, "My Lord Anthony has married Octavian's sister, Octavia."

A dizzy spell hit her, the land whirling away, leaving her behind, trees uprooting, flowers dying, and she moving through some dry and sterile land alone. Conscious of Laknefer staring at her, she stared back, her eyes hard. "Octavia? Is she not already married?" It was a Roman custom, families thus forging strong alliances, guaranteeing allegiance.

"Her husband died recently, leaving her a widow with three children."

"Then according to Roman law she can't remarry for at least a year."

"In her case the Senate made special dispensation."

"How fortunate for her that she's so in favor." Her heart slamming against her chest, she snapped, "You've seen her?""

"I have."

"And? Is she young, old, a gossip, a cheat, an ignoramus?"

He took a deep breath, his eyes darting away from her. "She's young, no more than early twenties, I'd gather. People say she is of spotless character. Everyone said nice things about her, pointing out she belongs to a literary circle and is quite knowledgeable."

She got up, unable to sit still any longer. Forcing a smile that showed what she thought of the lady and her attributes, she demanded, "What else?"

"She is sweet of temperament."

"And?" She glared at Laknefer. "Is she fat, short, ill favored? By the gods, man, speak or I'll have your tongue cut out."

"She doesn't wear a wig, but has a quantity of hair that she arranges in different ways each time one sees her. Long, natural hair, soft as down someone said, and in truth that is not far wrong." His eyes got a far-away look, and he stroked his beard slowly.

The words were like stones weighing her down. Anthony had not only abandoned her, he had taken up with another woman, a woman not only younger but also more beautiful, one who garnered the devotion of everyone who saw her, including the Queen of Egypt's own spies. She picked up the papyrus she'd set aside. "Is there anything more you wish to tell your queen, sir?"

"Only that the Romans shower My Lord Anthony and his bride with approval. They're going to Athens on a trip."

"Your tongue outdoes your common sense," she spat. "Get out of my sight."

When he was gone, she pulled the wig she sometimes wore from her head and threw it into the bushes. Tearing at her gown, she felt tears gather in back of her eyes and run like the Nile at flood stage. She had kept herself pure for Caesar, had put up with being a mistress in Rome, had bowed to Anthony's wishes, putting herself and her country at his disposal. But worst of all she had basked in Anthony's attentions, dreamed of a future together, their children and Caesarion ruling the world. She wanted to scream, but mindful of her position, she bit her lips until they bled. Calling for Iras and Charmion, one who would be deeply sympathetic, and the other who would share her anger, she went into the palace.

The next day, opening the shutters, she watched sun dance madcap along the waves in the harbor. Eternal darkness to Anthony! Her children and Egypt, the people who trusted and loved her were what counted. No matter that Anthony and his new wife sported around the Mediterranean, drawing accolades from the Greeks, she was the true Greek. Like her father, she would tiptoe a tightrope. And one day

Anthony, whose ambition outshone his duplicity, would look toward Egypt again, and she would retaliate.

Except for official communiqués, no notes came from Rome, but Laknefer reported Octavian took Anthony's ships but never gave him the troops he promised. Worse, within the year, as Anthony always victorious in battle moved like a conqueror throughout the world, Octavia gave birth to his child. Cleopatra clenched her teeth. In the future, she would use him as he had used her, and so, as the years passed, she said nothing, neither good nor bad, about him to Alexander and Selene. One day they would assist Caesarion and be her bulwark between Egypt and the Roman world.

Still, it hurt when she learned Octavian had betrothed his infant daughter to Anthony's son, Antyllus, who was Caesarion's age. An engagement bound Anthony's family and Octavian's family closer still. They would go to the baths and theater as a unit, sit as one at the games and races, celebrate festivals at one another's homes. She must do what she could to protect her children.

With the first weak light of day grabbing at night shadows, she wrote a formal letter to Anthony. The Queen of Egypt, reminded him of his affection for Caesarion and his love for his son, Antyllus. "Caesarion is bereft of peers, having no one of noble birth his age. I fear this lack of companionship. I suggest, My Lord Anthony you send Antyllus for a visit. It would be good for these two future leaders to know one another. In addition, he would have access to the best scholars and teachers in Alexandria. We await your answer and send best wishes for your continued good health and success."

No answer came to her formal request until Anthony's long-delayed campaign against Parthia was about to begin. A fast cutter sped into Alexandria with a letter. Addressed to her Serene and Sacred Highness, Her Majesty Queen Cleopatra VII of Egypt, Lord of the Living and Dead, of the house of Ptolemy and Selucid, it said, "Your most gracious invitation to my son is appreciated, but matters in the East cannot be delayed further. We ask Egypt to again ally herself with us in this most noble cause. We will winter at Antioch while making final preparations and look forward to seeing the Queen of Egypt. A suitable domicile will be prepared for her Majesty and her retinue. With all our best felicitations, good wishes and the blessings of the gods to your noble son Caesarion and Egypt's precious sun and moon. May they shine brightly forever."

So he called Caesarion noble and finally referred to Alexander and Selene. Rereading the letter, the formality of the salutation stabbed her with its significance. The Ptolemys and the Selucids. After Alexander conquered the world, the Selucids had settled the land that was now Syria, and her ancestors had married into the Selucid family. Was Anthony hinting that her children were not only heirs to the Ptolemy Empire but of the Selucid Empire also? Her thoughts flying, she envisioned an Egypt encompassing Judaea and Syria, but grander, including Rome as well. She called to Charmion, "Tell my Lord Chamberlain, we winter in Antioch."

Chapter XII

37 BCE

H ER FATHER HAD told her a day would come when she would know irrevocably that no matter what happened in her life, her eternal role would never desert her. Wearing the crown of Egypt and the multi-colored robes of Isis, she arrived in Antioch surrounded by staff in robes so rich everyone could see they attended no lowly commoner. Black eunuchs in blazing white, carrying casks filled with gold, added to her aura. No longer a girl queen, an innocent vying for Caesar's attention, she was a woman of power.

As word of her arrival spread, the city filled with her supporters. No matter that in Rome she was denigrated, here she was worshipped. In the Middle East, they idolized and loved her, and those in Antioch led the adulation. Twenty-two kilometers from the Mediterranean on the west and looking towards Parthia on the east, Antioch was perfect for an assault against the Parthians.

Aware of the standards of Egypt fluttering from her ships, of her jewels winking in the slanted sun, she listened as Anthony's envoy repeated Anthony's invitation to meet him at his headquarters.

"Tell Marc Anthony Egypt thanks him for his consideration, but we cannot accommodate his request this day. Her majesty is not the best of sailors and must find her balance on shore."

In the past he had witnessed her braced against the wind and spray, her hair streaming, her eyes bright, her laugh blending with the elements. He knew she seldom got seasick. Besides, the sea was smooth as glass, the shallows without ripples, water so clear it was possible to see fish darting to and fro. With a gesture, she dismissed Anthony's envoy, and preceded by eunuchs, priests, temple guards, and members of her court, her litter carried by Nubian slaves in red turbans, she was carried between Corinthian columns toward the center of town.

Throngs lined the colonnade. Not as large as Rome, nor as beautiful as Alexandria, Antioch's blend of architectural elegance— the classical lines of Athens blending with the onion-domed temples of the East—pleased her. The city, an important crossroads of the world, had traders and travelers going in all directions, and all understood, she came not as a god who would sport with Dionysus but as Isis the munificent and kind who, as Cleopatra the monarch, had the strength of a cobra. If Anthony wanted help with his campaign, he would have to deal with her on her terms for she arrived, not as a neglected love, but as an equal.

Hearing the people calling Isis' attributes in hushed tones of wonderment, she lifted her arms as if embracing them all. Isis, champion of the weak, the poor, the downtrodden, Isis bless us. Isis, look kindly upon us came from all sides. Surely, Marc Anthony was aware of her idolatrous reception.

Two days later, following protocol, she exchanged formalities with Anthony in a large room with many columns, her people and his adding to the moment with flowery phrases, everyone outwardly in agreement. Rain beat with regularity against the marble building and gathered in puddles between the stepping-stones outside. Inside the building a cold draft ran like evil along the floor. Cleopatra sat on a throne-like chair centered on a platform at a table laden with papyri, attendants close by. Across the width of the long room, Anthony sat on a similar platform and chair, putting himself on a par with her, a liberty only Rome would dare take.

In the past, Anthony, seldom used luxury for his own aggrandizement. Now bold touches of wealth showed in wall sconces of brass trimmed with gold, walls with silk hangings, incense burners inlaid with semi-precious stones. Despite the carpet on the platforms, Cleopatra was glad her Nubian slaves crouched to tend charcoal braziers at her feet.

At the appointed time, she leaned forward. "My Lord Anthony, daily I am reminded that you represent the might of Rome." She gestured. "Nay, I misspeak myself, you are the might of Rome." Her advisors, seated on low chairs to the right and left of her, the two scribes sitting at the edge of the platform, followed each word closely, but she kept her attention on Anthony.

Suppressing a smile, he inclined his head, and she saw that he was not anymore impervious to flattery than he'd been a few years ago. His trusted commanders and closest military advisers leaned forward, Anthony's history with Cleopatra adding a fillip to her words. Soon, they would begin whispering in his ear. She waited a few seconds and then, her voice clear as a temple incantation but sweet as honey, she said, "We all will be eternally grateful that the sword arm of Marc Anthony is lifted to bring peace to the region."

Again he inclined his head. "The Queen of Egypt is kind."

"Kindness is an attribute a Queen fosters when dealing with the lowliest of her subjects. But you are neither my subject nor lowly." Her eyes sparkling, her eyelashes brushing like cobwebs against her cheeks brought his approving smile.

"I see that the Queen of Egypt has not lost her ability to put things in perspective." He lifted a hand. "Marc Anthony would like nothing better than to retire from public life and dawdle at the side of a fishing stream, but the people of Rome have long memories, and they cry out for me to defeat Parthia."

"A ruler is always the servant of the people."

"Unlike the Queen, I have a reputation for bluntness. So I shall be true to my reputation and say that raising an army, training them, and keeping them supplied is not cheap."

"The Queen of Egypt can also be blunt. Has Rome not once again importuned Egypt and is not her divine highness in Antioch for the purpose of Egypt's assistance."

He gestured toward her. "The Queen's presence would grace any gathering, but assistance and indulgence in a cause so great cannot be taken lightly. We know that the…" he smiled, "munificence of the Queen of Egypt is legendary. Marc Anthony is not unaware of the debt of gratitude he owes the Egyptian people for their help to Rome in the past." As he had three-and-a-half years before, he lounged, one leg thrust out in front of him, the other bent at the knee, foot behind. At times he balanced on his spine, always at ease, the lazy, indolent look about him belying the words coming from his mouth. His intelligence, at times hidden beneath his rough exterior, shone now in the turn of his lips, the slow settling of his hands to the arms of his chair. His gaze remained fixed upon her, that warm and teasing look shining brightly.

Resolving not to succumb like a naive girl to his unuttered blandishments, she faced him with hard calculations that took into account all that had been and could be. "Egypt has been privileged to billet your legions in our country often, to entertain, to help, to educate, and to take counsel from Rome. We are always mindful that Rome is Egypt's number one friend, and Egypt has been happy to help her friend whenever she could." She paused so that the scribes could catch up. "But surely My Lord Anthony has heard of the drought that struck Egypt like a pestilence two years ago. Now that it is over my people demand recompense for any outlay of goods and services as well as gold that Egypt may give for this most worthy cause. We wonder what manner of compensation Rome expects to extend to its loyal friend, Egypt."

Marc Anthony's smile receding, he looked around the room, "As the Queen knows, I am only one of a triumvirate, too far from Rome for consultations with Lepidus and Octavian."

"I doubt that Octavian concerns himself with what My Lord Anthony desires. From all accounts he does not give overdue significance to matters of time." Thus, she reminded Anthony how Octavian had kept him waiting at Brundisium, and was positive

Anthony understood the insinuation for he frowned.

She rushed on. "Wherever the Queen of Egypt is, Egypt is there. I would think it no different for Rome. Egypt suggests Marc Anthony is complete upon himself. He is Rome."

His frown becoming a scowl, his eyes lost their baiting quality and showed momentary bewilderment. "The Queen's point is well taken, but what is it the Queen of Egypt wants? Speak plainly for I am a plain man."

For a moment it was as if they were alone. She recalled the impulsiveness lurking under his often playful, unpolished exterior. As his ministers and commanders whispered, she leaned back in her chair and said with studied indifference, "Egypt remembers ancient times and our ties with this venerable country where we hold this historic meeting. Syria, which is now under the gracious protection of Rome, has always had a tender place in Egypt's heart. Its Egyptian ties run deep. Ptolemys married Selucids, and their families ruled Antioch and all the land from here to Parthia, until Rome graciously offered its protection."

Anthony's mouth became a grim line and reflexively, he looked away from her. His people leaned over his chair and conferred with him. He listened and nodded before again peering across at Cleopatra, his eyes measuring.

The Syrians in the far corners of the room stirred, people whispered, others showed concern.

She smiled regally. "At one time, of course, Judaea belonged to Egypt also." Anthony sat bolt upright, and she realized he understood she wanted Judaea back.

"No, Madam, no, you ask too much. Herod is in Judaea, and there he remains." Anthony brushed off his advisers who tried to gain his attention, his frown growing deeper, directed at her now. "Would you have me forsake a friend? No, on this I am adamant."

Cleopatra smiled. "Then I take it, My Lord, that we are in accord about all the *other* ancient lands. They will, of course, revert to Egypt, the Queen and her heirs." There, she had alluded to his children. Let him do with the words what he would. She held out a papyrus. "I have a list of them here." She passed it to her ministers who passed it to his, they to him.

While he glanced at the list, his frown never leaving, her voice became a musical scale, ringing sweetly. "I also have a list of supplies we can begin to funnel into Antioch. It has been said that an army moves on its stomach, and Egypt would keep yours well fed. My finance minister is ready to turn over a chest of gold today to seal the bargain and give my Lord Anthony funds to purchase what supplies he needs."

He looked up from the detailed list, this land containing so many square miles for Anthony's son by the Queen of Egypt, this land containing so many square miles for Anthony's daughter by the Queen of Egypt. The dates the land belonged to, and the dates they were taken from Egypt were shown. "Gold?"

She nodded; her Nubians left, and within minutes came back with a chest they set before him. "I would not want a chest such as this to fall into Octavian's hands." She shrugged prettily. Anthony's glance went from the chest to the papyrus in his hand to her. "Octavian is… Octavian."

"Then we are agreed, Marc Anthony." She took his gaze and held it, seeing something she had not seen before. At Tarsus he had acted like a man with a lesser being, she a woman to tease with, to laugh with, to have pleasure with. Now, something else had been added, respect and honor, perhaps. It was clear he didn't resent her pushing him into a corner, but liked that she had played a man's game and succeeded. At Tarsus she had bedazzled him, and he her. Now she had shown him her intellect and asked for his esteem and consideration in return, and he appeared willing to give it.

Rising, he stood, and following a barrage of words and orders to his men, he bowed to her, the bow formal but relaxed. Speaking in a friendly tone, he asked about her entourage. Was everyone comfortable? Had the sun and the moon accompanied her to Antioch? Or were the heavens firm in their celestial locations?

Was he acknowledging Alexander and Selene publicly? Like a bird free to dip its wings, Cleopatra said softly, "When the sun and the moon are young, they do not travel well."

He nodded, and his gaze showed regard and understanding. She was pleased. Any more would not be fitting. Her heart swelled, a tightness caught at her throat. Before she could make a fool of herself talking about the twins in front of everyone, he spoke again. "Our ministers can finish here, while we stroll the garden and end our discussion in a natural setting." Without looking to see if she followed, he left the room. She followed.

Hand on her arm, he guided her along the portico past columns more Hellenic than Eastern, and bending down to her, interest apparent in each movement of his powerful body, each inflection of his voice, he demanded, "Tell me about my son. You named him Alexander, fitting for the son of a warrior. "

They passed a small group of Roman commanders who rapidly averted their glances. Without Anthony's presence, she had no doubt they would stare at her, possibly whisper about her. Pushing the thought underground, she said, "Your son is like you."

"How? Don't keep a man guessing." Anthony's voice betrayed his impatience.

"He has your appearance, your intelligence."

He smiled. "But, does he have the qualities of a leader?"

How could she know; he was much too young. "Oh, yes, he definitely has."

"How could it be otherwise, a child who sprung from such fertile soil?" His gaze zipped over her and he squeezed her arm. "And my little moon?

"In many ways she takes after her mother."

His expression softened. "Then I have no complaints." He smiled. "And you, Cleopatra, how are you?"

Abandonment could not be wiped out in a single afternoon. "I think Marc Anthony deals in words and actions tinged with fraudulent desire."

He chuckled. "If I'm a fraud, then you are, too, but we're in this together now, my sweet Cleopatra, and there's no backing out." He shook his head. "I have no illusions about where this is leading me. I step across the bounds Octavian wishes me to honor. He has little spine, but that won't stop him." He shrugged as if it were of little consequence and smiled at her. "I long to be free of him."

Did he expect her to believe he was severing ties with Octavian just because he'd said so? "You have my gold. Now I need your signature on the agreements." Pulling herself to her full height, she looked at him like she might at an Egyptian prisoner.

He laughed and said softly, for her ear alone, "That's not all you need, my ripe little woman."

"I'd forgotten how rude you can be," she snapped.

"I'm merely a man who has come back to his woman."

She whirled around to face him. "You dare to call me your woman after your rush into a Roman marriage? Hold your tongue, Marc Anthony, and recall whom you are addressing. I am not yours to command, merely the mother of your children. I am a queen, descendant of a line longer than Rome can ever conceive."

Surprise stamping his face, he shook his head and scowled at her. "Why did you bring me gold? What should I think of that, Madam?"

"That Egypt needs to be on the winning side. Reading more into it is a waste of time." She bit out the words.

"Your time, not mine. I have not forgotten you."

She raised her head, her chin high. "I have not forgotten you have obligations to our children. As for you…you, sir are merely a soldier."

"And, despite being a Ptolemy, you are merely a woman."

She knew she had hurt him when his words went cold, no passion, no enthusiasm, and his eyes became slits. If she were a man, would he hit her? Chilled to the bone, she turned away, the times she had wanted to crawl into Anthony's arms seeming like so many aberrations. Much of her life she had been alone, studying at the Museum, frequenting the library. Three men had entered her privacy. Her father had listened to her, drawn her out. Caesar had flattered her with his attentions, but he'd been remote, a mentor dipping into her life at intervals, demanding much, giving little. Only Anthony had treated her like a complete person, saying he loved her, allowing her to see his weaknesses.

The next day she hardly listened when Laknefer reported, but stood looking out to where the sun highlighted Antioch's library, its columns reminding her of home.

"Your Divine Majesty, the Roman, Marc Anthony, has sent a private message to Rome."

"You come to tell me that! He sends dispatches daily." She glared. "You are worthless as an empty tomb."

He shook his head vehemently. "No, My Divine Lady, this is no ordinary message. He is divorcing Octavia."

The room began to recede, the space around her go dim. She waved him away, and as the door clanged shut behind him, she dropped to her knees, a sheen of tears in her eyes. The gods had spoken. Anthony was throwing in his lot with her.

Chapter XIII

37 BCE

Thousands upon thousands of Anthony's soldiers crowded the streets, moving through the bazaars and ogling the women as if they had already achieved victory. Elite troops, raw recruits, and those ready to take supplies across the mountains or record what happened, swelled Antioch's ranks. When Anthony wasn't conferring with his commanders he visited his men in the field, moving through their ranks like one of them, keeping their morale high. His heroic deeds in battle were legendary, and when urged, he relived Philippi again and again, for his triumph there had made Octavian a laughing stock. As he drew closer to a line of attack on Parthia that suited him, supply lines in place, he occasionally dined with Cleopatra or spent an afternoon and always the night.

With the moon lighting their bed, she plunged like a sponge diver into the many layers of Anthony's personality, pushing at him with words, tantalizing him with her ideas, the breadth of her knowledge. Open to new ideas, nevertheless he resisted deep philosophical debate, wanting to get to the heart of a matter without examining every side of an issue. He knew what he wanted, and he dove toward that goal without undue thought of the consequences, trusting in himself. Once she carried a debate to a point where he muffled her voice with a hand. "You make music, my love, but it is not necessary to hear every word."

The largeness of his heart overwhelmed her. Still, friends, acquaintances, even his own kin when absent from him, apparently were forgotten. He spoke of none of them. With a mother's cunning, she mentioned Alexander and Selene often, but timed her anecdotes to when he would be most receptive. If she did not hold his interest; when he left, she and hers would be forgotten – again.

Although on guard, a renewed feeling of happiness filled her. Unlike Caesar, Anthony was blunt and plainspoken, not naturally fastidious. If his morning breath reminded her of the meal the night before, she would turn her head away, and he would pick his teeth and rinse his mouth before he kissed her. Without urging, he cut his finger and toe nails, had his beard trimmed, and when he wanted her to take the lead in love making, he scented himself.

But returning one day from the field where his troops practiced in mock battle, he wrestling with his men, he scooped her up before she realized what was happening. He reeked of the stables and the damp out-of-doors and no amount of nose wrinkling on her part would dissuade him. Abandoning his clothes in a rapid orgy of undressing, no washing away of dust and grime, his laughter told her his day had pleased him greatly. Afterwards, he called for a tub of hot water, put her in it and washed the sands of the drill field from her, his large hands gentle and soothing, his words soft with remembered passion before he followed her into the tub.

At times he was extremely playful, and she learned not to protest when he rousted her before the sun was up. As Caesar had been, Anthony was a superb horseman, and he delighted that she could keep up with him, galloping over the barren lands, tethering their horses near a stream where he could fish. Sometimes they fished, and sometimes they frolicked. He played games with alacrity, beating her as often as she beat him. He loved dice and gambling games, wagering large sums he lost with as good a mood as when he won. He took friends at their word, and the devious, baiting qualities she had seen in Caesar, and that characterized Octavian, didn't surface in Anthony

In January she realized she was pregnant again. As morning nausea hit her, and the Mediterranean whipped itself into its usual winter's fury, homesickness descended. It would be late April or early May before ships could ply the sea again. Although her physicians and her own knowledge told her nothing was wrong, she lacked the energy she had felt when she'd carried the twins. She tried to detect signs of aging. None showed, but could have. After all, she was thirty-two, almost thirty-three, and no matter that Anthony was twelve years older his vigor never flagged. He was bringing her an empire. With the lands he had already granted her, Egypt's share of the world would rival that of Alexander's conquests so many years before. Anthony was fair and would not cheat Caesarion out of his rightful heritage.

But, no matter how she couched the argument, he kept Judaea, the land she wanted most. It was a coup that he granted her a small portion of Herod's land, a place where fine stands of cedar trees grew, wood the building material and fuel Egypt needed most.

In mid-May, when the breezes blew warm, and the seas grew calm, Anthony went off to battle and she returned home. The wide streets, the grand buildings of the city and the wonder of her children mesmerized her. Caesarion, so tall and so eager to hear all she had to tell him, met her at the docks, and at the palace, the twins came running from their nursery when she arrived.

"In a few months, a very great man, your father Marc Anthony, will be here," she reminded them often. The air was ripe with promise, the future a branch on a mighty tree.

She waited eagerly for news of Anthony's progress, but when it came it was ambiguous. Although Anthony had persuaded neutral kings to take his side, parlays and talks ate into the time he needed to get to Parthia proper. Nevertheless as time passed, Anthony led Roman and allied troops toward the sleeping giant.

But then the scenario unfolded like a blanket filled with sand. An ally Anthony had depended upon, turned 50,000 horse soldiers on him. His soldiers fought gallantly but were slaughtered. His wagons, supplies and siege equipment were put to the torch. He lingered at Parthia's outer limits and waited until snow feathered down, but help from former allies never came. When snow started to collect, he began the long trek home over mountains and raging streams in increasingly cold weather. Repeatedly attacked by Parthia as well as one-time allies, his numbers kept declining.

Reading dispatches, Cleopatra paced the throne room and demanded answers. Everyone knew Marc Anthony was the best campaigner the world knew; his preparation flawless, his fighters strong and in vast numbers, he a lion. This rout made no sense. Her voice sharp as a dagger, she commanded Laknefer to explain.

Falling to his knees, he whispered, "Octavian used bribes, propaganda and fear to turn Anthony's friends against him."

She felt a sudden jolt to her belly, the baby within her kicking. But even as she wrung her hands in frustration, word came: Anthony, playing the magnanimous role he always chose, refused to call a former ally an enemy. The leader—who had deserted him earlier—impressed with Anthony's attitude, gave him food and supplies. Anthony, and three fifths of his army, waded through waist-deep snowdrifts and forded raging streams getting back to Antioch, where his men, shouting his praises, hoisted him to their shoulders and carried him into the city proper. He had snatched victory from defeat; he was their hero. Cleopatra rejoiced.

Although Parthia remained unconquered, like Caesar, Anthony had done the seemingly impossible. In the meantime tales of Octavian's treachery against Anthony grew. It bothered her that he shrugged it aside. "You were not defeated but made a strategic retreat," she wrote to him the night she gave birth to her third child by Anthony, a boy she named Philadelphus after a Ptolemy ancestor. Anthony, writing about the future, said, "I suggested to the king of Armenia that we should betroth Alexander Helios to his daughter. I expect him to see the wisdom of my overture."

Artavasdes had been far from fair in his treatment of Anthony in the debacle of the campaign against Parthia, but Artavasdes ruled a country strategic to the future. They needed him on their side. Yet, she feared Anthony's impulsiveness boded no good.

Three months later with ships, clothing and money, she re-joined Anthony. Gulls swooped and dipped, and the water lapped greedily at the shore when he met her at the waterfront. Walking beside him on the weathered boards of the pier, she stated, "You are more gloomy than the sarcophagi of my dead ancestors."

""I am beginning to doubt Artavasdes will respond favorably."

Three hours later, as she sat at her makeup table, he ran his hand over her head, messaging her scalp, his touch gentle. Parting the strands she had loosened from their confining pins, he began to comb her hair.

Truly surprised, she picked up a hand mirror and studied herself even as she watched his reflection. "So My Lord, what do you plan to do about Artavasdes?"

He stroked the length of her hair before meeting her reflection in the hand mirror. "Wait."

She fought down an impulse to tell him his proposal had been premature. First he should have wooed the king, softened his resistance to an alliance. She leaned her head back and looked up, seeing the crease between his eyes and knew she must not fight him on this but encourage him.

Yet, weeks passed with no answer from Artavasdes. It was as if Anthony, and his gesture of friendship with Armenia didn't exist, and rumor said Octavian had undercut Anthony's chances. His eyes glittering with anger and purpose, Anthony prepared for battle, and Cleopatra, set sail for Alexandria.

The sea had few ripples, reflecting only her own image, and in the free city of Damscus, the headquarters of the once vast Selucid Empire, the citizenry celebrated her link to their glorious past. The stay became a high spot in the journey; her stopover in Judaea far less grand. She didn't want to go, but she had to let Herod see her power and hear from her ministers the extent of her rapport with Anthony.

At the docks, a petty city official greeted her, and at Herod's request, traveled with her to his fortress city. The man spoke no Greek, and looked with askance on the vast retinue of retainers and royal personages traveling with her. She ignored him. In Herod's court, most of his people were of Greek descent, and only he followed the Jewish beliefs of his forebears. She would have allies.

Before she entered Jerusalem's Antonia palace, she put on a pectoral collar of such jeweled magnificence she was sure Herod would be envious. Already he seethed because Anthony had granted her a small strip of Judaea. Although, he met her with practiced grace and mouthed flowery words of formal diplomacy, his eyes showed nothing but distrust. She smiled with amusement.

Later, at a banquet and entertainment in her honor, she maintained a bright smile and said all the expected diplomatic phrases in Hebrew while her distrust of him increased. He had no compunction when it came to eliminating enemies. Knowing him most of her life did not make him a friend, although his mother–in-law, Alexandra, had always been her intimate. Once, Alexandra had talked about the curious state of love and politics, her observations so close to Cleopatra's own, she had never forgotten. Now, in the shadowy dining hall, she asked about Alexandra.

Herod's gaze held nothing but contempt. "My mother-in-law and I do not agree on many things." He glared at her.

She saw enmity if not outright hatred. Palace gossip said he had been instrumental in his uncle's death, and now his eyes, so perfect in their shape, were cold, and she shivered despite the overpowering warmth in the room, still air trapping the smells of greasy food and sweet wine. She could be the victim of an accident staged so cleverly no one would ever know. She left at dawn.

At Alexandria's busy docks, her people interrupted their work to acknowledge her divinity and royalty, and her city literally sparkled after the dust of Herod's Judaea. Yet, at the palace Laknefer's report made her stomach cramp. He said Octavia stayed on in Anthony's *domus* in Rome and cared for all his children, even Fulvia's. People called her a saint, and her brother, Octavian, had elevated her to a station equal with the Vestal Virgins, making her sacrosanct. They blamed Anthony for the failure of the marriage.

"Equal to the Vestal Virgins! How absurd," Cleopatra said aloud after Laknefer, looking like a cat dining on temple offal, left. Perhaps she should replace him. The Romans Vestal Virgins, keepers of the eternal flame, represented all of wisdom, all of good. If they failed their vows, they were buried alive. That Anthony's former wife had such a status did not bode well for Egypt.

With Anthony's support in Rome eroding, and open rebukes coming from lesser countries, Herod's open hostility to her couldn't be discounted. She must shore up her defenses, show the world Egypt was a power complete in itself.

Octavian had maligned her for years; now he was doing it more subtly against Anthony. Would Anthony be strong enough to withstand the pressure? If he returned to her, it would be a pearl in a string she was slowly fashioning; if not, she would show the world she was strong, a woman who could stand alone and guard the vast treasures of Egypt and not get lost in the doing.

The next day she announced Caesarion would be her royal consort, that his name would be placed upon the royal coins, and he would be called Ptolemy Caesarion XV; and this news should be relayed in all the forums, in all the countries, in all the world. But Anthony sent a communiqué both light-hearted and triumphant saying he had defeated Atavasdes and was on the way home to her. If his feelings were ephemeral, she would enjoy them, but if they were real, she would carry that love, that enthusiasm, to her grave, for deep in her heart, regardless of what he had done, might do, she loved Marc Anthony. The gods had ordained it.

Chapter XIV

34 BCE

CLEOPATRA AND HER children waited for Marc Anthony on the palace steps. Anthony, roaring his approval of his offspring, descended upon them like a Bedouin raider, querying Alex, flirting with Selene, and taking Philadelphus from his nurse, tossing him into the air in a whirlwind of action. Delighted, his children clung to his mighty legs and chattered so much Cleopatra put her hands over her ears in mock horror, and let happiness dispel anxiety as quickly as outliers took over an oasis. "You have captivated them," she said to Anthony "but it's time they continue their studies. Their tutors are waiting."

"They have captivated me, and I insist we dispense with lessons today." Boisterously, he took over, teasing and being the clown with Philadelphus, acting as if Alex were an older boy, and calling Selene his sweetheart. They rode his shoulders, sat on his lap, and raced through the gardens with him. Cleopatra was sure the children would be too excited to sleep that night, but Anthony vowed they'd be so tired they'd do nothing else.

When Caesarion arrived, his teen years bringing a dignity not unlike that of Caesar's, Anthony rose from his place at the table and clasped him warmly. "By the gods, you have grown," he said.

"I study my father's battles, and yours," Caesarion replied, distinctly and slowly as Cleopatra deemed proper for a future ruler. "I greatly admire the rout you pulled off at Philippi, sir."

Anthony sat back down. "It was not a bad battle." He dismissed his celebrity with a shrug. "Now we must discuss what to do with Armenia and the prisoners I brought with me."

Caesarion looked flattered. "It, too, was a great battle, sir."

My son has the makings of a diplomat, Cleopatra thought with pride. Anthony's success against Armenia, although magnificent, had been of much lesser stature than the battle at Philippi. Never unaware that money brought power, she knew full well the military significance of his latest deed. It was a show for the proletariat, Anthony returning with much of the Armenian treasury.

As evening shadows lengthened, and oil lamps were lit, he enchanted his children and Caesarion. She knew a keen edge of fulfillment watching Anthony play on the floor with the younger children while Caesarion sat near by watching. When dark made the room a shadowy, slightly cold place, Anthony sent the younger children to bed with kisses and protestations of love and again turned to Caesarion. "I was serious about the prisoners. What think you we should do with Artavasdes and his family?"

Caesarion said, "My father used royal prisoners in his triumphs. Perhaps we could do something like that."

A look of pride added to Caesarion's youthful eagerness, and for a while none of the three spoke. Cleopatra watched the candles burn down and sputter, saw the oil lamps flicker, and heard the whisper of bare feet on marble as house slaves, waiting for orders, gathered in the archway leading to the corridor.

"It's a thought." Anthony sitting on his spine, much as Caesarion did when Cleopatra forgot to reprimand him for slouching, stretched his legs in front of him. "It must be lonesome, no young men your age in the palace. I'll send to Rome for my son. Antyllus is about your age. Do the two of you good to be together." He glanced at Cleopatra, as if asking forgiveness for not sending Antyllus when she'd suggested the visit.

So this was his way of apologizing and showing they were together politically, socially, and personally. Whatever happened it was the two of them and their combined children—a family— conquering the world, the children following in their footsteps. A thrill of accomplishment, of skill and might, suffused her, like sun beating on desert sands, no escaping its power.

Two days later Anthony, wearing the saffron-gold robes of Dionysus, rode a chariot in a parade of the defeated. More Greek than Roman in his dress, actions, and popularity, Egyptians declared he was a god fit for a divine lady, a pharaoh, queen and goddess. They cheered this further evidence of the marriage of two gods. Shackled with golden chains, Artavasdes followed through the streets, his vacant-eyed wife, and two young sons walking with him. Effigies, paintings, and statues bearing religious significance, priests, poets, wild animals, and choral singers added to the mix as the parade, followed by Anthony's troops, wound its way between the throngs.

As the cooling breezes of autumn bent the date palms, and the eucalyptus trees swayed gracefully against a pale blue sky, Cleopatra waited at the temple of Serapis. Seated on a carved and jeweled throne of grand proportions, Caesarion seated as magnificently, her younger children near her, she had never been so happy.

Anthony's men prodded King Artavasdes and his family up the steps of the temple to her. Although dirty and disheveled, the deposed king glared, his gritty and bloodshot eyes filled with hatred and pride no matter his wife's robes were covered with dust, her hair limp, and their sons appeared like dirty-faced urchins. Yet despite this bedraggled facade, he stood king-like and proper.

Caesarion frowned and whispered, "Shouldn't he bow?"

"A king bows to no one," Artavasdes said, his head going higher, his gaze going from Caesarion to Cleopatra.

"You have chosen your words wisely." She nodded with respect and turning aside let Anthony's men take him away for the celebration began a time when days flowed like wine from a never-empty cask. Anthony was all things to her, and he and she were gods above the petty problems of the day. She paid little attention when Octavian and the Roman elite dubbed the celebration a mock triumph in imitation of Rome.

She was delirious with joy when in an event dubbed The Donations, Anthony made clear in a public speech he was on Egypt's side in all ways. He showered her and her children with lands he'd promised, land formerly in Roman hands. He also gave the children titles meant to cement their place in the world. While most were honorary, Caesarion's reminded the world he was Caesar's rightful successor. Cheers, echoing in Greek, Egyptian, Aramaic, Hebrew, and all the eastern languages, became a growl in Rome.

As Cleopatra basked in the serenity of the following days, Laknefer reported Octavian irritated his followers, had trouble keeping his troops satisfied, and got along with Lepidus like an alley cat. Lepidus's followers made sport of him while recalling Anthony's pleasant manner and fighting power. As long as he had the backing of the people, Anthony's position on the Triumvirate remained firm. Cleopatra felt assured of Egypt's place in the world and of a brilliant future for her children

As the bond between her and Anthony deepened, she indulged his liking for the risqué and naughty, even once allowing the obscene dances gossip said her father had favored. The story, repeated in Rome, was said to prove Cleopatra's debauchery and the licentiousness of the Egyptian court. Once, a dinner party becoming a repeat of many others, she suggested they go in disguise throughout the alleys and back streets of Alexandria, knocking on doors and pretending to be local people in need of a handout. Anthony delighted in the playful prank, but she kept track. If they received money, she had the royal treasurer return the money in triplicate the next day.

When Antyllus arrived from Rome, the children bubbled with excitement, as did Anthony. Shorter than Caesarion, more muscular, but as charming as his father, Antyllus, used to the give and take of soldiers as well as statesmen, laughed and joked with his father in a way Caesarion couldn't. Immediately, Caesarion's less effusive personality created a distance between the boys each envious of the other, showing disdain and looking bored

Remembering her own isolation as a child, once a week Cleopatra insisted on the children joining her and Anthony at dinner. Forced to be together Caesarion and Antyllus looked constantly for the other's weak spot. Witnessing the power plays between the boys, she said nothing until Antyllus sprinkled mouse droppings from a pepper jar on Caesarion's plate of food. Warning her son before he ingested the mess, she forced Anthony to acknowledge the problem. Later, he said, "Leave them alone, they'll work it out."

One morning as wind whipped around the palace, and a gray fog followed rain and didn't lift, Alexandra and her son arrived with a large and impressive entourage. Glad to entertain Hebrews who were not at odds with her, Cleopatra called to Iras, "Hurry with my hair comb, I want to be at the door when they arrive."

That night, in the great dining hall, she held a small family banquet, Anthony at one end of the table, she at the other, Alexandra and her son Aristobulus on one side, Caesarion and Antyllus opposite. Rain drummed against the palace, shutters were closed, coals burned in braziers, and everyone wore robes against the draft. Oil lamps and candles flared. Still visible in the flickering shadows the marble walls gleamed, the ceiling panels, a delight of gods and goddesses gilded in gold, cavorted for everyone's visual enjoyment.

It was a pleasant party, Anthony telling amusing anecdotes, everyone contributing to the conversation as serving maids and slaves hurried back and forth with trays of food. Alexandra, whose appearance was no threat, thought in ways similar to Cleopatra. Her son, Aristobulus, was as good looking and also as tall as Herod.

As Aristobulus spoke to Cleopatra in Hebrew, Caesarion and Antyllus listened politely for a while and then turned aside. Even though not understanding a word, both boys seemed impressed, along with Anthony who understood only the phrases and bawdy words of the barracks. Cleopatra translated glibly and quickly.

Alexandra shrugged. "I tell Aristobulus it's not polite to speak a language all don't understand, but I expect he was so engrossed he forgot."

"I apologize to all present," the young man said in accented Greek, even sketching a bow.

Antyllus shot a quick glance at Caesarion who was trying hard not to smile. He winked; Antyllus grinned.

Cleopatra said, "No need to apologize, I enjoy a chance to exercise my Hebrew."

Alexandra smiled. "Speaking of languages, I was in the temple balcony listening recently when Aristobulus read aloud from the ancient texts of our people. I was overwhelmed with maternal pride and intend to tell Herod. He needs a high priest and why should he seek further when Aristobulus is available?"

"Your son seems most suitable," Cleopatra agreed.

"A fact I'm sure Herod will recognize when others speak so glowingly of him."

"Indeed I shall," Cleopatra murmured, knowing Herod would not believe anything she said. Yet, it would be advantageous to have allies in the Judaean palace, and she would get Anthony to wield his influence. She gestured, and the wine glasses were refilled and fruit and nuts were set out along the table. "Perhaps your son would call upon the gods to join us in blessing this occasion." She leaned back with contentment. Tomorrow she would indulge herself with Iras and Charmion, Alexandra and her women. Slaves would massage backs and feet, pamper them with unguents and perfumes, and pretend not to hear while she and her best friends giggled, laughed, and gossiped like girls.

Aristobulus rose, and spread his hands as if in benediction, cleared his throat before launching into a singsong recitation.

Caesarion nudged Antyllus.

Speaking first in Hebrew, Aristobulus called upon the one god to bless the people present, and then switching to Greek, he called upon the spirits of all to blend in holiness and righteousness, his voice alternately piping and thundering until Antyllus and Caesarion went from raised eyebrows to outright grins and muffled their laughter behind cupped hands.

Cleopatra glared at them, but the boys seemed in accord, and pleased at that, she hid her vexation.

"You see his capability, his devotion," Alexandra said when her son finished and stood with bowed head. "He's a born priest."

"Such fervor cannot be easily dismissed."

Alexandra nodded vigorously. "The first time I saw him reading the ancient scripts he was but a mere boy barely weaned from the breast. Now he's sixteen, the same age the Romans are when they put on the toga of adulthood."

"When I put mine on I became a soldier." Anthony looked around the table. "Caesarion is of an age for it, Antyllus almost." He nodded at Alexandra. "I'll do what I can for your son."

Not long afterward, Herod appointed the boy head priest, and soon after Alexandra followed Aristobulus to Judaea.

The rains had ceased and pleasing warmth pervaded the land when a messenger came from Judaea. Cleopatra motioned the man forward, took the papyrus and skimmed its message. "I should have known," she said handing the scroll to Anthony. "Alexandra says Herod all but keeps her under house arrest. She's under surveillance, is seldom allowed to see Aristobulus, and fears for her life. She hopes to escape" She paused. "In the meantime...."

"In the meantime? " he asked, tossing the message aside.

"I beg you to do something."

He shook his head. "We have her word only."

She frowned. "She would not lie to me. Anyway..."

Anthony flung out a hand, stopping her words as he prowled the ivory porch where they often met, the vista down to the sea filled with swaying palms. "If she—and you—want me to kick Herod off the throne, I can't." He threw her a look of determination. Remember, Cleopatra, I took Herod's cities and groves and gave them to you. *And left him land-locked.* That's enough. You know very well I need Herod's friendship when I mount the final attack on Parthia." The stubbornness and strength that made him a leader of men, a fierce fighter showed in his stance, the look in his eye.

She spoke softly, "We're talking about people, not countries, my love."

Shaking his head, he met her pleading gaze. "I'll tell Herod to look the other way if your friend Alexandra wants to leave, but mind you, I'm not saying a thing for Aristobulus. She wanted him named high priest, and by the gods, he is."

She said nothing more, knowing they were in a high stakes game, and in Judaea she had run out of currency.

At the gibbous moon, Alexandra was smuggled out of Judaea in a wooden sarcophagus, and Anthony had barely returned to the palace from a fishing excursion when another message arrived from Judaea. Aristobulus drowned when bathing. Cleopatra shook her head. "Poor Alexandra. Aristobulus was barely older than Caesarion, and Herod killed him. Surely you will rebuke Herod."

"Rebuke him? For what? An act no one can prove?"

She whirled around, facing him squarely. "So, My Lord Anthony doesn't even reproach his friend Herod."

He shook his head and pouring wine into a glass spilled it over the table. " My god, woman, why do you think I wear myself out trying to build an empire for Rome, and yes, Egypt? For our sons, that's why.   By the gods, woman, I do everything for Antyllus, Alexander, and little Philly. Caesarion too. And you pick at me about Herod." He slammed his hand down on the table. "You want me to assassinate him? Kill him in hand to hand? I could you know. Don't forget, I'm a Roman, but I will not harm Herod." He glowered at her. "Now don't speak of it or Judea again."

She turned aside, his comment about Rome bothering her more than the rest. Octavian was speaking out against Anthony in the senate, from his couch at dinner parties, from the forum, and now the people of Rome were listening as he blackened Anthony's name.

He descended into a brooding silence, speaking to her seldom. Fearful, she had Laknefer intercept his letters to Rome, destroyed some, had others copied and sent the original on. In all the letters Anthony used a surplus of words to soften his anger at Octavian while also declaring his independence. Octavian answered none of the letters. Stung, Anthony sent Octavian a personal note.

Reading rapidly, Cleopatra stared at the rolled papyrus, her head pounding. Anthony declared first and foremost he was a man of Rome and asked why Octavian treated him so shabbily. Was it because he slept with the queen? After all, he had been with her off and on for nine years and didn't Octavian have liaisons with many women?

The words repeating in her mind, her heart pounding in her ears, a horrifying emptiness hit her, and dizziness swept over her like a plague. Had it all been a lie? Grasping the arms of her chair, with a supreme effort she slowly regained control. Anthony would always be, above all Roman, but he was with her, and she must make sure he stayed—for her, for Egypt and for her children.   She'd say nothing to him, but she'd be vigilant while waiting to see what Rome, and Anthony, would do next.

Chapter XV

33, 32, 31 BCE

WHEN OCTAVIAN'S WORDS in the Roman Senate grew heated, Anthony replied, the two leaders indulging in a war of words but accorded equal support in Rome. Anthony, not Octavian, was called upon when Media needed protection from Parthia. While Anthony seemed gratified at being chosen over his rival, Cleopatra viewed it as a symbol of Octavian's decline. He was again targeting her, spreading rumors and lies.

She was not surprised when Anthony, after advising, shoring up, and soothing the Medes, established military headquarters in Ephesus. Filled again with boundless energy and ebullient good spirits, he suggested she follow as preparations for a Roman campaign once more took shape. To insure Egypt proceeded on the path she wanted, she put friends in high government positions and hurried to join Anthony.

In Ephesus she stayed away from Anthony's military meetings and looked forward to spending time in the library. Second only to Alexandria's in the number of volumes, some from antiquity, the library had Greek manuscripts she wanted to peruse. But as Octavian's attacks on her escalated, it became clear she had to look out for Egypt's interests and counted on Anthony to mitigate any problems her presence would bring.

Trailed by bodyguards and attendants, she walked in unannounced at a campaign strategy meeting. Betraying nothing of his feelings, Anthony continued as if nothing had changed. Men with gray in their beards, men with smooth cheeks, exchanged looks, but no one objected, although few acknowledged her presence. She'd made it

her business to know Anthony controlled thirty legions of soldiers—
75,000 bivouacked near the city, with 25,000 light-armed infantry,
and 2,000 cavalry in addition to 800 warships while 300 merchant
vessels scurried in and out of the harbor.   Not since Alexander the
Great had the world known such sea power. She didn't need to remind
Anthony that Egypt's produce and money kept his mighty army and
armada going

In subsequent days she continued to sit in at strategy sessions, and
he said nothing. Although some of the allied generals looked askance,
once Anthony asked for her opinion and listened with respect as she
spoke. Several Romans frowned and others looked grimly at their feet,
but no one refuted her logic.

One day after she had spoken, a sharp-chinned, middle-aged
Roman who had barely contained his patience earlier, jumped to his
feet and glared at her. "I must ask, gentlemen, what is a woman doing
in a council of war? We are to discuss battle, not the latest way to apply
kohl."

Silence swept the room, and all eyes were turned upon her.

Glancing swiftly from one man to the next, she stood, and faced
her attacker. "Indeed I have authored a book about cosmetics, but I
have, gentlemen, run Egypt peacefully and, I might add, successfully
economically.   My country, my people, and I have a stake in the
outcome of this meeting." She smiled at the man who had objected
to her presence. "As you most correctly pointed out, sir, I am but a
woman, but need I remind you I am also a queen, and my country has
a large financial stake in this campaign?"

He shook his head, and sat, fearing, she supposed, Anthony's anger
for Anthony was looking at her with approval.

The grumbling ceased. Men who knew her, men who were not
threatened by her charm or position, nodded, showing regard for her
intelligence as well as her wealth. Still her detractors frowned, and the
meetings slowly became an armed camp between those who liked her
and those who, sneeringly, repeated Roman gossip.

"Perhaps it would be better if you stayed away," Anthony suggested
one morning.

"Are you speaking as the father of my children or a minion of

Rome?" she asked turning from her makeup table, her tortoise shell comb falling to the floor.

"Neither. I speak as a leader of men."

She lowered her head. "I bow in recognition of that fact." Slowly, she brought her head up and looked into his eyes, "But for Egypt's and our children's sake, I cannot stay away."

For a long moment he stared back at her, and then he sighed. "I cannot refute or deny your argument. You'll be pleased to hear I've made plain that the king of Judaea will not join us here."

Wiggling her toes and smiling in the predawn dark, she said sincerely, "I will stay away as much as possible."

Once on the way to the docks, her litter passing where Anthony met with his officers, he spied her chair and ran out. She thought, *I'll remember this moment always.* The air was soft, his eyes warm. At thirty-five, despite four children, she was still shapely, her face unlined. Beyond Anthony, a row of houses, lush with plantings, led to their abode, and happiness hummed through her like a harp string strummed by the gods as Anthony watched until her chair was a speck upon the horizon before he rejoined his men. Life had never been so good.

But in the spring, counsels arrived from Rome announcing only war between Anthony and Octavian would decide who would reign supreme. That day burnished sun cast long rays over the city. Waking with Anthony's love prominent in her mind, her skin glowing, her eyes shining, Cleopatra felt beautiful as well as confident   The Romans in the city, even the newcomers, backed Anthony. A stand against Octavian was planned for the Balkans. No matter what Octavian proposed, Anthony would triumph.

In late April she persuaded Anthony to go on holiday. At the island of Samos she took him to theater presentations, had him listen to choir competitions, and attend poetry readings, revels, and banquets of the annual spring festivals. Carefree, as a girl newly in love, she tasted with him the wines of life, feelings of unease coming only in Athens. Statues of Octavia appeared on the route into the city, ruining for her the sight of sun sparkling on whitewashed houses. Anthony's ex-wife had been loved by the Greeks and was indeed lovely. Cleopatra bit her lips to keep from crying out.

Anthony shrugged. "There's no denying, she was beautiful." Cleopatra shot him a questioning look.

"She was like a lovely candle that was never lit."

"No flame? Not even a spark?"

"Not the tiniest spark," he said, smiling at her.

She gave him a glittering, sidewise look. She'd never be jealous of another woman again. That night she sent a fast cutter to Alexandria with instructions for Antyllus and Caesarion, to return with their attendants. They were family, and she loved Anthony as a woman, a god and a queen, and nothing marred those thoughts, not even emissaries from Rome carrying messages from Octavian. He had declared war against Egypt, against her, not against Anthony and thus curried favor at home. "He wants you to leave me," she whispered to Anthony, the idyllic week coming to an end.

"Vain hope," Anthony muttered, making notes on an onyx tablet she had given him. "My men are loyal to me, not him." He looked up. "Don't worry about Octavian. He postures, uses words and symbols, but we have right on our side. I could whip him with both arms tied behind my back." He winked.

"Still, I think the boys should return to Alexandria where I know they'll be all right."

"Leave them," Anthony said. "I'll see that they're safe. In fact, you have no need to worry about anything. We'll rout Octavian before he lands a blow."

But it wasn't easy to ignore Octavian's diatribes against her. In the following months Roman poems, songs, jokes, riddles and communiqués said she had taken a noble leader and rendered him helpless. She had nursed on vipers, taken the poison into her system and spewed her evil over the civilized world.

Hearing the gossip, Caesarion scowled, his young face, so remarkably like Caesar's, wracked with worry. Despite Anthony's relaxed attitude, Cleopatra worried, and winter, dragged by with a few bright spots. The Macedonians issued coins with her likeness, feted her presence, and showered Anthony with praise. In Italy Anthony's bribes bought support in many regions, while it was reported Octavian scrounged for cash and credit. From all over, men joined Anthony. His supporters laughed often, saying Octavian would be easy to defeat. Only the Roman general, Agrippa, was anywhere near as capable as Anthony.

The night a lookout spotted Octavian's ships, Anthony and his top aides celebrated the coming rout, their laughter and carefree attitude infectious. Anthony went to sleep with a smile on his lips while Octavian's men swept down on Anthony's naval station at Methone and captured much of Anthony's fleet. In the morning Cleopatra learned Agrippa commanded Octavian's troops.

Anthony ran his hands through his hair and shook his head. "I should have realized Octavian would be a coward. He hasn't the mettle of a man." He barked out orders for defense, his voice cracking, his eyes glazed.

In the coming days the men slogged through rain and mud with Anthony attempting to hold off Agrippa's forays against their other naval station. Hounding and harassing Anthony's ships, splintering his defenses, giving him no time to go on the offense, he threw Anthony further and further off base. Cleopatra's supply ships were unable to get past Agrippa's well-placed armada.

Pacing her rooms, Anthony berated himself, repeating, "I should have known he'd send Agrippa and been prepared for it."

The truth of his words glared in the gray preceding dawn.

All day he moved troops, shoring up foundering positions, and winter howled and slipped slowly into a reluctant spring as Agrippa forced Anthony to stay on the defense.

One night, watching him pace the floor, Cleopatra jumped up and paced with him. "What is it?" she whispered.

"My god, woman, my men are starving! Food is scarce, morale has plummeted."

Her own meals had been meager, but the boys and Anthony subsisted on military rations. She slipped her hand into his. "We must remind the local people we can save them from Octavian's brutal rule."

Hollow-eyed, his mouth grim, Anthony studied her face before nodding. "I will take care of it."

The next day a long line of people approached the shore and slowly in the fog and rain, she made out details: men, women and children, carrying sacks of grain in their arms or on their backs, were marching toward the seashore. Anthony's troops whipped those who staggered and fell out of line. Few dragged their feet.

"Where do they come from?" she asked as a man pushed to his feet and stumbled into line.

"From the next town and the next. As far as necessary."

She turned aside.

"So you see the worst of war," Anthony muttered not going to where she stood, but turning a hard gaze upon her.

Since Athens she had viewed life through a prism rendering it shiny and clean. Now dull gray tarnish tinged everything Was Zeus conspiring against her, Anubis joining in? Armies were switching from Anthony to Octavian. Lately, while Anthony's generals fought Agrippa, Octavian sneaked in behind Anthony's lines. Soon he would be within striking distance of Actium where Anthony's remaining fleet stood waiting.

Since arriving, she'd been billeted in houses that rivaled the villas of Rome, but now a tent camp was set up on the south shore of the bay, and hers was erected. Across the waters, the lights of Octavian's headquarters flickered while Anthony's instant city on the banks overlooked the gulf and the riffling blue of the Mediterranean. Equipment and supplies were piled, horses hitched and corralled, and everywhere men and campfires dotted the area. Anthony's power was a bristling presence; Octavian's merely a threat.

Quickly, Cleopatra learned the rhythm of the camp. Couriers, running from one part of the vast tent city to another, kept everyone apprised of the latest actions. Octavian attempted to destroy ships Anthony still had in the bay, but he beat Octavian's troops back before any damage was inflicted. When he returned, armor dented but personally unscathed, his eyes shone brightly.

From her sprawling Egyptian tent she watched him slap backs, shake hands with officers and men alike. She had a finely woven rug placed on the floor of his headquarters, added a three-legged table, a folding stool. Sometimes, exhausted he'd fall asleep on his narrow cot without difficulty. Once she crept under the rough covers and shared the small bed with him. Without saying a word, he wrapped her in his arms and went back to sleep.

Not used to the cramped space, the hard bed, and the increasingly bad news, she slept little. Trapped on the ships bottled up inside the gulf, his crews grumbled and complained. Some came down with dysentery and other diseases. Some died. Few rowers were left, replacements couldn't arrive, supplies get in. Troops guarded meager stores and rations were cut again.

One of Anthony's head generals deserted, rowing across the waters to Octavian. Sitting in the headquarters' tent and slapping mosquitoes, she said, 'Too bad he's not a mosquito or he'd be dead."

From behind a rough table, charts of the area spread out in front of him, Anthony looked up, shrugged, his face smooth, furrows of doubt gone. "Probably he wants to hurry home. If the roles were reversed, I would certainly rush home to you." He smiled, his voice light and beckoned to an aide who sat at a table near the entrance. "Send the general's clothes over to him. I would have him join his *amor patriae* with his degrees of office."

"I care not whether he goes naked, " she cried.

Anthony shrugged again. "Enemies hate when you're nice to them. Anyway, he won't be the last man to dessert. Men look for the best deal. They think Octavian will give it to them."

Surprised by his apparent good spirits, she leaned toward him. "You aren't worried?"

"Not yet. I know myself and what I'm capable of doing."

Chastened, she looked away first.

But as additional generals deserted, client kings following and others whispering, Anthony hollered, "Enough! The next group who attempts to switch sides will be executed." Soon dead bodies hung from the stakes where they'd been chained. Flies and maggots crawled in the coagulated blood, and Cleopatra covered her nose with a silk scarf and never looked toward the parade grounds.

Like a caged animal teased into anger, Anthony launched a land attack against Octavian. But several of his generals, believing that in the long run Octavian had the best of it, deserted before the rout could take place. They took with them foot soldiers and cavalry officers, depleting Anthony's ranks.

Anger swept through Cleopatra like a brush fire. Octavian was defeating Anthony, not because Anthony was incompetent, but because of Octavian's duplicity and the unplanned for expertise of General Agrippa.

Returning to camp, sweat running like water from him, Anthony shook his head when he spied her. "Must I fight a pride of lions by myself? They declare loyalty to me but sneak out in the dark like carts rumbling out of Rome at dawn. By the gods, I won't have it." Defeat sat on his face like a carrion bird. Where multiple thousands of men had milled, now only a few thousand stirred up the dust around the tents. "They're like embalmers scurrying to leave before a tomb is sealed."

In late summer Anthony called a council of war. For sixteen weeks they had been besieged, cut off from supplies, facing the humiliating loss of officers and men. Those remaining in camp were ill or demoralized, their loyalty tested, each well aware of their numerical disadvantage.

A dozen men crowded around tables in the headquarters tent when Cleopatra entered, the odors of the camp following. Taking a seat next to Anthony, she listened quietly as he spoke, his voice a monotone, telling everyone what they already knew. Smoke from the campfires drifted in, and the generals and sea captains remaining in the inner circle wiped their eyes and coughed, and Anthony, his heavy shoulders slumped, his fingers playing with a papyrus, blinked. "We have to decide what we're going to do."

Several men stared at him as if he had taken leave of his senses. Canidius, head of the land forces, took a step forward. Although his tunic showed the wear of long usage, he made a commanding figure, his posture flawless, his voice firm. "I make a strong plea for drawing Octavian's forces deeper inland." The passion beneath his words showed, and it was evident he had thought through his argument. "We can cut Octavian off, surround him, show him how superior My Lord Anthony and all of us are in hand-to-hand combat. Yes, I'd like to annihilate that little rooster."

Anthony smiled, apparently liking the compliment and the idea. Others leaned forward, better to hear what was said. "We'd at least give them a damned good fight. *Non cuvis homini contignit adire Alexandria.*" Quoting Horace, he substituted Alexandria. *It was not given to every man to go to Corinth.*

Cleopatra felt as if it were a signal to her. But Horace's words could have many meanings. She kept her face bland as she listened to one speaker after the other. Only Dellius met her gaze, his as disrespectful as always. Once he had made a crude joke about her draperies, her rugs, her pillows, her vast array of personal items.

Anthony asked, "Where would you suggest we accomplish this?"

"In Macedonia. Or maybe Thrace. You, sir, have time after time proven your superiority on land. Why give up this advantage?"

Anthony spread out charts. "Show me."

Canidius pointed, his fingers stabbing at the terrain they would cross, showing where they'd encounter opposition, where they could expect help. A hot breeze riffled the tent flaps. "We could undoubtedly get our allies to back us. And it would be no disgrace to give up superiority of the sea to Octavian, not if we vanquish him on land." Anthony's superiority on land had been established long ago. Now only the sea captains looked askance as the others nodded agreement, added refinement of tactics.

A light appeared in Anthony's eyes, as yet another leader spoke, recalling Philippi. Smiles and excited chatter followed. He relaxed in his chair, and it was clear, he favored an assault by land.

The emptiness in Cleopatra's stomach wiggled snakelike to her chest. If Anthony led a land battle she and her people would be left, obliged to turn tail and run. She and Caesarion would have to hide, perhaps in the temple of Apollo. She had no doubt Antyllus would go with his father. But where was it written that Octavian would march out to meet him? Wouldn't it be wiser for Octavian to catch her and drag her and her child from their sanctuary and take them to Rome in chains? He had showed ingenuity thus far, and if he followed this pattern, he would not allow Anthony to draw him into a battle he would probably lose. She shook her head. "I worry about my ships." She kept her voice low.

"A ship can be rebuilt," Canidius said.

Not the gold stashed in its hold. Clasping her hands together so no one could see them shake, she searched for the right words. "The cargo can't." She looked straight at Anthony who alone knew what riches she carried in her flagship. For a moment, his gaze bit into hers before he nodded, and she knew he understood.

Canidius shouted, "Cargo! The woman worries about cargo while we worry about our very future." The furrows in his face deepened, his eyes hardened. "What can a woman know of war?"

She rose. "That cargo is why you are here, sir, and...."

He cut her off, a smile belittling her position.

"But you know nothing of war," Dellius murmured, so low few heard it, but she did, and everyone, sensing the uneasy moment, shifted, feet moving, clothes rustling.

His voice as powerful as the might of his sword, Anthony said, "I say let Her Majesty, the Queen of Egypt, speak."

Throats were cleared, feet shifted. A few men grumbled.

"Are you afraid to listen gentlemen?" she asked in her most soothing, yet needling way. Looking from one man to the next, her eyes as skillfully painted as if she were in her palace, she hoped to remind them of their own women and families at home.

Anthony gestured to her, and as she had done numerous times before, in her councils in Egypt, in hostile territories, among friends, but never before when she felt her life, her existence, her future and that of her children hung in the balance, she spoke. "If we lose my ships, gentlemen, we lose more gold than you ever knew existed, we lose the battles, we lose Egypt, and we lose Rome. To win against Octavian on land, is to win one battle. To exploit his position at sea is to give us an opportunity to regroup and fight him later. We are not talking a one-time triumph, a sword in an enemy's gut; we're talking futures, yours and your families, me and mine. With my help you can become richer than you ever dreamed. Isis will give you her divine protection. My way gives a future. Engage the enemy on land and what guarantee do you have that Octavian will even join the battle? He has no stomach for fair fights." She paused before adding, "He lies and cheats, and will do it again."

The sea captains present jumped to their feet, their own personal fortunes tied to bringing their ships home safely. One shouted, "On land, you must fight your way down the peninsula."

Publicola, foremost of the captains, murmured, "I'd never trust those blood-drinking cannibals along the way. Those bandit kings will spend your money and then join Octavian. You'd be cut off and alone. A land gamble would be a foolhardy undertaking."

Canidius shook his head and appealed to Anthony. "May the gods deliver me if I'm wrong, but you must see the wisdom of my arguments and fight where we're strongest."

Anthony crossed his legs as if he had all the time in the world. "And would we transport the gold with us from village to hamlet to town? And the Queen, who would guard her?"

No one met his gaze.

His voice ringing with reverence, a sea captain who had jumped up earlier, said, "I would deem it an honor to run interference for her Majesty's ship, "

Others spoke, voices raised excitedly now, the gods of the seas praised, Isis venerated.

When Canidius tried to speak again, Anthony shook his head and a stern look rode his face while his voice whipped like a leather thong. "Anyone who doesn't want to go by sea can leave now. But bear in mind, if you are with me, you are with me all the way. We live or die together, and if you leave, do not return or I will kill you."

No one moved and Canidius studied his feet before rising and bowing toward Cleopatra. "I respect Lord Anthony's decision and will go with his final plan."

Anthony rose. "At dawn we begin its implementation."

On the horizon a line of enemy ships were anchored. Four hundred someone said, and Anthony had only enough men to man 230 vessels, sixty of those Cleopatra's. A tight knot began to form in her chest, and rising she bid the men farewell and went to look for Caesarion, wanting her son near her this night.

Chapter XVI

31 BCE

SEPTEMBER 31, AT dawn, on a bluff overlooking the sea, as the sun tipped the horizon, Cleopatra stood staring out to sea. A simple white dress and a band with the uraeus of the cobra on her head, transformed her into Isis, patron of sailors, and as the shimmer of the sea receded from her view, her mind open to the gods, gentle Isis slipped in. She saw but did not see the camp, the people preparing for battle, striking tents, loading ships. A murmur of awed adoration rose, and from deep contemplation, she looked out to see people staring at her with exultation, sea captains and crews, Caesarion foremost among them. The sun, casting a pink oval in the east, turned her eyes into orbs of brilliance, catching light as mottled clouds in the west reflected eastern color.

Men who worshipped other deities, or spoke in the freethinking ways of the early Greeks, paused in their morning toilets to watch. Many Romans used religion as a social function, tossing off prayers to Mars, asking the deity to ward off evil, but belief was general, and Isis offered kindness and forgiveness. Everyone in camp watched with interest. Even Anthony conferring with his sea captains, Sosius and Publicola, had become speechless.

As the sounds of the camp mingled with the murmur of the sea, she started down toward her tent. Hardened legionaries made way for her with reverence and respect, and an ever-increasing silence followed her to her tent.

She slept until the bright sun of noon woke her. The camp had become a hive of preparation, men and equipment moving toward the beach. From a scrap of purpling shade, Anthony called out to her without first acknowledging her presence. Once more the strong man she remembered, he told her to get prepared. Naming the breeze that came up every afternoon, he explained, "We leave with the *maestro*." In full battle regalia, his breastplate shining, his helmet gleaming, he looked capable of anything.

Nodding toward Caesarion and Antyllus who waited a respectful distance behind Anthony, she whispered, "And the boys?"

He looked past her toward the sea and replied in a loud voice, "The boys will go with you."

His brow furrowed, Antyllus, shook his head, and a few seconds later, Caesarion did, too. "No, please, sir."

Anthony raked them with a gaze, his voice like the touch of a lash. "Don't argue. Caesarion, I depend upon you to guard your mother with your life. And you, Antyllus, I expect to carry out the orders of the captain, learn the ways of the sea. Now leave us."

As the boys moved away, Anthony stepped closer to Cleopatra. A sweet serenity still flowed through her, but worry sat stone-like on his face. The groove between his eyes was pronounced, his eyes turned inward. He lowered his voice. "We go one at a time through a gap in their defense, I first, your ships shall follow. As soon as we get through, yours will veer off. I will distract them long enough for you to slip away from Octavian and sail for home." His gaze came back to her, concern evident now in a softening of both sight and speech. "Is it clear?"

"I understand. But after it is all over and you have once again outwitted the enemy, will you sail for home, too?" Back to Alexandria, back to me.

"Of course." But his eyes had a vacant stare, his voice a hollow sound. It was as if he'd gone from her bed to a bed at the bottom of the sea. He stared toward the water breaking quietly on the shore.

She put a hand on his arm. "My lord."

He lowered his voice. "No matter what happens, stop for nothing. You and the boys must remain free. The future hangs upon all of us getting back to Alexandria safely."

The ramification of his words hitting hard, she nodded. Fleetingly, she touched his hands with hers, and then the thought came: if his ship went down in flames, he floundering in the water, she'd have to go on. But how? Their present closeness came, not with the exchange of passion, but building on it with day-to-day companionship and goals. She wanted, no…needed Anthony with her. She touched the golden medallion he wore around his neck, a good luck charm she had given him.

He leaned toward her. "May the gods guide you home safely."

"And may the gods of our fathers protect you."

He rubbed his cheek against hers so gently but firmly that it seemed to her more precious than the kiss he gave her at the last moment. It came swift and hard, and then he was gone. She knew she would see nothing more of him that day.

The bustle of the camp breaking up swirled around her, the place where thousands had dwelled was suddenly a place of trampled grass and forlorn trees, her luxurious tent struck last. With Caesarion, Antyllus, Iras and Charmion, she boarded, her flagship, the Antonia.

On the cliff, the leaves of acacia and olive trees turned in her direction, and she felt the first faint breeze that would go on to the grape orchards further down the coast. Along the shore, 20,000 legionnaires, followed by archers and slingers still loyal to Anthony, boarded the ships, the sound of footsteps carrying, no one speaking.

With Caesarion beside her, she stood on deck and watched Anthony's fighting ships move out. All had towers hastily constructed at bow and stern, braced for battle but looking unwieldy with sails added. The very survival of life as she knew it hung in the balance. As a band in her chest tightened, she took a deep breath and whispered ancient incantations to Atun, to Isis, to Osiris.

It was a warm day, the breezes making sweet the smell of campfires hastily doused, of voices calling, of snatches of prayer offered. And then, in a scorched earth policy that made her want to cry out at the waste of it, Anthony torched the ships remaining for he had not enough rowers to man them. Birenes, and the clumsier three-tiered tiremes, used mostly for ceremonial purposes, went up in smoke along with the lembi, the small swift ships containing no battering rams.

Foul black smoke rose like a bad omen, and automatically Cleopatra gestured to ward off evil. As the last ship was put to the torch, the others began to file through the narrow opening of the gulf. No one spoke. Only the dipping of oars, the soft commands, and the passage of the vessels through the water sounded.

It is not a day to die, she pronounced, pleased when her priests nodded. The auguries were with her and Anthony, and Octavian would be surprised, never expecting what they had planned. The thought pleased her. She smiled at everyone as sails, taken aboard for catching the breeze and outrunning Octavian's slower boats, were checked and rechecked.

Quickly, her ships went through the channel, the turquoise sea with the darting fish behind them. In the dark blue waters beyond, Octavian's large fleet, spread out in a semi-circle, waited. Four hundred vessels including liburnians, new ships with two banks of oars, designed for speed and maneuverability whether under oar or flying canvas. This staggering armada faced Anthony's one hundred and seventy warships, and Cleopatra's sixty merchant vessels and courier ships.

"We were betrayed," she whispered. Octavian's vast armada lay in position to annihilate her and Anthony.

"May the gods save us," Iras cried, clamping her lips tightly together.

The stunned face of youth facing treachery, Antyllus and Caesarion shook their heads in disbelief. "How can this be?" Caesarion cried, plainly puzzled.

"Who told on my father?" Antyllus demanded, his sturdy body balanced on legs far apart, hands clenched, muscles flexing. "Where is this traitor? I'll kill him myself."

She put her hand on his arm. "It makes no difference now."

The Captain nodded. "No my lad. Come help with the sails, for we must run at the first opportunity." Shouting orders, he moved swiftly away, Antyllus following.

"It was Dellius," she said as Caesarion looked to her for an answer. In Ephesus he'd accused her of bringing inferior wine to the troops, and when she'd retorted that no wine she preferred was inferior, he'd started a rumor saying she planned his assassination. The whole thing had been so ridiculous she had paid no attention, "I'm positive he reported to Octavian each move we planned to make." Fear knotted her belly, and she kept her gaze on Anthony's ships as his flagship, *Antonia*, came to a stop facing Octavian's fleet.

154

Her ships were close enough so she could see dim shapes and hear isolated words, shouted commands and then silence, the swoosh of water washing against wood. Time inched slowly forward. Neither fleet moved. Gulls swooped and dipped, and an occasional nervous cough echoed across the water. Still, no other noise disturbed the slight hissing rise and fall of the gulf, the battle to come seeming unreal in the peace of the moment.

Suddenly, one of Anthony's ships shot swiftly to the left, oars dipping in rhythm. In order to clash with Octavian his ships had to be farther out but not in the open sea where Octavian's superior forces could surround Anthony's remaining fleet.

Cleopatra clung to the rail watching, her nails biting into the flesh of her hands as Anthony's and Octavian's ships clashed, but they were so far away, at first she didn't believe it was happening. A flash of movement on the horizon, a disturbance on the surface of the water, a vibration and then straining she saw rocks and fire catapulted from ships, imagined arrows piercing flesh. Dry timber shot skyward in flames. Screams rent the air, and battering rams slammed amidships like sheep locking horns. Men locked in deadly hand-to-hand combat, screamed epithets, their words rising above the sound of the creaking vessels and sloshing sea. Tongues of flame licked the sky, and smoke darkened it, and the sea rushed in, claimed ships. Men floundered in the water. Cried for help.

But still Anthony's flagship stayed afloat while all the ships in the center of the arc–Octavian's as well as Anthony's–were taking water, sinking, burning to bits, casting men and objects into the sea faster than she could keep track. Weighed down with heavy helmets and shirts of mail, men bobbed helplessly. But a hole wide enough to sail through had opened up in the middle of the conflagration. "Make way," she called to the captain, pointing, and he brought their ship about so fast the breeze, swift now, filled the sails and sent them hurtling over the water to safety, the other merchant vessels following.

As the Antonia sped through the center of the battle, she refused to stay down. Smoke swirling in vast clouds choked her, and spying the blood and severed parts lining the decks of sinking vessels, watching men slide into the sea and drown, bile rose in her mouth.

His eyes big, Caesarion gripped her arm, and she looked up at her son and forced a look of peace on her face. "Remember, they die for us," she shouted as a burning mast splintered and fell, crushing men beneath it, their cries piercing the air. Her ships, taking hits, lobbed shots to protect themselves. Anthony's ship, beleaguered on all sides, sat dangerously low in the water while her own ship plowed through the melee mostly unscathed.

She searched for a glimpse of him, the foul taste in her mouth increasing. With a stiffening resolve, she put a steadying hand on Caesarion's arm. Antyllus, without missing a beat, was manning a slingshot, and. heart heavy, she sent her son to join him.

The quiet waters of the gulf, whipped to a fury by the carnage, her ship rose and fell while behind her Anthony left his flagship for another, a swifter, smaller ship and broke away from Actium as planned. "Thank the gods," she whispered as with the wind at his back, he sailed out of Octavian's reach. The battle had been bloody but involved few ships, and Anthony was safe.

Tears filled her eyes. No matter that they had lost most of their navy, they had accomplished what they had set out to do. They had saved the gold and were on their way home safely, their sons alive. Caesarion and Antyllus cheered, and a roar went up from all the ships clipping along, catching the counterclockwise currents of the Mediterranean helping them speed away. The tides were lower than the three-foot average and even the very salty spray that hit her face seemed welcome.

She laughed out loud for the first time since Athens. As Caesarion and Antyllus, at ease now, wrestled and pummeled one another, she wanted to join in. Tonight she would wrestle with Anthony, tickle him, as he often tickled her, swearing that she was much too serious. No, tonight, she would not be serious at all.

She looked back, expecting the rest of Anthony's ships not engaged in hand-to-hand combat to join them in the sprint to safety as planned. But none made it through the channel. Outnumbered and hemmed in, they surrendered after thirty or forty of their vessels went down in flames.

Three days later she and Anthony docked at the naval station under Anthony's rule at Cape Taenarum. "Octavian won the battle," he said, "but by the gods we did exactly as we planned." He lifted her into his arms and swung her around. "We've lived to fight again, and we will, my sweet love, that we will."

"Yes," she cried, her pride in his ability broad and deep as ever. They proved once again they could outwit the world. She sailed on secure in the belief that Anthony's large army, still extant under Canidius, would be there after Anthony rebuilt his navy, and that together they would show Octavian, Parthia, and the world

Before returning to the harbor at Alexandria, she had her ships decorated with flowers, had musicians play, wore her most elaborate jewels and fanciest gown. Cheers resounded all the way to the palace. But hearing the latest news, her elation faded into the fabled past.

Overtaken on land, Canidius had allowed himself to be swayed by Octavian's words. He had spared nothing while denigrating both Cleopatra and Anthony. Anthony's men deserted en masse.

At the palace Anthony looked out the window to the sea. "I have men who swear fealty to me and then stab me in the back. It's like Caesar and Brutus all over again. Now, it's down to Octavian and me."

"He doesn't have Egypt's backing. You do. Forget Octavian. Regroup."

"Need you attack me, too? Take bites from me, too?"

She turned away from his probing look. There was such a thing as being pragmatic, facing the new situation. "I'm sorry if it seems I belittled your abilities, my love. I'm not. My hand is always in yours. You have my love and support always." She had humbled herself, and she looked at him expecting to see him brace himself, become the strong and able man she admired. He didn't.

"Say no more about it, I believe you." He slurred his words, and his eyes remained troubled; his shoulders slumped. A fever seemed to have settled over him. He barely noticed her.

In the following weeks Anthony began to live a life that moved ever faster, spinning like a top, doing things at the cast of a die. He took part in chariot racing, horse racing, and gambled about anything and everything. Many nights he drank himself to sleep. Other nights, he stood for hours looking out to sea, watching for Octavian. Finally, he rejuvenated his old drinking club, calling it, "Those who are going to die together."

Cleopatra quit looking to him for suggestions. Recalling the praise showered on Antyllus for his seamanship, on Caesarion for his learning, she decided to do something to assure the Egyptian people and raise the boys' stature in their eyes. No matter what happened to her and Anthony, the children would carry on. Already Caesarion spoke three languages and was well on the way to being a diplomat. The pedagogues she conferred with said Antyllus's progress at the Museum went well. She would stage a ceremony to show that the boys were of age. Caesarion at sixteen, because he was part Roman, and Antyllus, although a little younger than usual, could don the toga of Roman adulthood.

When she told her idea to Anthony, he said, "Why not? One plan is as good as another. What more can they do to me, to us?"

At the ceremonies where both young men were named adults, he wore a solemn face, and as the Egyptian people knelt at Caesarion's feet, and the Romans lingering with Anthony helped Caesarion and Antyllus fold their togas properly, Anthony said little, moving through the ceremony as if sleep-walking.

It was as if a cold wind blew yet nothing but hot blasts carried from the desert. Anthony drank himself to sleep night after night. Lying alone, facing the god-filled sky, realization came to Cleopatra. Naming Caesarion an adult, she had played into the hands of Rome. They could wage war on him without compunction, call him names as they did her. She wanted to crawl into some safe place, but her father and Caesar were gone and Anthony was a changed man. He offered no talk of the future, nothing. At fifty-one he looked much younger, but he was far from young. Was it possible that she was thirty-nine? Her body was almost as slim as the first time he had seen it, and she wanted to lessen the sense of foreboding that slithered like snakes in the shadows, threatening them both. He can help me no more, she thought, a sadness enveloping her.

She began frantic preparations to ensure Caesarion's safety. If she hid him in the city, Octavian would roust him out, humiliate her publicly and kill Caesarion before her eyes. Of this she had no doubt. But if he ran now, left Alexandria, left Egypt... She had a pack train outfitted with swift horses and loyal retainers and alerted his tutor, Rhodon, to stand by.

The next day she called her eldest child, the son upon whom she'd pinned the future, into the throne room. Charmion, who had carried out the preparations for Caesarion's flight, waited at the far end of the room, but no one else was present. Candles blazed, and incense burned, and the alabaster and marble hall reflected a magnificence she had forgotten. It was here she had translated for her father; it was here she had welcomed the first delegation of Egyptians in her own right. Now her dearest son, so young, fresh and innocent walked toward her. Making her clamoring emotions submit to the gravity of the moment, she waited as Caesarion approached.

He trod a long scarlet carpet where suppliants had inched forward that first day of her reign. After her father died, she had wondered if she could render fair and just decisions as her people tremblingly came to the foot of her throne. Now, Caesarion, a puzzled look on his face, his walk that of a royal born and bred, looking so much like Caesar she wondered how the Romans could protest the reality of his being, drew within speaking distance.

She waved around her. "Remember this place where the Ptolemy name resounded with honor throughout the centuries. Remember this sacred throne that knew your grandfather, and all the kings and the queens who came before. Remember the great Ptolemy who fought with Alexander the Great. And remember, it will be your honor and duty to sit here after I am gone."

"I know, Mother. You've told me before." He spoke with the impatience of youth, the words softened with a smile.

She shook her head. "But now it is different. The throne and our country and people are under a great threat. Octavian means to destroy us, and I have no illusions about that. Unless My Lord Anthony can secure as large a force as Octavian, Egypt has no future, I have no future."

"Mother, what are you saying? The people of Egypt love you."

"I'm saying Egypt cannot turn aside a superior force of Romans. I doubt that Anthony can save us, even though he has made a gallant try. Now I rely on you."

"To do what?" A puzzled expression raced across his face.

"Save yourself so you can return later." She leaned forward slightly, wanting to take him in her arms, but nothing of this showed in her eyes, her bearing. "I want you to go up the Nile, traverse the desert and the ocean to India. Once long ago my father told me about this strange and distant land, told me about a route, but I'm not sure of the way, but I know it's possible even though it's a long way. Traders occasionally come from there."

He frowned.

She held up a hand. "With money you'll be all right. It will buy your safety with the Bedouins, buy you time in India. And you can return when you're older, when you feel able and ready. With the gods' permission, with Isis's protection, you will come back. This throne will await you."

He shook his head. "Mother, I don't want to leave you."

Oh, my child, I'd keep you with me if I could. She shook her head. "Caesarion, don't forget you're your father's son. You can do it. You'll have half the royal treasury with you. Use it wisely and it will keep you safe. In a year or two, whenever Egypt is secure again, I want you to return." She held out the scrap of cloth Anthony had given her years earlier. "This is from your father's toga. Take it." She held it out. "You must obey."

His face somber, he nodded. "I thank you and honor you, my queen." Unshed tears filled his eyes, and he fell to his knees and buried his head in her lap. "Mother, please don't make me go."

She smoothed his hair, cradled his head. "You must. You must do this for yourself and for Egypt. From the moment you entered my womb you were my heir." She studied him, her child who so gallantly controlled the tears leaking from his eyes. His legs, his body, so like Caesar's, her son held the future in his hands. "You must go." She tucked the scrap of cloth into his hands.

Taking it, he raised his head, tears still lingering in his eyes, but not running. A muscle in his cheek jumped, but nothing else betrayed his emotion. He started to get up.

"Stay down my dear son for the blessings of all who have ever sat on this throne and remember Isis, Osiris, and Horus watch out for you, and my personal wishes and thoughts go with you and stay with you always, my dearest, dearest son."

She touched him on the forehead and kissed his cheeks and then standing, she hugged him one last time, her son who towered over her, her son whom she loved like no other. Then she turned away.

She could tell he had not moved, hoping, perhaps she'd change her mind, but she kept her back turned. Finally she heard him leave, his footsteps echoing like a child's in the vastness of the throne room, dragging reluctantly, slowing, starting on again. She bit her lips to keep from calling him back. When she looked again, he was gone, and she knew the end was approaching.

Chapter XVII

30 BCE

OCTAVIAN MOVED WITH diabolical leisure through neighboring countries, adding supporters to his cause and men to his army. Any day he and his armada, his fighting men, his allies, and his clear superior power would arrive in the harbor, she knew, looking out toward the lighthouse each day. Desperate to continue the Ptolemy line in Egypt, she sent an emissary to meet and talk with him. As delicately as possible, the man explained that the queen was ready to abdicate in favor of her children. Egypt and Rome could carry on the type of relationship that had proved so workable in the past. She Cleopatra VII, Queen of Egypt, would retire from public life.

Octavian sent an answer shot with ambiguity, talking around but never addressing the issue.

"May the gods help us. What does he want?" Plans shot through her mind as fast as horses galloping to an oasis in the desert. Octavian was scrounging around for money, securing loans wherever he could. Her eyes glittering with purpose, she sent him a letter couched in all the flowery diplomatic language used by one head of state to another. With the letter she sent a chest filled with gold, and waited for an answer.

The days passed slowly, hot and hotter, and her tongue grew dry as dead leaves, but Octavian never answered.

Like a person looking at the familiar for the first time, she walked through the palace, seeing the size and grandeur of the rooms, feeling the pull of history. One way or the other she had to insure the continuity of the Ptolemy reign.

She wasn't surprised when Herod added his name to Octavian's list of friends, and only an iron will kept her from saying, "I told you so," to Anthony.

"What can we do?" Cleopatra cried to Anthony as Octavian drew ever closer.

He moved pieces on a game board before pausing long enough to regard her in a searching manner before pushing the table and the game board aside. "I cannot do less than you have done. I will offer to step down."

Antyllus traveled to Octavian with a message. His father would publicly humble himself before Octavian and go into private life if Octavian would spare the Queen and her children.

Again, no answer came, and Anthony's eyes wore the look of death. Sand scoured the outside walls of the palace and seeped in through closed jalousies. At night, the shutters open wide to catch the slightest breeze, Cleopatra slept little, her mind working furiously. One morning she knew what she must do.

She found Nicodemus in his office. At the top of his form, his buildings sparkling with incomparable beauty, the building honoring Anthony almost complete, he agreed to help her in a task that was surely beneath him. With rapidity he engaged men to build equipment to haul her remaining fleet of warships across the isthmus. She planned an escape from Alexandria at the same time she prepared for battle. She would follow Caesarion if possible, and if Octavian pursued her, she'd fight him on the far eastern front. Or take refuge in some lesser country where her money and reputation would give her clout. Throughout the years the people of Upper Egypt had loved her, worshiped her, telling wonderful stories about her goodness and ability, and despite Herod's perfidy the people of obscure eastern countries had always sided with her.

Nicodemus had wooden skids made for warships too big to travel by canal, and slaves hauled the fleet two days overland to the Gulf of Suez. Pleased, she scattered coin among them and whispered her planned exodus to Anthony.

"You must do what you must," he said, dismissing her explanations. "I must face Octavian here."

The next day, the palace unaccustomedly quiet, she woke late. His eyes skimming past her, Anthony brought her the news. Every ship, hauled from the water and carried overland and deposited in the water on the other side of the isthmus, had been sunk. Malchus, monarch of an Arabian kingdom, had once kissed her hands in appreciation when she kept Herod from overrunning his country. Now, he'd turned on her and burned her ships.

Stunned, she stumbled to a chair and sat staring at the scenes in her head. Once Malchus had begged and pleaded, fallen at her feet when he'd needed her help; now he had stabbed her in the back. Why were people doing this? Was treachery in the very air she breathed, in the vapors from the rising waters, in the stinging sand? Was the wind an ally of Rome? Had Isis deserted her? For the first time she understood Anthony's depth of despair.

She put her hand in Anthony's and he led her to the nursery where they sat watching and listening to their offspring. They were still there when Charmion brought more bad news. Herod had traveled to meet Octavian and, in his smooth and well-thought-out way, had additionally blackened Cleopatra's name.

Stepping aside so the children couldn't hear or see, she dug her nails into the palms of her hands and whispered to Anthony, "Have you nothing to say?"

He sighed. "What do I have, thirty, forty, maybe fifty ships, a few hundred, a thousand men? You ask for miracles, and I have none."

"Well, I for one will never give up. I do not let people spit on me and not spit back." She turned away, knowing that if she ran to the ends of her country, Octavian's men would hunt her down and drag her back to face him. No, she must hide and guard the royal treasure, for it was the only thing that remained, and with it she might save herself, her children, and Anthony.

Angrily, she rang the bell, and when Iras came running, she said, "I want everyone to know that if they betray me or mine, they will pay with their lives. Get the word out." She glared at Anthony. "Are you with me?"

His eyes shadowed and sad, he said, "Do any of us have a choice?"

Shocked once again, she stared at him and tears filled her eyes.

He put his hand on her shoulder. "I will protect you as long as possible, and go down fighting. Surely you realize that."

"I do," she murmured turning swiftly aside, not wanting him or anyone to see this moment of weakness. Only through strength could she survive, could Egypt survive.

Infused with a fierce protective love, she watched him walk slowly away. Then in a flurry of action she dictated a letter to the king of Media who had supported her and Anthony throughout the disastrous aftermath of Actium. Little Philadelphus who even now came to pull at her skirts and demand attention, was betrothed to the little princess of Media. "I am sending my sons Philadelphus and Alexander to you until things are settled here in Alexandria," she wrote to the king. Reminding him of the glories the liaison had already brought Media, she added that it was only the beginning of friendship and great prosperity for Media.

The King replied that if the Queen of Egypt got rid of his ancient enemy the king of Armenia, the king of Media would gladly extend his hospitality to include shelter to two princes of Egypt, the young sons of Cleopatra VII and Marc Anthony of Rome.

Her hand shaking, she set aside the papyrus. Artavasdes, the king who had spoken so bravely, who even now languished in prison had to be sacrificed. He had done her no personal harm and would leave a wife and children. She looked out at the harbor. Once it teemed with vessels, now only a few Egyptian ships bobbed at anchor, and Octavian, and Herod were on their way to Alexandria. "I have no choice," she cried aloud.

Anthony ordered the execution, and that night he and she whispered of times when their royal standards had flown high and the very air breathed words of encouragement.

The scramble to change sides continued, whole countries issuing proclamations of loyalty to Octavian. Now, men who had remained with Anthony began to dessert, and when he caught them sneaking past the palace walls, he had them flogged as a warning. Deserters were put to death, and anyone who mentioned the searing gossip that traveled from country to country and finally made it into the Ptolemy palace was beaten or tortured. Romans in high places exclaimed that

Anthony, who after all was still Roman and could be excused, should put Cleopatra to death.

"Should I arm myself against you?" she asked as if it were merely a joke. But her heart tripped crazily, and hot blood rose in her cheeks. Hadn't she seen families turn on one another, her own sisters and brothers fighting against her father and herself?

For the first time in weeks Anthony smiled broadly. "You have always been armed against me." He eyed her in a roguish way.

Still, she began moving the royal treasury to her mausoleum, sending slaves secretly. Her vast, two-story tomb stood near her father's and next to where other Ptolemys had been buried, including Alexander the Great. Huge marble buildings with splendid facades, they added to the grand design of Alexandria, and she would wait there while Anthony watched the sea.

In a whispered exchange late one night she told him what she'd been doing, and he whispered he'd die like he'd lived, a man. She realized he had no choice, but nothing had prepared her for the moment when he left her. His face bore deep lines of strain, but he walked with a purpose to the Pharos Lighthouse to watch for the arrival of Octavian's ships. It was a lonely spot, on the edge of the sea, and for days she heard nothing from him until Octavian and his army penetrated to the suburbs of Alexandria.

She saw Anthony and his few men drive Octavian away from the palace gates. Desperately, he and his small band beat back the superior forces, cutting them to pieces, smashing them like Alexander had smashed the oriental potentates' troops. At night, when he joined her, she was reminded of Caesar, similarly beleaguered, coming to her after his swim in the harbor. Anthony's face held the excitement of earlier days, and she praised him and with what might be her last act of largess, presented to the men who had fought gallantly alongside him, gifts of enormous wealth: a breastplate of gold, a golden helmet and other golden baubles.

She arranged a banquet such as Anthony hadn't had for weeks, doves in wine sauce, roast chicken, lentils and chickpeas, and dark, rich Egyptian beer. Death sat at the palace gates, and they tasted life while it lasted. Swordsmen sat at table with her and Anthony, all eating, boasting and laughing. Breaking off a piece of bread from a fresh loaf

Anthony held it to her lips, then handed her a glass of beer and together they sipped from it, the moment made magical by the sound of birds wheeling overhead. Only later did she see they were carrion birds.

The next morning, while the moments of the previous night still moved through her brain, Anthony's men cheered him. Yet, in a final act of treachery, some left. "The traitors!" she shouted.

"What will be, will be," Anthony said and sent a missive to Octavian offering to fight him single handedly, like a gladiator, winner take all. "After all, I am older, past my prime, while you are younger, in yours," he wrote.

Cleopatra knew such a contest would have to go in Anthony's favor; Octavian was no fighter.

This time Octavian answered. "There are many ways Marc Anthony can rid the world of himself. Therefore, I, Octavian, heir to the mantle of Caesar, will not waste my time on trivialities."

"How high and mighty he's become." Anthony's laughter, laced with derision., stopped abruptly, and a muscle in his cheek twitched slightly. Her love for him surging like a Mediterranean tide, Cleopatra turned aside in time to hear the latest news from Laknefer. A cohort of gladiators, Herculean men in their prime, declaring their admiration for Anthony, set out from Rome vowing to fight alongside him. They were waylaid on their way to him and killed by Herod's troops. Hearing, Anthony's eyes filled with tears.

Octavian's troops were everywhere in the city, tromping past boarded shops where rug merchants and jewelers had only weeks before displayed their wares. Food stalls were closed, fish markets went empty, and no one strolled the avenues, whole families cowering in rooms above shops or hidden in the elegant houses on the great boulevards. Ocatavian's troops controlled the streets.

With Nicodemus, Iras, and Charmion to help, Cleopatra quietly moved the emeralds, rubies, pearls, and other jewels in her collection to her tomb. Slaves had already transported chests of gold and silver, and all the objects signifying she was a queen of immense wealth. Ivory and ebony were piled high in the back of the tomb, cinnamon in barrels; gold coin overflowing the main room led to gilded chairs, plates of gold, and so many objects, two scribes scribbling furiously had trouble making a record. She had other slaves bring dry timber and kindling and pile it in the tomb even as Iras gathered food and bedding supplies, and Charmion checked once more on which poisons were most effective and how each affected those who ingested it.

All the while the specter of being dragged through the streets of Rome behind Octavian's chariot danced like an evil omen in Cleopatra's mind. She could hear the jeers and catcalls, could feel the stones beneath her feet.

The first night in the tomb with Charmion and Iras as company, sleep wouldn't come. As the moon slid like an augury through the upper windows, she whispered her fears. Always, as others weakened or ran like land crabs scurrying over the desert, they stayed with her, listened to her, supported her. Now, her greatest fear rattled like a human skeleton – to be taken to Rome like Arsinoe, to be treated like a nobody, spat upon, laughed at, derided, and called scurrilous names. "No, I'll never let them to do that to me," she whispered seeing moonlight as a gray path to the underworld.

Charmion touched her hand. "But My Lady you are a queen, the queen of Egypt. They can never take that from you."

"Romans have always done whatever they wanted to do. Octavian is no different. He needs to humiliate me, make me knuckle under, just as he wants to kill My Lord Anthony." She drew a ragged breath.

"Oh, My Lady, surely he wouldn't."

"He will." She glanced at the wealth piled up behind her. "For my sake, do not avoid the truth. This once, Charmion, and Iras, it is right and proper to speak what the gods already know. You and no others have been with me from childhood. You are my dear friends." For several beats of her heart, she heard nothing but Iras taking a deep breath, Charmion shifting from one foot to the other.

Then Charmion whispered, "Perhaps this once it is right and proper to address you as my dear friend but you will always be my queen."

Iras added, "Always."

"Thank you," Cleopatra whispered. Sighing, she added, "And thank the gentle Isis Caesarion has gotten away."

"You've made sure he's safe, My Lady."

"I'm positive of that, but I worry about My Lord Anthony. He is so brave, but so outnumbered." She shivered, and tears pricked her eyes. She fought them back before she sought the comforting arms of her ladies.

The next day, learning that Octavian neared the palace, she barricaded the entrance to the tomb and waited.

Her face hot and feverish, she slipped off her shoes, and walked barefoot over the cool granite and marble floor. Was Caesarion remembering to conserve his water supply? Surely he was past the step pyramid by now.

She lay down on the slab that would hold her sarcophagus. From outside a distant murmur of voices hummed like bees in a hive. She must not be afraid. Honey made bread fried in olive oil as good as cake. She closed her eyes. "Tell me when My Lord Anthony has beaten back that miserable little worm, Octavian. " Deliberately, she remembered the first time she'd seen Anthony. Without his Roman gear she would have known he was Roman. No matter where in the world they went, Romans were always easy to identify, even if they wore the same clothes, spoke the same language as the country they assimilated for they walked and talked with an assurance not given to others. Seemingly they cared not that their conversations were overheard. Their pride in being Roman rang louder than a thunderbolt. Anthony, no matter his devotion to her, to their children, had never stopped being Roman.

Her mind drifted. Nicodemus and Atennae had taken Cleopatra Selene into their home, and she had no doubt they would keep her safe along with their own children, raise her with them until Caesarion returned. Selene, with her Antonian blood was pretty as Anthony was handsome, but she had her mother's intelligence. Affable too, she usually brought a smile to everyone's lips. Certain her daughter would be safe, Cleopatra fell into exhausted slumber.

A commotion outside woke her, and pain shot like lightening from her chest to her jaw. Not Octavian already! She tried to sit up, but had no strength, her body like a dead weight, her muscles seemingly useless.

"Here, My Lady, my queen." Charmion rushed over, Iras following. They took her arms and helped her to a sitting position.

"Thank you, dear friends. You remind me of my duty as you have throughout the years. A queen must live life for others and not for self.

It is what I've endeavored to do." She put her feet to the floor. "Not always successfully."

"Exceedingly well, if I may be so bold," Charmion said.

She smiled acknowledgement of the words as the disturbance outside increased. Not daring to open the barricaded door downstairs, she hurried to the second floor window and looked down. A messenger standing below cried out that Marc Anthony had offered himself in death to Octavian in place of her.

The stabbing pain in her chest gripped hard and moved like evil up her jaw again. "No!" she cried, pressing her hand to her heart and calling down, "Such a thought renders me dead even as I live." Octavian must be storming the palace. She should have insisted Anthony come with her. Oh, by Atun, by Zeus, by all the Gods of antiquity, where was he? Surely he would come to her. She glanced around. Should she set fire to the royal treasury, melt down the gold, burn the cinnamon and the ebony to ashes, render the jewels worthless? But, of course, Octavian would never permit that. At the first puff of smoke he'd send troops.

A renewal of strength and purpose flowing through her, a laugh escaped her lips. "Can't you see that poor little skinny boy-man? I doubt he's ever seen anything as magnificent as the palace." Through the years of Ptolemy reign it had grown, the complex of buildings dominating Alexandria, with the Museum where foreign scholars came to learn, the library that was the envy of the world, the parks and terraces nearby the sprawling residence. "I hope he doesn't allow his men to piddle in the corners." She giggled.

Iras joined her. "Oh, My Lady, you make it all seem right."

"It will be, Iras, it will be."

"You must keep up your strength, My Lady." She held out a tray of fruit.

"I am a prisoner, Iras, bread and water only."

"Oh, My Lady, please don't speak like that."

"It is the truth, a self-imposed truth. I am but a prisoner." She nibbled bread, sipped water.

The heat of searing day seeped through the open upper window. The sun shone brightly, laying a path of light across the floor. She stepped out of the ray as she moved across the floor, thoughts of night pervading her thoughts. "It will not be the first time Romans have taken over the palace." She shrugged. "And we always got it back."

Charmion's smile matched hers.

"And will again," Iras added, her smile wobbling.

Quietly, she brought up things they had done as children, she and Charmion instigating the tricks played on their tutors, Iras going along. As they talked, Anthony's name repeated like a chant through her mind. He was her mortal and immortal love.

A shout and holler coming from below brought her to the present. She recognized an agonizing cry full of grief and ran to the window and leaned on the sill. A clutch of servants stood below, and a man she recognized as having been in Anthony's family since he was a child, looked up. "My Divine Lady," he said, a frown cutting his wrinkled face.

Speak out," she cried, her bowels cramping, her heart thudding like the Roman cavalry.

Tears were leaking from the corners of the old man's eyes. "It's about my Lord Anthony. They told him you were dead, and he fell on his sword."

"No!" She cried, shaking her head, but knowing it was true. It was the noble thing to do, but it had come too soon. She didn't want to believe it; she couldn't believe it, wouldn't. "No, no."

He took a step closer to the building. "He still lives, and begs to be with you, My Lady."

"By all that's holy, bring him to me." she cried and waved the old man off, watching as he half ran and stumbled out of sight. A lessening of the pain gripping her came so suddenly she smiled. Of course Anthony would survive. Was he not a god? Even if he died of the wound, he would live. *And so would she.*

"May the gods grant him wings," she whispered, pacing the hall, waving her arms and hands as if waving away the evil of Ptah and the underworld while brushing away the tender ministrations of Iras and Charmion, her friends, her companions, her helpmates.

Within the hour two slaves carried Anthony's litter to the front door, but Nicodemus had made sure it would be difficult to open, even from the inside. With Charmion and Iras, she struggled but it would not budge. To dismantle the door would take forever, and Octavian would surely catch them in the act, and all would be lost. No, they must hoist Anthony up through the second floor window. Dreading it, knowing it would cause him more pain, she issued instructions, and Charmion lowered a rope.

Taking hold of one end, and with Charmion and Iras backing her, she began to pull Anthony and his litter up to the second floor. How heavy he was, how unwieldy the litter, but even if Charmion and Iras were not there, she would manage it. She had to.

Anguished cries pushed past Anthony's lips, and she cried in sympathy, straining and pulling until he was inside. Her breath sounding like a trumpet in her ears, as gently as possible she helped ease the litter to the floor and went to her knees beside it. "Anthony, my love," she whispered, leaning over him, taking his hand in hers, holding it against her heart. "You're with me now. It's all right. You're safe, my dearest."

His eyes fluttered open and focusing with difficulty, he looked up at her, his gaze encompassing her, taking her in as if he were holding her. A small smile crossed his lips. "You never give up, do you my little queen."

"No," she agreed, shaking her head, smiling at him.

His fingers tightening briefly on hers, his voice weak, he whispered, "Will you bring me a glass of wine?"

"Oh, my dearest, yes. Whatever." She touched his cheek, her hand light and loving. For so many years he had lived in her thoughts, supported her, been her love, and now blood ran from his side and pain turned his face into a travesty of itself.

Iras handed her a goblet and Cleopatra held it to his lips. "Here, my darling." As he swallowed, color returned to his face.

"I did all I could," he said and touched his tongue to his lips.

"You did *everything* you could," she whispered. "You were never defeated, never."

He opened his eyes wide and looked up at her as if memorizing her face. "Did I tell you how beautiful you are?"

Tears filming her eyes, she shook her head.

"You are, you are my right hand, my strength, my…" he whispered words lost in a bubble of blood. His eyes glazing and then clearing, his gaze stayed with her. "Take care of the children. Antyllus, too. He is a good boy."

Guilt raced through her like a runaway horse. "The children are safe," she said, avoiding his eyes. *How could I have forgotten to secure Antyllus's safety, too! May the gods forgive me.*

Anthony's eyes fluttered and closed. "Don't leave me."

She strained to hear the words. "Oh, Anthony, my dearest, I'm here. I won't go anywhere. I'll never leave you." She pressed kisses to his cheeks, his slack lips.

"I go," he whispered, struggling to open his eyes again.

"We will be together again, Dionysus," she said, leaning over him, her hair framing his face. "Of this, I promise."

His eyes flickered open. "Remember…."

"Tarsus?" she encouraged, but his mouth went slack, his eyes glazed. He was gone, and though she sought to put the breath of life into him, his lip tasted only of death. "Oh, no, oh no," she wailed. It was too soon. She had so much to tell him, to ask him, to discuss with him. She wanted once more to lie at his side, speak of what had been and what was to come. "No!" she shouted. "He cannot be dead. I want him alive." Frantically she gathered him into her arms, pressed his head to her shoulder.

"My Lady." Charmion put her hands on Cleopatra's shoulder. "Please let him go."

They unwound her arms from his body and lifted her to her feet.

She had thrown in her lot with Anthony, and now he was gone, and she was alone. She sagged in their arms and wailed her grief until harsh, hard footsteps in the back of the tomb made her push her dearest friends away and spin around.

A Roman, in full armor, stood staring at them, a look of triumph on his face.

She fainted.

Chapter XVIII

30 BCE

W HEN SHE CAME to, she realized she was a prisoner in her own palace. Outside her doors and in the gardens, guards stood at attention. She'd been hauled like a common thief from her tomb. Crying, and wailing, she had scratched and fought until they beat her into submission. Thrown into a cart and taken to the palace, she'd scraped her face and arms, and a fever had set in. She had floated away, awakening at times to find Iras and Charmion sponging her burning body with cold water, their words of reassurance humming in her ears, days slipping by.

She woke to hear priests chanting and to smell the incense, and to see the flickering lights. Rising, she let her friends dress her, and then she called Octavian to her. He stood patiently, staring at her as if at an apparition as she begged and pleaded with him to understand that she had to attend Anthony's burial. And then debasing herself, she'd fallen to his feet and pleaded. All the time he'd said nothing, and she had floated in and out of understanding, knowing only that he agreed, she was to see Anthony entombed.

Throughout it all she dwelled in a fog, imagining that Anthony spoke to her, reminding her that one day they would be together always. Already he was with the gods, walking the celestial sky, his love whispering on the wind. Something brought her back to the present, the sun-sharp sky and the paved street at her feet, and the sandals Anthony had fastened upon her once, pretending to be her slave, teasing as only he could tease, laughing at her, with her. But now she would hear his laugh no more until…. And then the fog grew thick, the darkness closed in again.

Now, a great sadness enveloped her, but lifting her head she saw the sun like a ripe lemon, the juice spilling over a honeyed land, and it was good. She would join Anthony soon, and for a while Egypt would languish, years might pass, but Caesarion would return to reclaim what she and Anthony had sought to preserve. My dearest son, she whispered, for surely she had taught him well.

The next day, she rose before her ladies, they jumping to their feet when they heard her.

"Oh, My Lady, it is good to have you back again," Charmion cried, rubbing sleep from her eyes.

Iras came running from the chair where she'd slumped.

Cleopatra knew a vast tingling of her nerves and an extraordinary awareness of every sound, every smell. Always she had known Charmion was the taller of her two friends, that her hair had streaks of blonde, witness to her Macedonian heritage, that petite Iras had hair the color of night, but she'd never thought of it, never thought about them separate from her. She'd accepted their love and devotion as a given. Now she noticed everything about them, about the room, about herself. She felt the meshing of muscle and mind, saw the remnants of a splendor she's taken for granted. We come in with nothing, we leave with nothing, she thought asking if one of them would get her a little wine and the other would fill the tub. "I need to prepare. The day we talked about has arrived."

"*That* day, Your Majesty?" Charmion asked.

"Yes. It is a fine day to leave, don't you agree?"

Iras glanced toward the window. "It is a fine day, My Lady, not hot, not cold, the breeze carrying nothing but pleasant sounds, sweet scents." Yet she shivered.

"An excellent day to take into eternity," Charmion agreed.

How dear they are, she thought as Iras brought the wine, spilling only a drop as she handed over the goblet. She pushed the visions plaguing her aside. She had no fear of death; Isis who was Aphrodite, would shortly join Dionysus and they'd dance the skies forever, but she feared what Octavian would do if he knew her plan.

As Iras filled the vast sunken bathing pool with perfumed water, she stood still while Charmion helped divest her of her soiled garments and lay out fresh. Once she had gamboled in the bath, and Anthony laughing lustily had joined her, and they had with joy become one as they had so often.

Now, she used the pool to cleanse the illness from her body, and to review the past. She had guided Egypt through famine and prosperity, put down traitors and raised up supporters, and always she had increased the royal treasury. She had dealt kindly with friends, given opportunities to women and talented peasants, and meted swift punishment to those who deserved it. She had been a principled monarch, bending when necessary. Satisfied, she called, "Have you put out my clothes?" It was hard to stay focused; she longed to be gone. "You know which ones." When they found her, she must look like a goddess and a queen.

"They are ready, Your Majesty."

Your Majesty. Charmion had seldom addressed her that way. In school she and Iras had called her Princess or Cleopatra. After she'd ascended the throne, Charmion and Iras had routinely said, My Lady, but nothing ever as formal as Your Majesty. "Do I have any jewels remaining, or has Octavian stripped me bare?"

"The rooms closer to the main entrance were ransacked, but luckily, they hadn't come this far when we were returned." Charmion attempted a smile that went off center. "I hid some things."

"Are they regal enough?"

"Whatever you wear is regal, My Lady."

"Oh, Charmion, Iras, I've been blessed by your friendhip." She shook her head in gratitude as she stepped into the tub and after bathing, drying and being perfumed and rubbed with unguents and powder, she let them put henna on her hands and feet. At her dressing table, Charmion lay out the jewelry, as Iras dressed her hair, dropping the comb and apologizing before she got control. Parting and smoothing strands, she piled locks on top, in back and alongside Cleopatra's cheeks in a becoming and fashionable style, adding combs and pearls as Charmion unearthed them from secret drawers.

Cleopatra kept her gaze on the outside world. Ships again moved in the harbor, ships from Syria, Greece, Macedonia, and Mauretania as well as Rome. Fishmongers cried their wares, and glassblowers plied their trades. Their voices, and those of other merchants, rose above the rattle of chariots and the babble of children in the gardens. The smell of the sea was clean and crisp. Was it possible that she had truly lived thirty-nine years? It seemed only yesterday when her father had told her she would be queen. True to his prophecy, the whole world had bowed to her. She had known riches and fame and been loved by the two noblest men of Rome. Now, her son was almost as old as she when she became queen. It was time to join the gods.

The thought increased her growing sense of peace. She studied her reflection in a hand mirror as Iras applied the makeup that transformed her. When she was done, she said, "Please, tell Nicodemus it is time for the figs I favor. A large basket of them."

Iras's hand flew to her breast, makeup brush slipping from her fingers, her eyes big. "So soon?"

She nodded. "We must hurry before Octavian learns how well I have recovered."

Charmion placed a diadem upon the makeup table and turned away. "I'll tell the guards."

She took Iras's hand and said softly, "It will be swift, my friend. Hardly no pain, and then we will all be together again."

Iras whispered, "The eyes, when the snake puffs his hood." She shivered. "They have always frightened me."

"Don't look. I won't. Think instead of the joys to come. You, Charmion, Anthony and me."

"Yes, My Lady, I will try."

"We will help one another as we always have. Here, drink some wine; it will relax you." She poured two more glasses, gave one to Iras, sipped the other herself. She had gone over all the options; this was the honorable way out. She took Iras's hand. "Come to the window and see what a grand day it is."

They were standing there sipping wine and whispering less than an hour later when Nicodemus arrived with the basket of figs.

"Thank you my dear friend," Cleopatra said for the guards' ears, "I grew up eating figs daily, and I haven't had any for weeks."

As soon as they were gone, she turned her head away from the basket Nicodemus placed upon a table. "Tell me about my daughter."

Moving closer to the window, drawing him with her, aware of the pulse beating in his throat, of the look of sadness permeating his face, of her own thoughts rushing faster than she could speak, she shook her head.

He attempted a smile. "She asked for you."

She squeezed his hand. *So much to say in so short a time.* "Take good care of her for me. Tell her I go to join my celestial husband, but that I will always be with her. When the sun marches across the sky each day and the moon comes out at night, I, Isis, will be there always. But until she joins me, you and Atennae are to be her mortal parents, and she is to look to you for counsel."

"I will do that, my Queen." His voice was solemn, and a tremor shook his body.

"Oh, Nicodemus, my dear loyal friend, guard her well."

"With my life."

She kissed him on the cheek and handed him a note she had written herself. "See that Octavian gets this. It is instructions for my burial."

Tears coming to his eyes, he bent his head and kissed her hands.

Impulsively, she lifted his hands and held them briefly against her cheek. "Now go," she whispered.

Bidding Charmion and Iras farewell, he bowed deeply in Cleopatra's direction, before leaving.

The light was beginning to go out of the world. The flowers in full bloom were beginning to wither, while the water in the fishpond, untended during the recent weeks, had turned green. She turned back to the room, as if seeing its brightly colored murals and tapestries, its marble and alabaster, its frescoes and tiles for the first time. Glancing at her reflection, she saw that her eyes were un-naturally bright and her lips, her cheeks, her brows, as Anthony had said. For the first time in her life she felt truly beautiful, and she moved with a firm, purposeful step. "It is time," she said, and let her friends help her don the dress of Isis, the form-fitting gown that showed her body as shapely as a girl's but unmistakably that of a queen and a goddess. They fit the bracelets and the jeweled collar around her, fastened earrings in her lobes and set a diadem of sparkling emeralds on her head.

Iras said, "I should be the first. In case we miscalculated."

The years together were melding into a montage of never-ending scenes. Cleopatra hugged her. "Dear Iras."

"First, let us see that nothing is out of place. That the room is clean and pure, a fitting abode for your final trip." Iras put antimony and kohl and makeup wands into the makeup case.

Charmion smoothed the covers on the bed and plumped the pillows. "It looks most fitting," she pronounced, her voice scratchy.

"Then I go," Iras murmured. Her eyes registering willingness as well as fear, she approached the table where the basket of figs waited. "But first, my most noble queen, I would see you as Octavian will when the guards discover us."

Cleopatra stretched out on the golden couch she had selected for her bier and looking to Charmion, she said, "It is up to you to finish the tableau, mark an end to the scene. Always I have depended upon you, and I do once again. We have shared much. But the hours in life are few, and of them, this must be the greatest."

"It will be My Lady, " Charmion promised, her voice cracking but her head high.

Biting her lip, Iras pushed her left hand deep into the basket.

"Dear friend," Cleopatra said, "dear Iras."

Iras steadied herself, but soon a look of relief passed over her face. "It was no more than a prick," she said and slowly settled to the floor, her head against the foot of the couch.

"Kiss me quickly, Charmion, and then make sure I am gone before you join Iras and me." Her gaze took in the basket in Charmion's hand. "Do what you have to do, and then toss the contents of the basket out the window. I want no unseemliness to remain, nothing to mar the symmetry of the room and our being."

"I promise, Your Majesty. Nothing will be awry." Charmion kissed Cleopatra's cheek.

"Such cold lips for a heart so warm and beating within your flesh. It is as if you were already on your way. As we all are." Her gaze went to the basket where the figs began to jiggle and an asp stuck its head above the fruit. "You will have to work fast, but I know you are more than capable, my dear friend. I do it now." She held out her arm and fixed her gaze on the window beyond Charmion. The sky was so deep a blue it was almost like the sea, but clouds, unlike anything she had ever

seen in summer moved like feathers across the sky. Feeling two quick
pricks, she stiffened her arm and kept her gaze firmly above until the
blue began to dim. She closed her eyes. No one must see her staring
sightlessly and mute. Thank the gods Caesarion was safe.

* * *

Octavian's men found Iras breathing her last breath, Charmion fast
approaching it, and Cleopatra dead. Standing at the head of the bier,
Charmion attempted to adjust Cleopatra's diadem which had shifted.

"Charmion, was this right?" they asked.

Charmion steadied herself against the bier and made her voice a
trumpet that would resound throughout the ages. "It was entirely right
and fitting for a queen descended from so many kings," she said before
she, too, died, having adjusted the symbolic crown of Egypt so that it
sat squarely on the dead queen's head.

Epilogue – 30 BCE Octavian's Triumph Through Rome

F ORCED TO HURRY along behind an effigy so startlingly like her mother, Selene stumbled and tears erupted. Her mother never walked with a snake hanging from her arm. No, her queen mother had been a woman who praised her when she did well, and frowned when she didn't, and made her feel unique, like her father.

Stepping in dung, hearing the mocking, frightening crowd, she wanted to sit down, refuse to move. But would they kill her if she didn't keep up? Tripping, she caught her balance with difficulty.

"There, there, little princess," a deep voice said, and she looked up at a man whose eyes were so tender, she wondered if she were dreaming. He reminded her of Caesarion or maybe Antyllus They had killed Caesarion, called him ersatz Roman, dragged Antyllus out from behind a statue of Caesar and beheaded him

"My name is Juba, and once I, too, was hauled through Rome in a Triumph. My father, the king of Mauretania, had been killed, and I was alone. I never forget I am Juba, II, heir to the throne and you must never forget you're Cleopatra Selene of Egypt."

She studied his kind face and the thought came, her mother had said royalty married royalty. When she was older she could marry him. Now with the crowd roaring, she didn't want him ever to leave. She put her hand in his and held on tight.